Diners, Dives & Dead Ends

A Rose Strickland Mystery

Terri L. Austin

HENERY PRESS

DINERS, DIVES & DEAD ENDS
A Henery Press Book

First Edition
Trade paperback edition | July 2012

Henery Press
www.henerypress.com

This is a work of fiction. Any references to historical events, real
people, or real locales are used fictitiously. Other names, characters,
places, and incidents are the product of the author's imagination,
and any resemblance to actual events or locales or persons, living
or dead, is entirely coincidental.

ISBN-13: 978-1-938383-00-7

Printed in the United States of America

To Jeff, the love of my life.
Thank you for making dinner all those nights I sat in front of the computer. I couldn't have done it without you.

ACKNOWLEDGEMENTS

I owe my thanks to a lot of people who helped make this book a reality. To Emily Collins, my swim buddy and fellow critter, thanks for NaNoWriMoing with me. See what you started? To all my KCACG ladies—Kim Gabauer, Christina Wilson, Lindy Dierks, Paula Gill, Dawn Lind, and a special shout out to Heidi Senesac. Thank you for your friendship and holding my feet to the fire. To Shannon K. Butcher, an amazing writer and mentor—you've helped me more than you know. Thank you, Cheryl O'Donovan, for all your guidance. Kathy Collins, Alta Durrant, Sara Attebury, Sarah Skolaut, Janice McClain, and Barbara Herrin thanks for reading for me and inspiring me to be better. To Ann Charles, a kick ass writer, thanks for reading and blurbing. You are awesome. To Kim Carruthers and Sarah Lovewell, my beta readers, thanks so much. You guys rock. To my fellow chicks in the hen house, Larissa Reinhart and Susan M. Boyer—it's been fun taking this journey with you. To John Snethen, thanks for all your help on all matters legal and illegal. Jeff and Colter, my go-to guys, first readers, and favorite husband and son—you two put up with my nuttiness and were my biggest cheerleaders. Even though you looked ridiculous in those skirts. But keep the pom-poms, you never know when they might come in handy. And gratitude to my daughter, Austin, who let me have her name—you're not getting it back, so forget it. A big thanks to Kendel Flaum for all your hard work. Thank you all. You're the best.

Chapter 1

Mondays were known for two things at Ma's Diner: we poured lots of extra coffee and the tips sucked. After my last customer left, I counted out my money. Twenty-three dollars and sixteen cents. Hmm, food or gas?

I walked behind the counter and had just started to refill ketchup bottles when my friend, Ax, walked in. The bright afternoon sunshine flashed on his wallet chain as it slapped against his thigh.

Axton Graystone—his real name, I swear to God—was usually cheerful, goofy, and extremely mellow due to his natural disposition and the boatloads of pot he ingested. But when he stopped by the empty diner that afternoon, he was twitchy and nervous.

He plopped onto a stool in front of me and swung his overstuffed backpack onto another. His knee bounced up and down like a toddler on a sugar binge and he tapped his fingernails on the counter. "Rose, I need you to do something for me."

"I'm not giving you my pee." Axton had a couple of possession misdemeanors. Now the administration at the college where he worked made him take a urine test once a month.

The keys in his pocket jangled with every bob of his knee. "No, not that. I need a favor." Worry lines creased his forehead and his pale blue eyes were more bloodshot than usual.

I glanced up from my ketchup transfusion, leaned over and stared into said bloodshot eyes. I sniffed the air around him. "You're not stoned. Are you drunk?"

Roxy Block, my fellow waitress-slash-bestie frowned. "I thought he was always stoned." Roxy was in a pissy mood. She'd quit smoking the day before and it was not going well. For any of us.

"Where were you last night?" I asked him. "I thought we were going to watch *War of the Worlds*. I made those pizza rolls you like."

"Jeez Rose, I told you a million times, it's *When Worlds Collide*. It won an Academy Award. It was like, a visual masterpiece." *Tap, tap, tap.* He rapidly beat out a rhythm on the counter.

"Whatever." I reached over and laid my hand on his, forcing him to stop tapping his nails.

Axton hopped down from the stool and went to the picture window at the front of the diner. With his hands on the glass, he glanced up and down the street—left, right, then left again. His breath made a big foggy circle next to the closed sign.

After I twisted a lid on the last bottle of ketchup, I walked to the tables around the small dining room, putting a bottle on each. "So where were you?"

His shoulders jerked at the sound of my voice. "I went to a club. Look, Rose—"

"Like a dance club?" I interrupted, a bottle dangling between my fingers. I'd known Axton forever. We'd gone to school together from first grade through high school at Huntingford Prep and the only club Axton ever attended involved Starfleet uniforms and speaking Klingon.

"I'm trying to picture you dancing." Roxy smacked a piece of nicotine gum as she pushed a broom across the black and white checkerboard floor. "And in my mind it looks more like a seizure." Roxy wore a very short, red pleated skirt, a frilly white blouse, and white platform shoes. A lacy headband held back her electric blue hair. Her outfit was not a side effect of cigarette deprivation. She always dressed like that.

Axton glared at her. "It was a private club. Invitation only." He looked back at me. "That's not the point." He shoved his hands into the pockets of his baggy jeans that were almost white from too many washings, then stomped back over to the counter and jumped up on the stool.

"It wasn't the country club, was it?" I gave a little shudder. "I hate that place. I thought you did, too." I turned to Roxy. "The last time we were at the country club, he set off the fire alarm and the entire place had to be evacuated."

Roxy smiled around her wad of gum. "That figures."

"Dude, that was a long time ago. And no, it wasn't the country club. It was...exclusive. Seriously, can you do me a solid?"

Axton at a *Star Trek* convention? Yes. Axton, at an exclusive anything? Uh-uh. Something was way off here.

Today he seemed wired for sound, but normally he was just wiry. From his thin, five-foot-seven-inch frame, to the patchy tufts he called a beard, to the dishwater, chin-length waves that swirled around his head. The man loved all things Tolkien and cheesy sci-fi movies. Private clubs where admittance was by invitation only? Uh, no.

"Ax, what is going on? And why are you so hyper?"

His gaze darted past me, to the last glazed doughnut on the cake stand.

Roxy walked up to the counter. "Bet you went to a titty bar. You know the strippers invite everyone, Axton." She reached out and patted his back. "Not just you."

He blew out a breath. "It was not a strip club."

Roxy rolled her eyes and tried to blow a bubble. She wound up with a string of gum stuck to her upper lip.

Axton looked longingly at the doughnut. "Can I have that?"

I lifted the glass dome. "Take it."

He grabbed it and snarfed it down in two bites. "Thanks. I haven't eaten all day." He rubbed his hands together, wiping crumbs from his fingers.

"Hey, dumbass, we just cleaned that counter." Roxy picked up a rag and swiped at the crumbs.

With a sigh, I took the rag from her hands. "I'll finish this. Why don't you take a break?"

She raised a brow. "Like a cigarette break, you mean?"

"Like a fresh air break." I spun her around and gave her an almost gentle nudge toward the kitchen.

Once she was gone, I faced Axton, pushed aside the salt and pepper shakers, and leaned on my forearms. I gave him a narrowed-eyed look designed to make him spill all his secrets. "What did you do last night and what kind of favor do you need?"

"Can't tell you where I went, but I need you to take my backpack for a day or two. Keep it someplace safe."

Now I knew something was wrong. Axton without his backpack? That'd be like Linus without his blanket. Ax toted that thing everywhere. He probably slept with it. "Are you in some kind of trouble?"

"No, no trouble." His knee bobbed even faster than before. "Will you help me out?"

He gazed at me with an emotion I didn't recognize. Anxiety, maybe? "Sure, Ax, whatever you need."

His shoulders sagged in relief. "It'll only be for a day or two. Thanks, Rose." He came around the counter and pulled me into a hug. "I've got to get back to work." He quickly walked to the front door.

I followed him out of the diner, the aroma of coffee and cinnamon trailing behind me. I held up my hand to shield my eyes from the afternoon sun. "Call me later?"

His smile didn't reach his eyes. "Sure." Climbing into his Honda hatchback, he waved as he drove out of the lot.

A brisk wind kicked up and I rubbed at the goose bumps on my bare arms.

Stupid me, I should have never let him drive away.

Chapter 2

I walked back inside and scooped up Axton's backpack, taking it into the kitchen with me. As I opened the swinging door, the smoky tang of bacon grew stronger. My boss, Ray, scrubbed the grill, and the dishwasher, Jorge, clinked plates as I moved past them into the pantry. I dropped the bag at my feet. It weighed a ton.

I sat on my haunches and unzipped it. So help me, if Ax stashed his pot in here, I was flushing it. But as I dug into the pack, I found it drug free—unless you counted the flannel shirt that almost gave me a contact high after one whiff. There was also a hardback copy of *The Hobbit*, two tech magazines, a laptop, a small tool kit, and a rectangular computer doodad the size of a deck of cards. Nothing unusual. At least not for Axton. I wondered why he left this with me. What the hell was going on?

I stuffed everything back inside and took a case of syrup off the shelf. I removed the restaurant-sized bottles of imitation maple goodness and stuck the backpack in the large box, closed the lid, and hoisted it back in place. Then I made some room next to the salsa and decided the condiments could play nice for a couple of days.

Roxy found me a minute later, with my hands on my

hips, staring at the syrup box. "You must be really bored," she said.

"Yep." I followed her out of the pantry and into the dining room.

"Do you want to do something tonight or are you studying?" She walked over to the windows and pulled down the shades.

"I'm going to study with Janelle, go to bed, then get up and do it all over again. It's glamorous, I know." I lifted a shoulder. "But that's just how I roll, my friend."

"Your life kinda sucks."

Sadly, she was right. Truth was, my life had become pretty predictable. My classes were beyond boring and I spent weekends either drinking watered down beer with Roxy or watching sci-fi movies with Ax. Sometimes when I got really wild, I did both at the same time. Not exactly living on the edge.

My name is Rose Strickland—Rosalyn to those who named me. I inherited my blue-green eyes from my dad, my A-cup boobs from my mom, and my blonde hair from them both. Where I got my wicked sense of humor and independent spirit was anyone's guess, but the last two traits pissed my parents off to no end.

When I was eighteen, they shipped me off to the college they had chosen for me. A small, private, all-girls-all-the-time school. I hated it. After my freshman year when I insisted on changing schools, my parents insisted I leave their home and pay for college myself.

Fast forward five years, and I now was a student at Huntingford City College—not the most prestigious college in Missouri, but nearly affordable on a waitress's salary. I took a class or two each semester in an effort to figure out what I wanted to do with my life. This semester, I figured out I did not want a career in ethics or accounting. I don't know what a career in ethics would be anyway. Nun, maybe?

I was a twenty-four-year-old former rich girl who didn't know what she wanted to be when she grew up. But for sure, it wasn't a nun.

"Well, at least I have a date with Scotty this afternoon. That's something to look forward to." I untied and folded my apron before laying it on the counter. Scotty, my too adorable, five-year-old nephew had challenged me to a game of Hungry Hippo. Oh, the foolishness of youth.

Roxy popped her gum. "Why was Axton acting all weird today?"

Good question. "I don't know. But he wanted me to keep his backpack for a couple of days."

She raised a pale brow. "Remind me again why you like that stoner so much."

"Axton's one of the good guys. He was there for me when I needed him. He's true blue."

But he had been acting weird today. I decided to call him later about this backpack business. He must have had a good reason to give it to me. I just wanted to know what that reason was.

Grabbing my purse, I poked my head into the kitchen and said goodbye to the boys, then walked out to the parking lot with Roxy. As I waved to her, I saw a black SUV with tinted windows drive by. The back passenger window was down and I caught a glimpse of a man staring out at me.

Roxy followed my gaze. "Someone thinks you're tasty." She wagged a finger at me. "And remember, don't study too hard. Boys like girls with big tits, not big brains."

"Unfortunately, I don't have either."

I hopped into my piece of shit car and sped out of the lot.

Scotty waited for me at the door of my sister's mini-manse. By the time my feet hit the narrow porch, he was out of the house and launching himself at me like a missile. I stumbled back from the surprise attack, but kept upright as I bear hugged him.

"Hey, Sport, how are you?"

"Good. I want to go to the park. Can we go to the park? Please, Aunt Rose, please?"

I looked down at the tow-headed love of my life and smiled. "Sure. But you need a jacket."

He flew back into the house and I followed at a slower pace. My sister, Jacks, her blonde hair in a twist and her pretty face makeup-free, stepped into the marbled foyer.

"Did he talk you into taking him to the park?"

"Yep."

"You're such a softy, Rose."

Rose Strickland, part-time student, full-time softy. "How can you say no to that sweet, little face?"

"He sure has you fooled."

Scotty, soccer ball in hand, sped down the stairs as fast as his short legs could manage. "Got to go, Mom. See ya." Then he ran out the front door and I swear my hair blew back from the breeze that kid created in his wake.

"See ya." I gave my sister a finger wave.

Scotty and I walked to the park, which was a block

away. The large houses in this neighborhood sat on small lots, with the occasional tree dotting the yard. It was early October. Only a few leaves had changed color, but the weather was in flux. Cold mornings gave way to mostly warm afternoons. As the sun started to fall, so did the temperatures.

The park was a hotbed of elementary action—swings, jungle gyms, those little cartoon characters on springs—all teeming with screaming kids. More nannies than moms stood off to the side and sat on benches, watching the mayhem.

Scotty ran ahead. "Let's go."

I ran after him to a relatively clear spot on the edge of a wooded area. We spent half an hour kicking the ball back and forth, until I kicked it too far, and it whizzed past Scotty into the woods.

"I'll get it, Sport. You stay right here."

I trotted off, my eyes scanning the ground for a sign of the white and black ball. I finally spied it wedged against a sapling. I picked it up, and when I straightened there was a man in a dark suit standing a few yards in front of me.

I gasped and dropped the ball. It rolled toward him, hitting his shoe. He did some fancy maneuver with his foot and suddenly the ball was in his hands. With long fingers he twirled it in the air. "Tell your friend Axton I'm looking for him. Tell him I want what's mine." His voice was deep— smooth and polished. The afternoon sun at his back made it impossible to see his face clearly.

My heart started to pound, and despite the fact my legs felt wobbly, I walked toward him. "Who the hell are you?"

"He'll know." He threw the ball at me and I caught it

without thinking.

"Aunt Rose?"

I spun and saw Scotty a few feet behind me. When I turned back toward the mystery man, he was gone. I searched the trees for any sign of movement, but he'd disappeared. I didn't know what Axton had gotten mixed up in, but you could bet your ass I was going to find out. Whatever it was, it involved strange men lurking in the woods. I'd read enough fairytales to know that was never a good sign.

I slapped on a smile and walked toward Scotty. "It's time to go home, Sport." The stranger had me spooked, but I didn't want to freak the little guy out, I just wanted to get him safely home.

"But I still want to play." There was a hint of whine in his voice.

I took off running. "Bet I can beat you," I yelled over my shoulder. I let him catch up and win the race back to the house. As I ran on shaky legs, my eyes continuously scanned the area looking for the stranger in the suit.

I called Ax, but kept getting his voicemail—which consisted of Ax quoting the opening lines to the original *Star Trek* in a horrible William Shatner voice—and I wound up leaving him a dozen messages.

I knew if I sat around my apartment I'd brood, so I decided to stick to my schedule. And most Monday nights you could find me studying at Janelle Johnson's house.

In her mid-thirties, Janelle had smooth, dark brown skin, an enormous, gravity-defying rack, and long, thin braids that skimmed her ample butt. We bonded over fetal pigs in biology class last semester. She had gone back to school after her husband cheated with a woman he picked up at Kentucky Fried Chicken. Janelle came home early from her afternoon shift at the Quickie Mart and found them eating fried chicken—and each other—in Janelle's bed.

We lounged at her dining room table, studying for an ethics test. And by studying, I mean gossiping and eating.

I'd told Janelle about Axton, the club, the backpack, and the strange man.

"That Axton's always been a little squirrelly."

"No, he's a sweetie. But something was up with him today. And the guy with the suit? Creepy."

"Ask him about it." She handed me a bag of pretzels.

"Oh, believe me, I will." If I ever got a hold of him.

"So, Asshat has the kids tonight," Janelle said.

I nodded, making an effort to get my mind off of Axton and the strange man and focus on her story. But I kept peeking at my phone, willing it to ring.

"Chicken Licker told my daughter," she poked herself in the chest with a long, blue acrylic nail, "*my* daughter, she could get her ears pierced this weekend. Oh hell no. Over my dead sexy body." Asshat was of course her ex-husband and Chicken Licker his Kentucky Fried girlfriend.

"What did Asshat have to say about that?"

She rolled her eyes. "What does he ever say? Nothin'. I told Chicken Licker if she got her bony ass anywhere near my child's ears, I would make my foot a permanent part of her anatomy."

I munched on a pretzel. "I wouldn't want her bony ass near my ears either." Just then my phone rang. I recognized the number and quickly answered.

"Rose, it's the Axman."

"Thank God, I've tried calling you a million times. There was a strange man looking for you."

"Listen—"

"I can barely hear you." I put a finger over my left ear and held the phone closer to my right.

"Can you come and get me?"

"Ax, what is going—"

"I need a ride, man. Can you come or what?" Something about his tone sent chills up my spine. "Aw, shit. Rose..." I heard clattering, like something hit the phone.

I sat up straight. "Axton? Where are you? What's—"

His phone cut out before I finished the question.

I looked at Janelle. "Something's not right."

"See? Squirrelly." She sipped her Coke. "Where is he?"

"I don't know. Can I use your phone to call him back? My battery's almost out."

Janelle waved vaguely at the phone on the counter. I dialed Axton's number, but my call went straight to voice mail. Dread swept over me. "He's not answering."

I walked back to the table, closed my books, and shoved them in my backpack. "I need to look for him."

"You want me to go with you?"

I zipped my bag. "No. I'll drive around, see if I can find him. He's probably fine." I tried to reassure myself, but even as I said it, I didn't believe it.

Axton Graystone was in trouble.

Chapter 3

I drove toward Axton's house, way south of Apple Tree Boulevard. The Boulevard—mysteriously named as it was devoid of apple trees—was the dividing line in Huntingford. To the north, subdivisions with names like Stony Gates, The Cottages, and Crabapple Estates surrounded manicured golf courses or large man-made lakes. South of Apple Tree contained the historic district of Huntingford. Or as most people called it, the crappy side of town.

Axton lived in a tiny, white clapboard two-bedroom, one-bath home with his stoner roommate Joe Fletcher. Joe worked sporadically. Mostly, I think he sponged off Axton.

I pulled into the driveway behind Axton's blue Honda. A huge sense of relief washed over me at the sight of his car. That phone call really freaked me out. I didn't know what was wrong, but I wasn't leaving until he told me everything.

I bounded up the front steps and knocked on the door. After about a minute, Joe answered.

Joe was a little taller than Axton but just as thin. His brown hair was shaggy and greasy and he always wore a purple tuque with strings that fell on either side of his head. Even in the summer.

"Rose, hey man. Like, mi casa es su casa." He made a

sweeping gesture with his arm.

I hadn't been inside Axton's house very often and frankly it was not an experience I wished to repeat. It was dusty and smelled like old bong water. I stepped in and glanced around. A guy with a long ponytail and chin stubble sat on their old corduroy couch. He was completely engrossed in a video game that involved shooting people. Nazis, by the look of it.

"Where's Axton?"

"In his room." He waved toward the hall, his attention fixed on Ponytail and the video game. "Dude, you totally shot the shit out of that dude."

Ponytail nodded. "Hell yeah I did."

I walked down the short hall, knocked on Axton's door and waited. Nothing. I tried the door handle, but it was locked. I jiggled the knob. "Ax, you in there?"

No answer.

"Hey Joe," I yelled.

Joe shuffled down the hall to stand next to me.

"Axton's door is locked and he's not answering."

Joe shrugged. "Don't know, dude."

"Do you have a key?"

He scratched the top of his head. "Um…I don't think so."

I pounded on the door and shouted Axton's name, but still no response.

"Are you going to kick the door in?" Joe asked.

"Not unless I have to."

"Cuz that would be awesome. But, like, better if you had on a tight leather jumpsuit and boots that came up to your cootchie. All superhero style, you know?"

I walked back down the hall and out the front door. I made my way toward the side of the house until I stood outside of Axton's room. His light was off but the window stood open, the curtains fluttering inward from the light wind.

Joe followed. "Hey, maybe the Axman escaped."

I wrapped my hands over the window ledge, and bracing my feet against the house, hoisted myself up. Throwing one leg over the sill, I ducked my head and toppled into Axton's bedroom, then quickly scrambled to my feet.

With my hands stretched out in front of me, I stumbled around in the dark and stubbed my toe as I searched for the light switch. When I finally found it, I flipped it on and took a good look around. There was an unbelievable amount of crap scattered everywhere, but no Axton.

A knot formed in the pit of my stomach. Where the hell was Ax and why hadn't he taken his car?

I tromped back to the living room and asked Joe a few simple questions, like 'When did Axton come home? Was he acting strange? Did he say if he was going out tonight?' All I got back was, "Dude, I don't know." Not terribly helpful, Joe.

I gave Joe and Ponytail specific instructions to call me if Axton called or came home. They nodded as they munched on cold pizza and watched me with glazed eyes. With a sigh, I left the house and got back in my car.

I drove around for hours, stopping at all of Axton's favorite hangouts: The Burger Barn, The Slaughter House (a local watering hole), Howard's Hot Dog Stand, The Carp (a bar that featured live music), and even The Sizzler, Axton's favorite restaurant. He was nowhere to be found and no one had seen him all night. I kept calling him, but he never answered.

I got home close to eleven o'clock. Worry clawed at me as I climbed the two flights of stairs to my studio apartment. Something was wrong with Ax, I felt it in my gut.

I dropped my stuff on the small bistro table in the corner then curled up on my orange futon, but I was too edgy to sit still, so I stood and paced the room. Axton gave me his backpack for safekeeping. Why? He was obviously hiding something, but there was nothing unusual inside of it. Did it have something to do with his computer? And what about the strange man? Did Axton have something that belonged to him? And why did Ax sneak out of his window and not take his car?

My head ached from asking myself the same questions over and over. Should I call the police? Should I wait to see if he showed up tomorrow? I didn't know what to do.

Axton and I didn't have much in common on the surface. I vaguely remembered him as a goofy kid from school. We hadn't been friends, but our parents moved in the same social circles. But five years ago, when we ran into each other at the city college, it was like I saw him, really saw him, for the first time.

I had been feeling so hopeless and isolated after moving out of my parents' home. All my old friends had gone back to their expensive schools, my sister had newborn Scotty to take care of, and I went to work at Ma's Diner. I'd gone from country club tennis courts and a Lexus convertible to shopping for food at the dollar store and using a bus pass. I'd never even made my own bed and suddenly I had to figure out how to pay rent on a dump of an apartment. I was completely lost.

Until I met up with Ax.

With his sweet smile and love of Godzilla movie marathons, he kept me going. One day at a time. He held my hand through it all, offered to lend me money—which I could never bring myself to take—and brought me pizza. Lots and lots of pizza.

For a while, he was my only friend. And I would have lost my way without him.

He was an affable, tech-loving doofus who liked to spark up a bit too frequently and I was a rebellious smartass who could barely pay my bills. We were both misfits, not to mention bitter disappointments to our respective parents. I loved him like a brother. And if he was in trouble, I had to help him.

But I couldn't do anything about it tonight. With a sigh, I took my hair out of its ponytail and massaged my scalp. In my Post-it sized bathroom, I washed my face, brushed my teeth, and pulled on a t-shirt my ex-boyfriend, Kevin, left behind. It was puke green and bore the name of his band, TurkeyJerk.

Boyfriends like Kevin might drift in and out of my life, but Ax was my constant, the one man I could count on. And now he was missing.

I blew out a breath. Well, I was just going to have to find him. Whatever trouble he was in, I would help. Maybe it was my turn to save him.

Chapter 4

The next morning I awoke to my phone ringing instead of my alarm. "Axton?" I asked, after fumbling with the receiver.

"It's Ray. You're late. You sick?" My boss's gruff voice got me up in a hurry.

I looked around the room, my gaze finally landing on the clock. Six-fifteen. "Damn." I hauled ass out of bed. "I'll be there in fifteen minutes."

He grunted in reply and hung up.

After throwing on a pair of semi-clean jeans, a bra and a wrinkled, long sleeved t-shirt, I brushed my teeth and pulled my hair into a sloppy ponytail. Then I grabbed my bag and made it to work in ten minutes.

"Sorry I'm late," I yelled through the kitchen door. The smell of fried eggs and cinnamon French toast made my stomach growl. Tying a blue and white gingham apron around my waist, I got to work. I wanted to make sure Axton's backpack was still safely hidden away in the syrup box, but there wasn't time. The early crowd was in full swing.

Ma's Diner was a hole in wall. A little brick building with no sign, a place you'd drive past and never notice. Ma's served breakfast. Period. If you wanted a sandwich, it better be an egg sandwich or you were out of luck. We were open seven days a week, excluding Thanksgiving, Christmas, and Easter, from six to one. And if you came in at twelve fifty-five, you took it to go.

Ma's hadn't changed much since it opened in 1956—I'd seen the pictures to prove it. Wallpaper patterned with big baskets of fruit was now yellowed and dingy. Ten rectangular tables topped with pink Formica speckled with little pieces of gold glitter were scattered throughout the room, and none of the chairs matched.

Ma came in five times a week. At almost eighty, she still waited tables like a pro. Her real name was Marty, but I'd never heard anyone call her that. She was a favorite with the customers, especially older ones who liked to sit back and shoot the shit. Ma would talk to them about the good old days when her husband, Frank, was alive. But what she loved to do most was drink black coffee and complain to her son, Ray, that he never did anything right.

Lucky for me, Ma had come in that morning, as evidenced by Neil Diamond's greatest hits playing over the speakers.

When we hit a lull around ten o'clock, I poured myself a cup of coffee and leaned my elbows on the counter in front of Ma. Sitting on one of the four counter stools, a food service order form in front of her, she sported a red sweatshirt with a yellow rhinestone cat on the front. Spikes of white hair stood out at odd angles on her head and large-framed trifocals were perched on the bridge of her nose. She tilted her head up with her eyes cast down to the paper in front of her.

"So, why were you late, toots?" she asked.

"Sorry about that. Forgot to set my alarm."

"Late night studying?" She put down her pen and took a sip of coffee.

"I should have been, but I was out looking for Ax. He's in trouble, Ma." I updated her on all things Axton. "I'm really worried about him."

Roxy poured herself a cup of coffee and stood next to me. "What's the big deal? This is Ax we're talking about. I mean, where would he run off to?"

"It is a big deal, Rox. Giving me his backpack? A strange man lurking in the woods leaving cryptic messages? Something is off."

As I spoke, Ray carried two plates out of the kitchen. He set a ham and cheese omelet in front of me and a cinnamon roll in front of Roxy.

"Thanks, Ray," I said over my shoulder.

"Uhm."

"You put too much pepper in the gravy this morning, son," Ma said to his retreating back. "Boy always uses too much damn pepper. Anyway, call Axton's office and see if he came in this morning."

"I figured I would. I'll call his brother, too."

Roxy polished off the last of her cinnamon roll and stared at her empty plate. "What am I supposed to do now?"

"What do you mean, hon?" Ma asked.

"I want a cigarette. What do you people do after you finish eating? What is there to do besides smoke?"

Ma peered at her. "Your job?"

Scowling, Roxy picked up a rag and began wiping down tables.

I finished eating and went back to work. We had a

steady flow of customers until one o'clock when Ma flipped the closed sign.

As soon as my last customer was out the door, I hustled to the pantry. I pulled the syrup box off the shelf and hauled out Ax's backpack. Sitting cross-legged on the floor, I started with the outer pocket and found a disposable lighter and a small package of tissues. I shoved them back and unzipped the main compartment, drawing out each item and inspecting it thoroughly. Nothing had suddenly appeared overnight. It was still just ordinary Axton stuff.

I set the laptop on the floor and booted it up, but without his password, I didn't get very far. I tried his birthday (January 13th), his favorite movie (*Avatar*), his favorite comic book series (*X-men*), characters from his favorite book (*Lord of the Rings*), and even "George Lucas is a god." Nothing.

Frustrated, I stuck everything back in the bag, placed the bag back in the syrup box, then put the box back up on the shelf. There must be something on the laptop. But since I couldn't even log on, that was a bit of a problem.

I walked to the dining room where Ma scrubbed down the counter and Roxy swept the floor. "I just checked Ax's backpack again."

Ma raised her penciled brows and Roxy stopped smacking her gum.

"Nothing. And I don't know the password for his computer."

"Bummer." Roxy resumed her chomping.

"Go ahead and call his office, toots."

Since my phone had limited minutes, I used the wall phone next to the kitchen and called Ax's cell number first. His voicemail was full, so I tried his office number. It rang six times before someone answered. When I asked for Ax, I got a 'No, he didn't bother showing up today' before the phone slammed down.

I dug under the counter for the phone book to find Packard Graystone's number. Axton and Packard—okay seriously, what had their parents been thinking with those names?—were estranged. But I still wanted to talk to him in case he'd heard from Ax.

Packard's home number wasn't listed in the white pages, but his office was listed in the yellow ones. Pack was a dermatologist and the receptionist wouldn't let me talk to him unless I made an appointment. I might have raised my voice when I told her Pack's brother was missing, but she didn't seem to care. I grrred at the receiver.

I finished helping Ma and Roxy with cleanup, then drove to Axton's house to check in with Joe. Because he spent most of his life buzzed or better, I thought talking to Joe in person, rather than over the phone, would be the way to go. And maybe I could press him about that exclusive club Axton talked about.

Without bothering to knock, I opened the front door and found Joe sitting on the sofa watching an episode of *Bewitched* with a bag of potato chips on his chest. A glass bong sat on the scarred coffee table along with an empty pizza box. Crushed beer cans littered the carpet. Joe wore the same clothes from the night before: a t-shirt with a picture of the St. Louis Arch and ripped jeans. And his purple tuque, of course.

"Hey, Rose." He shifted his eyes from Elizabeth Montgomery to me and back again. "You ever wonder how Samantha does that nose twitch thing? I've tried to do it, but

I can't." He demonstrated his attempt at the nose twitch thing. He looked like a rabbit with a cocaine habit.

"Have you heard from Axton?"

"Um, negative." He stared at the TV, bringing a chip from the bag to his mouth without sparing me a glance.

I reached over, grabbed the remote control from his lap, and turned off the television.

He gazed at me, his brow furrowed. "What'd you do that for?"

"Axton hasn't shown up for work, he hasn't been home, and he left the house last night without taking his car. I'm worried about him."

He reached for the remote control, but I tossed it over my shoulder and heard it thunk against the wall. "Joe…Axton is missing."

"Dude, that was so uncool."

"Focus. Where did Ax go the other night? The club, where was it?"

"Um, can I have the remote back, please? I need to see if Samantha's mom turns Darren back into a dude."

I leaned down, my face inches from Joe's. "She does."

He blew out a breath and I winced. "Man, I hate spoilers. You are seriously harshing me."

Straightening up, I closed my eyes for a second. I obviously needed to go about this in a different way. I settled myself on the edge of the sofa and patted his shoulder. "Joe, we need to find Axton. I'm afraid he's in trouble."

He nodded, seeming to understand. Okay, we were making progress.

"Did he tell you anything about the club? Anything at all?"

With his mouth hanging open, he lowered his brows and rolled his eyes upward. Awww, he was trying to think. Mostly though it looked like he was trying to poop. "I know he said something about an invitation."

"Right," I nodded. "Do you know where he was going?"

"Um…some club? It sounded kind of boring."

"Where was the club, Joe? Think really hard, because this is important."

He scrunched up his face and closed his eyes. When he opened them, he looked like a sad puppy that had peed on the carpet. "I don't know."

"What about last night? What did Axton say when he got home?"

"He told me to save him a piece of pizza." He gestured toward the empty box. "And like, I totally would have if he hadn't skipped out."

I sighed. "Where did he go last night, before he came home, I mean?"

He shrugged his bony shoulders. "Sorry, Rose. Can I have my remote back? *I Dream of Jeannie* is on next. I love her, man."

I rubbed my temple. I was starting to get a headache to go along with the pain in my ass named Joe. "Sure. I'm going to check out Axton's room, okay?" Not waiting for his reply, I walked down the hall.

After climbing through the window last night, I'd unlocked Ax's door. I hadn't wanted to search his room then, because it seemed like such an invasion of his privacy. Today it seemed like a good idea.

It was even more of a wreck in the daylight and the

sour, musty smell hit me hard, just like it had the night before. The bed was unmade and I had trouble telling whether the sheets had once been white or if they had always been that shade of gray. Little mountains of clothes were piled up across the floor.

I surveyed the room and tried to figure out where to start. The desk was as good a place as any.

It was one of those discount store models you put together yourself. The top was cluttered with jewel cases filled with burned CDs and gaming magazines. I looked in the cubbyholes and found a bag of pot—no surprise there—and not much else. I flipped through the gaming magazines to make sure there were no loose papers between the pages.

Glancing around the rest of the room, I realized was going to have to touch that bed. My whole body shivered and I took a deep breath, wishing like crazy I had thought to bring gloves.

Under the bed were dust balls and spank mags, featuring women with novelty breasts the size of beach balls. I did the same thing and shook them to be sure there were no loose papers inside. Some of the pages were stuck together. I gagged a little. I lifted the twin mattress and found bubkes, as Ma would say.

Next I carefully made my way to the small bookcase where books had been haphazardly shoved on the shelves. All science fiction—natch—and as I thumbed my way through the pages, I noticed a theme. Most of the covers depicted large breasted women in skimpy outfits. Some wielded swords, some stood tall, their legs in a wide stance, their ginormous breasts thrust out. Axton *really* liked the boobies.

The closet yielded nothing but a few faded t-shirts, one

pair of khakis, and a dirty pair of tennis shoes on the floor. A cardboard chest of drawers held his socks and a lone pair of underwear.

I glanced around the room one more time, trying to take in anything that might hold a clue, and spied two pairs of jeans tossed in the corner. I picked my way through the dirty boxer bombs to get to them. Holding up the first pair with two fingers, I felt around in the pockets. Nothing. But in the front left pocket of the second pair, I found a folded yellow Post-it with the words NorthStar Inc. written in Axton's blocky handwriting.

I smiled. I didn't know if this was a clue, but I felt kind of excited.

With the paper tucked in my pocket, I scooped up all the burned CDs from the desk and slipped them into my purse. I doubted they contained any clues to Ax's whereabouts, but I wanted to be sure. I left the bedroom and went into the living room for one last attempt at Joe.

"Joe?"

"Mmm?" he didn't look away from the TV.

"Joe?" I said, louder this time.

His glassy gaze drifted my way. "Hey, Rose, you still here?"

"What did Axton wear to the club?"

He blinked, and seemed sharper, more alert for a moment. He grinned and snapped his fingers. "He had on this jacket, like you wear to funerals and stuff."

"A suit jacket?"

"Yeah, and *pants*."

"Slacks?" In all the years I'd known Ax, I'd never seen him in a suit. I didn't even know he owned one.

"Yeah, not like jeans or anything." He stared at the wall next to my head, the glazed look back in his eyes. "Yeah," he whispered. "Kind of like the dude who dropped by earlier."

"What?" My heart hammered in my chest. "What dude?"

"Some tall dude who looked in Ax's room."

I stomped over to the TV and shut it off, then blocked it with my body. "What tall dude?"

"I don't know, man. A guy showed up and asked for Ax...," he looked up at the ceiling, "this morning?"

I buried my face in my hands. So help me God, I was going to strangle this moron with his own hat strings. I took a deep breath. "Joe. Start at the beginning. A dude came to the house. What did he look like?"

He scratched the top of his head. "Like a funeral guy, I told you."

"What did he say? Tell me exactly."

His stomach rumbled and he looked up at me. "Huh, did you hear that?"

"What did he say?" My jaw was clenched so tight, I could barely move my lips.

"Man, chill. He said Ax had something important and he needed to search the Axman's room. Like you did."

I stepped closer to Joe. "Did he find anything? Please Joe, please focus."

"No..." he tilted his head to the side and closed his eyes for so long I thought he'd fallen asleep. Then they popped open. "No, I don't think so."

"Are you sure?"

"Ah man, I don't know."

I could tell I wasn't going to get any more out of him, no matter how much I pushed. "Joe," I said slowly, "I want you to call me if the man comes back."

"Sure." He dug into the chip bag and brought out a handful of crumbs. Half made it into his mouth and the other half landed on his shirt. "No problem."

I stared at him in frustration. I had no doubt Joe would completely forget our conversation, let alone his promise to call, if this guy showed up again.

As I left the house and made my way to the car, I dug in my purse for hand sanitizer, pouring half the bottle into my palm. The bright blue October sky was completely at odds with my dark mood. There was just a little breeze, a nip of fall in the air. Still, I was freezing.

I now knew Axton wore a suit to a club, had the name of a company that may or may not, in any way, be related to Axton's disappearance, and knew a man had searched Ax's room before I got there. It had to be the same mystery man I'd met in the woods. What was this guy looking for? And what would happen if he found Ax before I did?

Chapter 5

On TV they say you must wait forty-eight hours before a person is considered missing. I hoped that wasn't the case in real life. I knew Axton was missing and I needed him back.

I drove to the better side of Huntingford where the police station resided. The old station had been an historical landmark, but the city built a new one fifteen years ago. It was now a generic brick box.

As I walked through the doors, my feet met industrial grade dark green carpet. A large framed aerial view of the city hung on the off-white wall to the right. Except for a few people in police uniforms milling around, it wasn't at all what I imagined a police station would look like. Where were the criminals handcuffed to chairs? Where were the hookers in bad wigs? I didn't think we had a large hooker population in Huntingford, but I still felt a little let down.

I walked to the window near the front door where a uniformed female officer sat behind a desk and stared, unblinking, at a computer. "Can I help you?" she asked in a bored voice.

"Uh, yeah, I'd like to report a missing person?" My hands felt clammy and I wiped them on my jeans. I didn't know why I was nervous. I hadn't done anything wrong.

She looked up at me then. Her gaze took in my hair, face, and red t-shirt. "Who's missing?"

"My friend, Axton."

With a sigh, she stood. She wasn't very tall, but she was sturdy, like a fire hydrant with big boobs. Just Axton's type. "How long has your friend been missing?"

"Since last night."

She sighed again and sat down. "I can take an information report, put his name in the database. If you want to make a missing person report, you need to wait forty-eight hours. Thank you." She dismissed me and returned to her computer.

"He called me for help, but we were disconnected. He gave me his backpack. He's never without his backpack." I did a little jazz hand move, trying to get my point across. "He left his home without his car and no one's heard from him. He didn't show up for work today. Don't you think that's suspicious? Because, personally," I pointed to my chest, "I find that very suspicious. And there's a man in a suit looking for him."

She held up her hand to stop me. "Ma'am, you need to lower your voice."

I took a breath and nodded. "Sorry. I'm just very concerned. This isn't like him at all."

"Give me his name and DOB and I'll put him in the system."

I did, and she tapped on the keyboard and fiddled with the mouse for a couple of minutes, and then eyeballed me. "He's got two misdemeanors for marijuana possession."

"So?"

"Most likely he'll come home soon. They usually do. If you haven't heard from him in forty-eight hours," she stressed that part, "then you can make a report."

This time I didn't argue with her, even though irritation churned in my stomach. I was about to turn and leave when someone called my name.

"Rosalyn? Rosalyn Strickland?"

A man walked toward me from the main hallway branching off the foyer. He had very short brown hair with a hint of wave to it. He carried a briefcase and the tailored navy suit he wore complemented his light blue eyes. Not my type, but yummy in a corporate way.

He caught up to me and smiled. He was handsome before that smile appeared, but after... Let's just say there were dimples involved.

"It is you. Hey," he said.

"Hey yourself," I said, not knowing who the hell he was.

"You don't remember me, do you?"

"Um..."

He laughed. Those dimples returned, and they were darn cute. "I'm Dane Harker."

I shook my head. "I'm sorry..."

"We went to school together until I moved away in eighth grade."

"Ah, okay." I still had no idea who he was.

"I sat right behind you in Mrs. Henky's sixth grade class. I wore hideous glasses, had a mouthful of braces." He pointed to his face.

Then I saw it, the nerdy boy who used to shush me. He'd really changed. "Right, Dane. How've you been?" I suddenly was very conscious that I hadn't yet showered, wore no makeup, and my blonde hair—one of my best features—was pulled up in a half-assed ponytail. I touched it nervously. I wondered how he even recognized me.

"I've been well." His smile widened. "So what are you doing here?"

A light bulb went on over my head. Maybe this guy could help me. "Are you a cop?"

"No, an attorney. I was here to see a client."

"Oh."

"But I know some. Cops, I mean. Do you have a parking ticket or something?"

"No, nothing like that. Thanks, though. It was good to see you." I turned toward the door, but his voice drew me back.

"Rosalyn. I may not be a cop, but if you tell me what's wrong, maybe I could help."

"I don't think you can. And I couldn't afford you anyway." My gaze slid over him, from head to toe. "You look expensive."

He laughed. "I am expensive. But for an old friend, I'll give a discount. I haven't had lunch yet and I'm starving. Buy me burger and I'll listen to your problems." He shifted the briefcase from his left hand to his right and glanced at his watch. "I have forty-five minutes."

I shrugged. "I could use someone to bounce ideas off of."

We wound up at The Burger Barn down the street from the police station. I got the Barnyard burger with special sauce and tater tots and Dane got a triple Moo with curly fries. Once we tucked ourselves into a yellow plastic booth, our food in front of us, Dane took the lead.

"What are you up to these days, Rosalyn?"

I raised my chin and sat up a little straighter. "I go by Rose. I take night classes at the city college and work at Ma's Diner as a waitress."

"Wow, I haven't eaten there since I was a kid. Are the pancakes as good as I remember?" He got a faraway look in his eyes.

"Yeah, they're delicious." He hadn't even flinched. A point in his favor. Usually when I mentioned my occupation to people from my old life, they shifted their eyes away in embarrassment, as if I'd blurted out I had a yeast infection instead of the fact I served flapjacks for a living.

He pulled himself back from short stacks of yesteryear to the present. "What kind of trouble are you having?" He had his burger in one hand, a curly fry in the other and alternated bites, burger, fry, burger, fry. Seemed he had a system.

"My friend, Axton Graystone, is missing and the police won't take a report until he's been gone forty-eight hours."

He nodded. "That's standard procedure. And I think I remember Axton. Scrawny kid, blond hair?"

"That's him."

Sucking on his strawberry milkshake, he narrowed his eyes. "Is Axton related to Packard Graystone?"

"Yeah." I swirled a tot in pool of ketchup. "They're brothers."

"I see Pack at the country club from time to time. He's got a mean golf swing. How long has Axton been missing?"

"Since last night."

"Have you contacted his family?"

"Not yet." I shared all the crazy of the last two days

including the Post-it I found and the man in the woods.

"You have no idea who the mystery man is and all you have to go on is this NorthStar Inc.?" He'd finished eating and now leaned back, wiping his hands on a paper napkin.

"I don't know where Ax is or where he went last night or if NorthStar has anything to do with his disappearance. And I have no clue why this guy wants Axton."

He propped his elbow on the table and looked at me like he could see right through me. Uncomfortable with that level of scrutiny, I shifted in my seat.

"Do you want me to look into this company for you?"

"I told you, I can't afford you."

His light blue gaze never left my face. "You've already paid me with a Moo burger," he said with a smile. "I haven't had a Moo in years."

The way he said Moo sounded naughty. I stared at a cartoon picture of a cow on the wall next to us. "Sure, that would be great." I glanced back at him. "Why are you doing this for me?"

"It's the least I can do." He gathered up the trash and put it on the tray.

"No, the least you could do is nothing." Why would some guy I barely remember go out of his way for me? And no, I wasn't always this suspicious, but the last couple of days made me wary.

"Fine. I may have had a very small crush on you back in the day. It was probably all that time I spent staring at your head."

"You were always telling me to shut up."

"You were noisy," he said. "And it got you to turn around and look at me."

I laughed. "That's diabolical." I grabbed my purse, pulled out a pen and a piece of paper then wrote down my home and cell numbers. "Here."

A half smile teased his lips. "See, I got your number."

"Yeah, and I've got yours." I scooted out of the booth, dragging my purse behind me.

Dane did the same, except without the purse, and slipped on his suit jacket. He pulled a white business card and a gold pen from his pocket and wrote something on the back of it. "Here are my numbers—business, home, cell. If you need any help or get into trouble, give me a call."

I shoved his card in my pocket as we left The Burger Barn, then crossed the street at the light. A large black SUV with tinted windows slowed to a stop across the road. I remembered seeing one just like it outside the diner the day Axton disappeared.

Black SUVs weren't a rarity. I saw them all the time. But ever since Axton gave me his backpack, I'd been paranoid about everything. I blinked as the car drove off and thanked Dane for his help.

As I watched him walk away, the wind tugged at the edges of his suit jacket and lifted his tie, which he caught and held down with one hand. Tilting my head, I admired the view. He sure hadn't been this cute in grade school.

Standing in the middle of the street, Dane turned around. "Hey, be careful. You don't know what kind of trouble Axton's in and I don't want you to wind up missing, too."

Chapter 6

My phone was beeping when I got back to my apartment. I dropped my purse and yanked the phone from its charger, hoping it was a message from Axton. It wasn't. It was from my ex-boyfriend, Kevin.

Punching the delete button, I put Kevin from my mind and tried to work up the courage for what I had to do next. I reminded myself I was doing this for Axton.

I took a deep breath and dialed the number.

"Hey, Mom," I said when she answered.

"Rosalyn? What's wrong?"

"Nothing. Why?"

"Something truly catastrophic must have happened. Why else would you be calling?"

I went on cheerfully as if she hadn't said anything at all. I found this was the best way to deal with her—really the only way that didn't involve heavy meds or jail time. "Do you happen to have Packard Graystone's phone number? You know, Axton's brother?"

She clicked her teeth. "Yes, Rosalyn, I know who Dr. Graystone is. Why on earth would you need his phone number?"

I rolled my eyes and held back a sigh. Nothing was ever easy. "Axton's gone missing and I was wondering if Packard had heard from him. I just want to be sure Ax is all right. Oh, and I need his mom's number, too."

"I don't know if I feel comfortable with this, Rosalyn. You might worry them unnecessarily. He's probably out *getting high*." She whispered the last two words.

"Fine, Mom, just forget it."

"All right, Rosalyn, calm down. There's no need to get upset."

"Do you have their numbers or not?"

"I don't know. It may take some work to get them."

She waited two beats for me to tell her how grateful I was. I left her waiting.

"Be here for dinner tomorrow, eight sharp. I may have them by then." And she hung up on me.

Well played, Mom. Well played.

The campus of Huntingford City College covered three acres of land. There were a total of six trees, the leaves of which had started turning red and gold at the tips, and one gently rolling hill amidst its four squat buildings.

I won't bore you with the specifics of my ethics test. I was bored enough for all of us. As soon as class let out and I cleared the door, I called Axton's home number. The minutes on my phone were racking up and my bank account was not going to be happy.

"Speak," Joe answered, followed by a wheezy laugh.

"Joe, it's Rose. Have you—"

"Rosalita. Hey man, didn't I see you the other day?"

"No, Joe, it was this afternoon. Have you heard from

Axton? Or the man in the suit? Did he come back?"

"Negative, Rosary." He wheeze-laughed again and hung up.

The wind picked up to a gust and the temperature dipped as I walked past the lighted parking lot toward my car, which was parked on the street. I had just thrust my hands into my jacket pockets when a hand grabbed my arm and jerked me backward. I yelped and struggled to pull away. Fear flooded my system. The yelp became a scream. I spun around, finally yanking my arm out of my assailant's grip.

Two good Samaritans hollered from across the lot, a thin African-American guy with a backpack in one hand, a cell phone in the other, and a woman in her forties wearing a baggy sweater over a broomstick skirt. They sprinted toward me, but my attacker didn't flee. He just stood there, his hands raised in surrender.

"Are you okay, hon?" The woman's gaze shifted between me and my assailant.

"This man came out of nowhere and grabbed me." I got a good look at him for the first time. A little over six feet with attractive bland features and clunky black glasses. He wore a white button-down and khakis.

"I'm sorry," he said, "I didn't mean to scare you, but you're Axton's friend, right?"

I glared at him. "I don't know you."

"We've never met. I just started working with Axton in the IT department. I've seen a picture of you on his desk. I'm Steve, by the way. Steve Gunderson." He held out his hand. I didn't shake it.

I stood on the sidewalk, my heart still pounding, my body still shaking from the sudden rush of adrenaline. "What the hell were you thinking? You don't accost people in a dark parking lot. Especially women you don't know."

The guy with the cell phone finally spoke. "Are we good here or what?"

I took a deep breath. "Yeah, I think there was a misunderstanding."

"I'm so sorry," Steve said to me. He turned to the man and woman who'd come to my rescue. "Sorry. I shouldn't have touched her like that. I just wasn't thinking."

The woman jabbed her finger at him. "You don't grab women, period. It's not cool."

Steve nodded. "You're right. Will never happen again, I swear."

"Thank you both," I said.

The man mumbled something as he walked off and the woman gave Steve one last dirty look before leaving.

I turned to him. "You scared the crap out of me."

"I'm sorry. I just don't know your name."

I was still irritated, but told him anyway. "It's Rose."

He wrapped both hands around the strap of his messenger bag. "I'd been working late and was ready to go home when I saw you. What's the deal with Ax? Eric's pissed that he didn't come in today. We had a real problem with the servers being down and had to reroute through a proxy server which filtered stuff out."

"I'm sorry?" I had no idea what he was talking about. My lack of understanding—and interest—must have shown on my face.

"I'm boring you, aren't I? Yeah, my girlfriend never wanted to hear shop talk, either. Well, my ex-girlfriend, really. We just broke up."

"Oh, sorry," I said after an awkward pause.

"Thanks." He stared at me for a moment. "You know, you don't really seem like Axton's type." I think he realized he might have insulted me, or Axton, or the both of us, so he tried to backtrack. "What I mean is—"

I held up my hand to stop him. "I'm not Axton's girl-friend."

"Oh, I thought…I mean he has a picture of the two of you on his desk, so I just assumed…"

"Axton's my friend." I felt a mixture of sadness and guilt as I said it. I hadn't pressed him about the backpack. I should have insisted he tell me the details about the club. I knew he'd been acting unAxton-like in the diner, but I'd let it slide.

A blast of wind whipped my hair skyward. "Wow, it's getting cold out here." I rubbed my hands along my arms.

"I'm sorry, you're right. Can I walk you to your car?"

"Yeah, thanks." We walked toward the street in front of the campus. "Hey, Axton went to a club the other night. Do you know anything about that?"

"No."

"Did you notice him acting weird yesterday? Nervous?"

"No."

I went through my spiel—backpack, mystery man, yada yada. Maybe I should record this little speech because repeating it was getting old.

"I can't get into his computer," I said. "Do you think you could?"

"Yeah, probably." He ran a hand through his hair. "But are you sure he didn't just leave for a few days?"

While Ax had taken off a time or two in the past, he'd always called to let me know where he was and when he was coming home, and he'd always taken his backpack. "I'm sure. Do you want to meet up tomorrow and take a crack at Axton's computer?"

"Like for dinner, or something?" He smiled. "I know this Italian place, they make an authentic osso buco—"

"How about I bring it by after I get off work?"

Steve's smile lost a few watts. "Sure. You know where the IT office is, right?"

"Basement of Blake Hall. I'll see you tomorrow."

As I drove home, I kept checking my rearview mirror to make sure no one followed me. Yep, definitely becoming paranoid.

Feeling drained and more concerned about Axton by the minute, I slogged up the stairs to my apartment, sifting the keys in my hand to find the right one. But before I could slide it into the lock, a mountain of a man opened my front door. He loomed above me, his dark hair slicked back from his face. His crooked nose had been broken in at least three places and a long jagged scar ran close to his left eye.

He said nothing, but a deep voice from inside my apartment said, "Come in, Rosalyn."

Chapter 7

It was *the* voice. The one belonging to the mystery man from the woods.

I gulped and stood there, too scared to move forward, too shocked to turn around and run. The man at the door snatched my arm and pulled me into the apartment, slamming the door behind me. He plucked the keys from my hand and tossed them on the bistro table.

I sidled to the left, with my back against the wall. I kept him in my peripheral view while I studied the man standing in the middle of my apartment. He was the exact opposite of Scarface. His blue-black hair was combed away from his perfect face. His gold eyes—not golden-brown, just gold—glittered in the faint glow of my yard sale flamingo lamp. With light honeyed skin stretched over strong cheekbones, he was beautiful—like fallen angel beautiful. He wore a dark suit and overcoat. He scared me a lot more than the other guy. It was obvious he was in charge and Scarface was just there for back up.

I didn't know what he wanted or if he planned on hurting me, but I made up my mind then and there that I wouldn't go down without a fight. And I wouldn't let him see how afraid I was either. But between you and me, I think

I wet my pants just a little.

"Hello, Rosalyn. Oh wait, you like to be called Rose. Please, have a seat." He gestured to the futon.

"Thanks, but I think I'll stand, you know, since it's my apartment and all."

I felt a massive paw on my shoulder. "Sit," Scarface said. His voice sounded like crunching gravel.

I twisted out of his grasp and my backpack slid to the floor. I side-stepped away from him, bumping my hip into the closet doorknob. Since I was scared shitless, the pain barely registered.

The boss waved two fingers and shook his head. "Let's be civil, Henry. Why don't you wait in the car?"

As soon as Scarface Henry left, the mystery man began prowling around my apartment. He slid his fingertips across the bistro table and snagged my keys, twirling them around one finger. Then he paused and looked at the red rose keychain Axton had given me as a joke. "Original." He dropped them back on the table.

Crossing my arms to hide my shaking hands, I glared at him. "What do you want?" I kept hold of my bravado, but my knees were knocking so hard I thought I might topple over.

He walked to the kitchenette and looked at the paper hanging on my refrigerator. Scotty had colored a picture of me—my head was ten times the size of my stick body. The mystery man tapped the drawing. "I can see the resemblance." Then he strolled to the cluster of cheap frames arranged on top of my dresser. He picked up the picture of Roxy and me. We had our arms thrown around each other and were making smootchie faces at the camera. He put it down and moved to the next photo. The one of Scotty when he was about ten minutes old. I rushed toward him and tried to grab it, but he held it just out of reach.

"Put it down." I grabbed the soft woolen sleeve of his overcoat and pulled, but he didn't move. I peered up at his face, and he stared back at me. Our gazes locked and held for a moment.

He leaned toward me. He smelled citrusy and spicy at the same time, like oranges and sandalwood. "I want my property." His voice was silky steel.

I let go of his arm and stepped back. "I...," my voice cracked. "I don't know what you're talking about."

"Don't play games, Rose." He set the photo down and walked to the futon, gracefully folding himself onto it, his arm spread along the back. "You'll lose."

"I don't know what you're talking about," I repeated, my voice stronger this time.

He looked at me like he was waiting for something. Eventually, he nodded. "Let's pretend that's true, and for your sake, I hope it is." His gaze flickered from my face to my breasts and back up to my eyes. The whole process took less than a second, but I had the feeling he'd categorized and labeled me in that brief instant.

"Why don't you just ask Axton where the hell your property is?"

He didn't move a muscle, but I noticed a shift in him. His eyes seemed sharper and tension ran through his body.

I hadn't realized until that moment I'd been holding my breath. Air whooshed out of my lungs as relief and hope shot through me. "You don't know where Axton is, do you?"

"Why don't you stick to serving pancakes and focus on your classes. A C-minus in accounting? Tsk, tsk." He shook his head in mock disappointment.

Hearing him casually discuss the details of my life made me almost dizzy. I stood straight and lifted my chin. "You seem to know a lot about me. In the interest of fairness, why don't you tell me about yourself? Like, who the hell are you?"

"I'm not interested in fairness. And your interference could be detrimental to Axton's health."

I took a step toward him, my fists clenched. "If you harm one wiry hair on his head—"

"You'll what, sling hash at me? If I wanted to hurt your friend, you'd never find the body." Then he laughed.

Anger rose up deep inside me, crowding out the fear. This smug asshole broke into my home, threatened Axton, and was sitting on my own damn futon laughing at me. I saw red.

I leapt on him, lashing out with both hands and popped him one in the mouth. All of the frustration, anger, and fear I'd bottled up since Axton's phone call bubbled to the surface. "You'd better not hurt Axton, do you understand me?"

He calmly pinned my hands and held them behind my back, pulling me forward until my breasts smashed against his chest.

I tried to pull away, but he held fast. "Let go of me."

His eyes darkened to an antique gold. "Only if you promise to behave yourself."

I didn't want to behave myself. I wanted to pound my fist into his face a few more times. I leaned my head back, then drove it forward, trying to head butt him in the nose. But he saw it coming and jerked his head to the side at the last second. My forehead grazed his ear.

"That's enough," he said.

I struggled to free myself. With both of my hands restrained in one of his, he thrust his other hand into my hair, firmly holding my head still.

"I said enough."

My breaths came in choppy gasps, my heart beating so fast I thought it might burst. I stopped moving. My body was plastered against his, each shallow breath pushing my breasts even further into his chest with every inhalation. His lips were soft against my cheek, his breath fanned my ear. We stayed like that, pressed against each other, for what seemed like a really long time. It was probably only a minute, but it was intense and awkward.

"Are you okay now?" he asked.

"Yeah." He slowly released me. I scrambled off him and walked backward until I hit the wall. Neither one of us spoke, we just stared at each other. His chest heaved like he'd run a four-minute mile. I was glad to know I wasn't the only one affected by that little exchange. Gradually, my own breathing returned to normal.

When I thought I could talk without panting like a dog, I said, "What's to stop me from calling the cops?"

"That wouldn't be in Axton's best interest." He stood and buttoned his coat as he walked toward me, coming to a stop when his toes bumped mine. "And I'm not a man you want to fuck with."

After he left, I stood there for several seconds before hurrying to the door, locking it and sliding the chain in place.

Tomorrow I was going to get new locks. I doubted it would keep him out if he wanted to get in, but it would make me feel better. I moved my dresser in front of the door and huddled up in the corner of the futon, fully clothed, until the next morning.

Chapter 8

I took the quickest shower of my life just before five a.m. The two men probably wouldn't come back and catch me wet and naked, but why take chances. After throwing on some clothes, I made a full pot of coffee, guzzling down most of it.

It was still halfway dark when I left my apartment and crossed the parking lot. Jumpy and alert, I scanned the area, but didn't see anything out of place. Of course I hadn't seen anything out of place last night either and look how well that turned out. I hopped into my car and slammed the door, making sure it was locked before I started the engine.

There weren't many cars on the road this early, but my eyes darted around the gloomy streets looking for anything suspicious. By the time I got to Ma's I was a shaky mess.

I greeted Ray and Jorge as I walked through the kitchen before making a beeline to the restroom. Ma and Roxy exchanged a glance as I hustled past. When I stepped back into the dining room, I pulled a clean apron from the hook and put it in on.

"Rose, honey, are you all right?" Ma asked.

I gave them a recap of my crappy night. They both made "o's" with their mouths.

"And the thing is, this guy who broke into my apartment didn't say what he's looking for. But I have to find Axton before he does." I realized I was talking so fast my words jumbled together, but I couldn't seem to stop myself. And I flailed my hands like a loon. "Whoever he was, he was scary. Hot, but scary. No, forget hot. Hot has nothing to do with it. Just scary." I finally paused to take a deep breath. "Sorry. I drank almost a whole pot of coffee."

"No, really?" Roxy asked, around a wad of gum. "Why didn't you call me?"

To be honest, it never occurred to me. I was so used to handling things on my own, I never thought of calling anyone for help. Besides, what if the two men were watching my apartment? I didn't want Roxy in their crosshairs, too.

Ma pursed her lips, causing her wrinkles to deepen. "Did you call the police?"

"No, this guy made it seem like a bad idea. But I am going to report Axton missing. I'm just not going to mention anything about this guy. That's the right thing to do, right? But what if it isn't? Oh my God, what am I going to do?"

"Okay, honey," Ma led me to the nearest chair, gently pushing on my shoulder until I sat. "No more coffee for you. Now, do you have any idea who this man was?" She pulled out a chair next to me and plonked her bony butt on the edge of it. She put her hand over my knee, which was bouncing like a jackhammer.

"I don't know. I don't know who he is or what he does, or how he knew everything about me. I have to find Ax." I reached out and grabbed Ma's hand. "And I haven't heard from him since Monday night. I've racked my brain, but I don't know where he could be."

"It's going to be all right, Rose. Axton's probably just hiding out somewhere."

I shook my head. "Where? I know where Axton goes and what he does. What if he's…" I couldn't even bring myself to say it, but it had been circling my brain since last night. What if Axton was lying out there, hurt and unable to get to a phone? What if he was dead?

"No, Rose," Ma said forcefully, squeezing my fingers. "He's just fine, do you hear me? He's fine. You have to believe that."

"Okay." I wanted to believe it.

Ma glanced out the window at the line of people standing outside the door. "Why don't you go home today, honey?"

"I'm too wired. I need to work. I need the money. And I can't go back there until I get a new lock."

Roxy, uncharacteristically quiet, bit her lip. She looked worried. And if Roxy looked worried, that was saying something.

I cleared my throat, got up from the table, and put a smile on my face. "You know what? It's going to be fine." Neither Ma nor Roxy appeared convinced. "Really. Just fine. I'm going to find Axton. End of story. See? I have a plan." I had no idea what that plan would entail, but those were just details. I moved to the door and flipped the open sign.

I don't think in the five years since I'd worked at Ma's I had ever been quite so speedy. I felt like I was on fast forward. I forced myself to be cheerful to customers as I whirled around filling coffee, taking orders, helping Roxy and Ma get their food out. My tips had never been so good. But it didn't last. Before noon, my caffeinated high crashed and left me cranky. When a customer sent back his omelet for the second time, I nearly burst into tears.

Ma stood next to me at the kitchen pass through with a carafe of coffee in her hand. "Roxy and I will finish here. She said you can go to her place and get some sleep. Ray will come by your apartment later and put on a new lock."

"Bu—"

"I'm not asking you, Rose, I'm telling you. You look like shit warmed over, toots."

"Gee, thanks."

"Just telling it like I see it. Now get out of here. I'll take that jackass his omelet."

"Okay."

Roxy came up behind me, took my elbow, and ushered me into the kitchen where she took her apartment key off her key ring. "Take a shower and try to get some sleep. You can change, too, if you want. Sweats and stuff are in the third drawer of my dresser."

I got a little teary. "You're a good friend, Rox."

She rolled her eyes. "Jeez Louise, you are one hot mess today." She spun on her heel and left the kitchen.

I went to the pantry and pulled the syrup box off the shelf. I dug out Ax's backpack and stuck his laptop and the shiny computer doodad in my own backpack. I still needed to take it to the IT office for Steve to look at. Then I put everything back and walked out to the kitchen.

Jorge stopped me before I left. "Are you all right, chica? Do you need to come stay with me and Marisol? You'll have to sleep on the floor in the baby's room. Marisol's brother is sleeping on the sofa until his wife takes him back."

"Thanks Jorge, but I'll be okay."

He hugged me with one arm decorated with colorful sleeve tattoos. "Let me know if you change your mind."

Now I really was about to cry. I took off my apron, grabbed my jacket and said goodbye as quickly as I could before I broke down completely.

I let myself into Roxy's apartment—well, you could call it an apartment if you were being generous. I had a studio with an economy kitchen. Roxy's place was a room with a hotplate. A rack with wheels held most her clothes. A sewing machine was set up along one wall and a *Sailor Moon* poster hung on the door.

Her bathroom was the size of a small closet with light pink tile that had been popular sometime during the Eisenhower administration. But it was clean and organized and the shower felt good.

I put my bra and panties back on, and from Roxy's dresser I chose a Hello Kitty t-shirt and a pair of worn sweatpants that were a little short on me.

I sat crossed-legged on the bed and pulled my hair into a ponytail and wondered what I should do next. Quitting at this point was not even an option. I had to find Axton before The Bossy Jackass did—or BJ as I was starting to think of him. Axton had something that belonged to him. It had to be related to that club Axton went to. And it had to be in the backpack Axton gave me. The computer stuff was the only option, unless BJ was jonesing for a used copy of *The Hobbit*.

Exhausted and out of ideas, I sighed and crawled under the blanket and decided to rest for an hour.

I must have slept harder than I thought because when I awoke, Roxy was sitting on the other side of the bed reading a paperback book with a Japanese anime drawing on the cover.

"Hey," I said around a yawn. "What time is it?"

"After four. Ray got your new lock put on and left the keys with your landlord." She flipped a page. "You make a funny noise when you sleep."

"Like what? Do you mean snoring?"

"More like a soft humpf, humpf. You do it over and over and then you stop for a while."

"Are you serious?" I scanned her face to see if she was teasing me. She was not. "So I'm a humpfer. That's what I am I guess." No one had ever told me that I made noises when I sleep. "Was it annoying?"

"I got used to it after a while. So, what's the next step in getting Axton back?"

"I need to take Axton's computer to Steve."

"Who?"

"Right, I forgot to tell you about him." I filled her in on Mr. Grabby. "Then I'm going to have dinner at my parent's house so my mother can harass me and hopefully give me Packard Graystone's phone number. I doubt Axton told his brother anything, but it wouldn't hurt to make sure."

"Sounds like a plan."

"Not a great one."

We sat in silence a few moments. The only sound in the apartment was Roxy slowly and quietly—at least for her— chewing her nicotine gum. The stillness finally broke when my stomach growled.

"I'm going to go see Steve." I stood up, folded my

jeans, and slipped on my jacket, promising Roxy I would wash her clothes and bring them back. I left feeling much better than I had that morning. The coffee was out of my system, I'd slept for over three hours, and my apartment had a new lock, thanks to Ray.

On my way to the campus, I picked up sub sandwiches for Steve and me. It was the least I could do, since he was helping me with Ax's computer. Plus, I was starving.

The college was fairly quiet. Most of the day students were gone and the night classes didn't start for at least two hours. I snagged a great spot in the parking lot for a change.

The basement of Blake Hall was dimly lit with gray concrete floors and ugly green subway-tiled walls. Wedged between the men's room and the supply closet, the tiny IT office was crowded with multiple desks, numerous computers, and two guys.

Both men looked up at me when I opened the door, a sandwich sack in my hand and my backpack over my shoulder. Steve sat in the back corner and Eric, whom I had met before, sat in the middle of the room. The empty desk at the back wall was Axton's. A wave of anxiety rolled over me when I saw it. Ax should be sitting there, fiddling with… Well, whatever computer stuff he fiddled with. I missed him.

I smiled. "Hello."

Steve jumped out of his chair. "Hey, I thought you'd forgotten."

"Sorry, I'm just running late."

"Rose, this is Eric."

"Yeah, I know. Eric and I sang a karaoke duet at last year's Christmas party." *Islands in the Stream*. It wasn't pretty.

"Where the hell is Axton?" Eric asked. "We were in

deep shit yesterday with that server." In his late thirties, Eric's spare tire was little bigger than the last time I'd seen him and his hair was definitely thinner.

I raised my eyebrows at Steve. "Didn't you tell him?"

"I kind of forgot."

I turned back to Eric. "Axton's missing. He gave me his computer for safekeeping, but I can't get into it without a password." I tilted my head sideways in Steve's direction. "Steve said he'd try to get into Axton's computer and see if there's anything that'll help me find him."

"Missing?" Eric ran his hand over his stubble-covered cheek and frowned. "Are you sure he didn't just leave for a few days? He's done that before, you know."

"Only for important stuff like Comic-Con or a Trekkie convention," I said. "I always knew where he was. Besides, he wouldn't leave behind his car or his backpack."

Eric's frown deepened. "Have you called the police?"

"Yeah, but they won't let me file a report until he's been missing forty-eight hours."

"Are you sure he's not on a bender?" Eric asked.

"He is not on a bender." Why wouldn't he believe me? Axton wasn't off on an adventure or out getting stoned, the guy was missing. "There's a strange man looking for him, says Axton has something that belongs to him. Do you know what Ax was up to? Do you know anything about a club he went to a couple of nights ago?"

"He didn't mention it." Eric reached his hands out to me. "Let's get a look at that computer."

I shrugged at Steve. He frowned and shrugged back.

First I handed the backpack to Eric, then I handed the food to Steve. "I brought you a sandwich as a thank you."

Steve adjusted his glasses. "That was really thoughtful of you. Thanks."

Eric dug Axton's computer out of the bag and booted it up. "Where did this internal hard drive come from?" He held up the shiny rectangle.

"I don't know. I wasn't even sure what it was. There's another sandwich in the sack, Eric. You can have it."

He grabbed a sandwich out of the bag, unwrapped it, and peeked beneath the bread. "Bring ham next time."

I rolled my eyes. "You're welcome. How long do you think it will take?"

"Don't know. May take a few minutes or I may have to run a program. Maybe longer if the hard drive is encrypted." He finally glanced up at me. "You want to come back tomorrow?"

I grabbed my backpack from Eric's desk. "Yeah, thanks. I'll probably be here around two-thirty. By the way, if you find anything about NorthStar Inc., pay special attention to that, would you?" I stuck my hand in my purse and brought out all the burned CDs I'd taken from Axton's desk. "You might look at these, too."

"Okay. And Rose? You better find Axton soon or he won't have a job to come back to."

Chapter 9

When I got home I was disappointed there were no messages from Axton or Dane. There was, however, one from Jacks telling me she was excited I was coming to dinner. That made one of us. And yet another message from Kevin, which I deleted.

Girding myself for dinner with my parents, I straightened my hair, put on some makeup, and donned a pair of black slacks and nice flats. I took one last look in the mirror and made a face.

My parents lived in a subdivision called The Greens, which skirted a golf course—of course. In an effort to downsize, they bought this home a few years back. My childhood home boasted a two acre plot with easy access to horse trails, which we never made use of because we had no horses. My mother was allergic. This newer, smaller house had four bedrooms, five baths, a media room, a state of the art kitchen, and a game room. But it was less of a home, more of a showplace. A sterile, gorgeous showplace.

I parked on the street in front of the house—I didn't want to hear about my car leaving oil stains—and walked to the front door. My sister's SUV was already in the driveway. I glanced at my watch. Two minutes early. I admit I felt a little smug when I rang the bell.

Barbara, my mother, answered the door with a glass of wine in her hand. Her champagne blond hair perfectly coiffed, her slacks and blouse fashionably chic. "Hello, Rosalyn. You're late." She turned and walked toward the living room, leaving me on the front porch.

I found my family gathered in the ivory and beige living room. Standing by the empty fireplace with a drink in one hand, my father talked hospital politics, gesturing with his glass. My brother-in-law, Allen nodded, a look of concentration of his face. Their plaid shirts, khaki pants and sweater vests were almost identical. Allen, with his sandy blond hair and handsome features reminded me of a younger version of my dad. What that said about Jacks, I didn't want question too closely.

Jacqueline sat on an ivory chair with a glass of white wine in her hand. Although she was six years older than me, she didn't look it. She wore her expensive blonde hair several inches shorter than mine and kept herself trimmed and toned by working out at the country club gym. I, on the other hand, kept my girlish figure by not being able to afford a lot of groceries and got my hair cut at Huntingford Beauty Academy.

When she saw me, Jacks set her glass down on the marble-top coffee table and hopped up to give me a hug. "Hey, you," she said, embracing me. "I haven't heard from you since Monday."

I hugged her back.

Barbara, her head tipped to one side, gestured with her wine glass. "Don't feel bad, Jacqueline, I never hear from her."

"I called you yesterday, Mom."

Her lips thinned. "Only because you wanted something fr—"

"Rosalyn." My dad set his glass on the mantle as he walked toward me. He leaned down and kissed my cheek. "Your mother said something about Axton Graystone?"

Barbara put a hand to her temple. "We can discuss that unpleasant subject later."

My dad nodded. "Would you like something to drink?"

"Yes, please." I was going to need it to get through the evening.

"No," my mother said, "she's late. There's no time for drinks." With that, she walked to the kitchen. "Get Scotty to the table, Jacqueline," she said over her shoulder.

Jacks raised one brow. I sighed and shook my head. The maternal unit was in fine form tonight.

"I'll get Scotty, hon," said Allen. "Good to see you, Rose." He smiled and headed to the game room.

My father drained his glass. "I'll go help your mother."

Left alone with Jacks, I grinned. "I ran into one of my old classmates yesterday."

We walked slowly toward the dining room. "Oh really?" She linked her arm in mine. "Who?"

"Dane Harker."

"I've seen him around the club. He's a hottie."

"I didn't remember him at first. But the dimples—"

"Oh, those dimples." She gave a little sigh.

"Apparently he had a crush on me in sixth grade."

"Where did you meet him and is he still pining away?"

"The police station and nope, I'm pretty sure he got over his crush a long time ago."

"Just think about how romantic it would be if you married your childhood sweetheart."

"We weren't sweethearts and nobody's said anything about marriage."

"You never know." She turned to me and frowned. "Were you at the police station because of Axton?"

"Yeah, I'll give you the details later." And I would have to give her the abbreviated version, because there was no way I'd tell Jacks about seeing BJ in the park. I didn't want her to worry about leaving Scotty in my care. He would always be safe with me—I'd take a bullet for that kid.

"Tell me now."

Barbara popped her head out of the kitchen. "Rosalyn, are you going to sit down? Or should we continue to wait on you?"

Grinding my teeth, I sat next to Scotty.

"Look, Aunt Rose," he said with a wide grin. There was a hole where his front tooth should have been.

I ruffled his hair. "Hey, Sport, where'd it go?"

"I lost it," he said. "And I got five whole dollars when the tooth fairy took it. So I'm trying to make this one come out too." He wiggled another tooth.

"Well, good luck with that." I unfolded my beige linen napkin and placed it on my lap.

My mom and dad brought platters of food from the kitchen and took their seats at the table. On the menu: salmon. I hated salmon. My mother knew I hated salmon. She was definitely bringing her A-game.

Everyone settled in and began passing the food. I piled my plate with rice and grilled vegetables, but passed the salmon off to my dad.

Barbara noticed and attempted to raise an eyebrow. Since she had regular Botox injections, she was not entirely successful. "Is there something wrong, Rosalyn?" She delicately wiped the corner of her mouth.

I blinked and tried to look serene. "No, I don't think so." I took a small bite of rice.

"Was there something wrong with the salmon, dear? I noticed you didn't have any. You're not turning into a vegan, are you?"

"No, of course not, mother."

She pursed her lips. "Then why won't you try the salmon?"

"Barbara," my father cut in, "if she doesn't want salmon..." he trailed off with a shrug.

Taking a deep breath through her nose, she sucked in her cheeks. "But the salmon is delicious."

"Mmm. It is delicious, Barb," Allen said. *Suck up.*

"And the wine is great. What is this wine, Dad?" Jacks asked.

"It's—"

"Salmon is good for the heart. Isn't that right, darling?" she asked my father. Well, since he was a podiatrist, he should know.

"Yes, dear, it is," he said, before lapsing into silence.

"Did you hear that, Rosalyn?"

"Yes, I heard. Salmon—it's all the rage with the kids these days."

Barbara set her fork on the side of her plate. "Why must you be so contrary?"

"She hates salmon. She said that the last time she was here, Grandma," Scotty said. "And I don't like it either."

I bit my lip to smother a grin.

My mother picked up her fork and continued to eat. She didn't say another word.

I winked at Scotty. He smiled back. Darn, that kid was cute.

"So," Jacks said with a little too much enthusiasm. "How's school, Rose? You're taking ethics now, right?"

I opened my mouth to answer, but wasn't quick enough.

"Are you concerned about the ethics of serving your customers heart attacks along with their biscuits and gravy?" my mother asked. Each word was a bullet shot through a tight smile. "So useful, these little classes."

Wow, Jacks was really crappy at defusing. I pierced a carrot. "You're right as usual, Mom."

No one said much after that, and only the clinking of silverware broke the uncomfortable silence. The tension was almost painful.

Eventually the torture came to an end. My mother, Jacks, and I cleared the table while Scotty went back to his video game. Allen and my dad retired to the media room to watch TV.

"Rosalyn?"

"Yes, Mom?" I grinned, baring my teeth.

She held a glass in one hand and a dirty plate in the other. "Why don't you go relax? After all, you clean tables for a living. I'm sure you don't want to do it on your off hours, too."

"Don't be silly. Since I'm a pro, it will go that much quicker if I help."

Jacks' nervous gaze shifted between my mom and me.

"Why don't you both go relax? I can do it." She hurried into the kitchen.

As we cleaned up, my mother chatted with Jacks, freezing me out entirely. She considered this a punishment. I considered it a reprieve.

After we filled the dishwasher, Jacks left the kitchen with the sorry excuse she needed to check on Scotty while my mother and I stood in silence.

"Did you get the phone numbers for Mary and Packard?" I finally asked.

She raised her chin in the air and stared at me with her lips pursed before walking to the small desk attached to the countertop. She pulled a piece of paper from the top drawer. "I want you to know that I'm doing this against my better judgment. You can't hound these people."

"Darn, hounding and grain alcohol are all I have going for me." I took the paper. It had Mary's new married name, her address and phone number, as well as Packard's number and address.

She acted as if I hadn't spoken. "Packard is very busy. He's on the city council, you know."

"So?"

"There's talk of him running for mayor."

"And?"

She closed her eyes for a second and sighed. "Axton is nothing but trouble, and why you continue to be friends with him is beyond me. He ruined my birthday party with his drugs."

Ah, the infamous country club fire alarm incident where Ax toked up in the bathroom. "That was four years ago. Seriously, when are you going to let it go?" My guess was never.

"Furthermore, Packard doesn't need some drugged up relative causing him problems."

My turn to ignore. "Thanks, Mom," I said, waving the paper. I almost made it to the stairs when her voice stopped me.

"Why can't you just for once do what is expected of you?"

I turned to face her. "What exactly is expected of me in this situation, Mom?"

"He's probably somewhere getting high. Just stay out of it. It doesn't concern you. You'd be better off trying to get a good job and make some decent friends."

I clenched my teeth and took a deep breath. "Axton is decent. He's the sweetest, kindest, most generous person I know, and he's in trouble." I stepped forward and lowered my voice. "And I like my job, thank you. Just because you were too good—"

She made a slashing motion with one hand. "As far as I can see, you've had a pretty good life. We gave you the best of everything so you could make something of yourself, but you're throwing it away with both hands."

I rubbed my eyes. We'd had this conversation a million times. We could have it again tonight, but it wouldn't change anything.

I turned and left the kitchen, made hasty farewells to my dad and Allen, gave Scotty a kiss on the head, and promised my sister I'd call later in the week.

My mother stood on the front step, her arms crossed, and watched me drive away. I felt unsettled, sad and angry at the same time.

But in a way, she was right. Although I'd rather stick a shrimp fork in my eye than admit it to her. Lately, I felt like life was passing me by. I'd been coasting.

I diddled my time away, taking classes like Film Appreciation and Sex Throughout History for the past five years without any direction whatsoever. I couldn't decide what to do with my life, and it scared me I might never figure it out.

I blew out a breath. What I needed was action, not introspection. I wasn't going to find Axton by driving around feeling sorry for myself.

I pulled into a Quickie Mart and asked for directions.

Packard Graystone lived on the outskirts of Huntingford in a development so new half the houses were under construction. Silhouettes of backhoes and earthmovers, their jagged claws hovering in the air, bordered the neighborhood. I got lost driving down partially finished streets that led to nowhere. Kind of like my life.

The luxury homes all looked the same in the dark. Cookie cutter housing for the professional set. I finally found Packard's house—two chimneys, two bay windows, and a four car garage—in the middle of a cul-de-sac. A white SUV sat in the driveway and most of the lights were shining from inside the house.

I grabbed my purse and keys, marched up to the front door, and knocked. Axton's niece or nephew—I couldn't tell which because it had one of those floppy haircuts and long eyelashes—answered.

"We don't want any," he/she said and started to close the door.

I wedged my foot in the gap. "Get your dad, kid." Ax never talked about his brother or this kid. Axton was on the outs with this family, even more so than I was with mine. But it was going to drive me batty. Was this kid a boy or girl?

The child looked at me, then my foot, and proceeded to yell at the top of its lungs, "Dad!"

Packard walked toward the door, wiping his hands on a green and white plaid dishcloth. He resembled Axton, but where Axton was small and scrawny, Packard was taller, beefier, and almost fifteen years older. The wiry blond hair was obviously a family trait, but Packard wore his short and full of hair product.

"May I help you?"

"Hi. I'm Rose Strickland." I waited, but there was no look of recognition on his face. "I'm a friend of Axton's."

"Jordan," he said to the kid, "go finish your homework."

Darn, I still didn't know if that kid was a boy or a girl. Jordan could be used for both, right?

When the kid zoomed out of sight, Packard narrowed his cold blue eyes. "Listen," he pointed a finger at me. "I don't know who you are or why you're here, but that little shit has nothing to do with me."

Chapter 10

My mouth hung open a second before I snapped it shut. "When you say 'little shit' are you referring to Ax?"

"That's right."

His brotherly concern was underwhelming. "Axton is missing. Like really missing. I'm filing a police report tonight because it's been forty-eight hours. He's in trouble, Packard."

He threw the dish towel over his shoulder and rubbed his forehead. "Is it a drug thing?"

"No, and he's not really into anything but pot."

"Hey," he said, "pot is a drug. It's an illegal substance."

I rolled my eyes and sighed. Packard was working my last nerve. "Yeah, yeah, I know, but this isn't a drug thing." I peered over Packard's shoulder as a tiny woman walked up behind him.

"Pack, what's going on? Who is this?" she gestured in my direction. Her brows drew together over light brown eyes.

"She says she's a friend of Axton's."

I smiled and held out my hand. "Hello, my name is Rose."

She stared at my hand a moment before shaking it. "Hello, Rose. Where's Axton? Is he with you?"

"She—" Packard started.

"He's missing," I said, "and I'm very worried about him."

"Would you like some coffee?"

"Sheila, I don't want to get involved in this."

She gently shoved him aside and opened the door wider. "You are involved, Pack. He's your brother."

I stepped into the house.

"Thanks," I said, leaving Packard standing by the door. The faint scent of dinner lingered, leaving a garlicky smell behind. Whatever they had, it was better than salmon.

The foyer walls were decorated in soft earth tones and rose into cove ceilings. The wrought iron banister on my right twisted toward the second story.

"As you heard, I'm Sheila." She walked further into the house. "This way."

I followed her to the homey kitchen. Copper pans hung on a rack above the island range. Hot pads and a newspaper lay on the granite counter.

Sheila grabbed a mug from the cabinet next to the sink and poured me a cup of coffee. "Cream or sugar?"

"Yes to both, please." I heard Packard walk in behind me.

"You'd better sit down," he said.

It was a half-assed invitation, but I took it and hopped up on one of the stools at the island. Sheila passed me the mug and I took a sip. "I take it you haven't heard from Axton?"

Packard grabbed a stool next to me and Shelia leaned against the sink. There was a long pause. "Actually, he did call me a couple of nights ago," he said.

"Monday night?"

"Yeah." He waved his hand dismissively.

My stomach fluttered. "Is he all right? What did he say? Where is he?"

Packard held up a finger. "First of all, I could hardly hear him. And second, he never said where he was."

"Did he call from his cell?"

"I don't know. I guess." He shrugged a beefy shoulder.

"You didn't tell me Axton called," Sheila said. "What exactly is going on here, Pack?"

"I didn't tell you because this isn't our concern, Sheila."

"What did he say?" I wanted to beat this guy like a piñata until he spilled all the information he knew.

"He said he needed help. I assumed it was financial and told him no. Either that or he was arrested again. Then we were disconnected. I assumed he hung up."

"You do a lot of assuming, Packard," I said. "Are you sure you didn't hear anything else? Background noises, other voices?"

"God," he snapped, "I already told you no. I didn't hear anything else. It was a ten second phone call."

Sheila crossed her arms. "Again, what is going on?"

I gave them the scoop on Axton's vanishing act and ended with BJ and Henry breaking into my apartment. When I finished, both Packard and Sheila were silent.

I sipped my coffee and waited.

"He gave you his backpack, but you don't know why?" Sheila asked.

"The only thing I can figure is there's something on the computer or the internal hard drive. His boss, Eric, is working on it."

"And this man who broke into your apartment, he wanted Axton? Did he say why?" Sheila asked.

I thought back to Gold Eyes prowling around my apartment, touching my stuff, making threats. "No, but I need to find Axton before he does."

"He's probably a dealer. Axton's been arrested twice, for God's sake," Packard said.

"Oh come on, Pack," Sheila huffed out a breath, "he was caught with a joint. It's not like you've never done it."

"Hey," he pointed a finger at her, "I haven't made a lifestyle of it." He was big with the finger pointing.

And okay yes, Ax had been arrested at routine traffic stops last year. Got popped once because of a joint and once with a dime bag.

Since Sheila was the only one who seemed to give a crap, I directed my comment to her. "This isn't about drugs and Ax always tells me if he's going somewhere—even if it's for a couple of days. I really just came by to see if you'd heard from him." I turned back to Packard. "That's all he said? You're not leaving anything out?"

He sighed. "No. Axton and I aren't exactly close. If there was something wrong, I'd be the last person he'd tell."

"And yet, he called you." I set down my mug, picked up my purse, and dug around for a pen and paper. "Thanks for the coffee. If you hear from him again, here's my home number and my cell."

"Is there anything we can do to help?" Sheila asked.

"If I think of anything, I'll call you. I thought I'd give your mom a call, too. See if she's heard from Ax."

"Absolutely not. She's an elderly woman and I won't

have you dragging her into this."

Sheila sighed. "She's in the middle of the Mediterranean anyway. Month long cruise."

Must be nice. "Then I'm off to file a missing person report."

Packard swiveled toward me and shoved a finger in my face. "Wait a minute, you can't go to the police with this."

I wanted to grab his finger and twist it, but I batted it away with the back of my hand instead. "I told you, it's been forty-eight hours."

"This can't get out. The press will be all over it." I remembered my mother said Packard was thinking of running for mayor. Well, guess who wasn't getting my vote? I was beginning to understand why Axton didn't talk to his brother. Packard was an ass.

"Oh my gosh, Pack, I can't believe you," Sheila said. "You've gone insane, you know that?"

"I have a certain reputation in this town—"

"Maybe so, but he's your brother," Sheila said.

The two continued to argue as I ducked out of the kitchen, down the hall, through the front door and back onto the brick stoop. I wondered if they even noticed I left.

My last stop for the night, despite the fact it was after ten o'clock, was the police station. I didn't care about Packard or his self-aggrandizing reputation, I just needed help looking for Axton.

Unfortunately, I left the police station feeling helpless and dejected. It had been a complete waste of time. I told my story to some bored desk cop who typed it into his computer. I was starting to get the impression the police weren't that concerned about a missing stoner. But this wasn't just any stoner we were talking about. This was my missing stoner. Axton. My bud, my rock, my expert on dorky sci-fi movies from the fifties. I missed eating off-brand pizza rolls with him, missed listening to him lecture about the graphics of game design. I missed him translating English words into Klingon. *Sa'Hut* was his fave. That's buttocks to you and me. I just missed him, period.

As I drove home, I was hyperaware of other cars on the road—making sure no one followed me. And when I reached my parking lot, it took ten minutes to work up the nerve to run from my car to the building. I didn't like this feeling, as if someone was watching me, waiting for me. It was exhausting.

The next morning at the diner, Ma was in bossy mode. "No, Jorge, you need more sugar in the glaze."

Jorge smiled. "Okay, Ma."

Ma nodded in satisfaction and moved over by the grill to stand next to Ray. "Are you using too much butter, son?"

Ray grunted.

I pulled an apron around my waist and tied it. Although no unwelcome visitors showed up last night, I still hadn't gotten much sleep. I tossed and turned and jumped at every little noise while my brain spun in circles over Axton. I was tired and cranky, but I slapped a smile on my face. "Good morning, everyone."

Jorge waved, Ray mumbled something, and Ma walked over and hugged me. "How you doing this morning, toots?"

"Not so well. I still haven't heard from Ax, I made a police report last night, and Axton's brother is an a-hole."

"I have a feeling things will turn out all right." She squeezed my shoulder. I wished I shared her optimism.

Roxy walked through the back door and snarled. She chomped on a wad of gum and I noticed she had a nicotine patch on her arm. She wore a skimpy plaid skirt and short-sleeved red sweater. She looked like a crazy Catholic school girl who would kick your ass with her thick-soled combat boots, even after you coughed up your lunch money.

"How's that patch working for you?" I asked.

"How do you think?" She slammed out of the kitchen.

"Perfectly," I said to the swinging door.

I worked steadily until around eight, when Dane came into the diner. He looked out of place in his designer suit and leather briefcase. He smiled when he saw me.

"Hey, Rose, you have a minute?"

"Sure." I filled my customer's coffee cup, then walked behind the counter. Dane followed. "You're not staying to eat?"

"No, I have to be in court in an hour. Have you heard from Axton?"

"No, but he called his brother a couple of nights ago asking for help. Then they were disconnected. The same thing happened when he called me."

"I found out some information on NorthStar Inc." He pulled a manila envelope out of his briefcase. "It's a company that owns a few local bars and other small business-es in town."

"Thanks." Although my hands itched to open the envelope, I stuck it under the counter. I had too many customers and couldn't afford to get distracted.

"Sure. Rose?"

"Hmm?"

"Are you going to pass this information off to the police?"

I quirked my brow.

He sighed. "Yeah, that's what I thought. Just promise me you'll be careful?"

"You bet."

He narrowed his eyes at me. It was almost as if he didn't believe me.

"I swear," I said, raising my right hand, "I will be careful."

"If you need anything at all, just call me, okay?"

"Thanks, Dane. I really appreciate all you've done."

"So have I redeemed myself for shushing you all those years ago?"

I stepped closer to him and in turn he leaned his head toward me. "Nope. You still have a lot of kissing up to do."

He leaned down further, his lips tickling my ear. "Kissing up, huh? Sounds like torture. But if that's what it takes…"

I slapped at his shoulder.

He dimpled and strode out.

I smiled for a good thirty minutes after he left.

The diner was hectic for the next couple of hours. Ma ran to the warehouse store while Roxy and I held down the fort. Traffic finally slowed down by midmorning. When only two customers remained, Roxy bussed tables and I wiped down the counter. I was scrubbing away when my ex-boyfriend, Kevin, walked through the door.

He wore ratty jeans and a blue t-shirt stretched across his broad shoulders. He was tall and cute with dark brown hair that stood up every which way and had ear gauges the size of quarters. Exactly my type. Unfortunately, we had no chemistry. That fact was obvious to me, but to Kevin, not so much.

"Hey, Rose."

Roxy stepped out of the kitchen with an empty bus tub and leaned against the stainless steel counter beside me. "Hey, Roxy." Kevin tipped his chin in her direction.

"Rox, I think my stragglers could use some more coffee," I said.

"Sure." She set down the tub, grabbed the coffee pot, and walked to the table by the front window.

"What are you doing here, Kevin?" I asked.

"It's Spaz now. I changed my name to Spaz. Like, legally and everything."

"So is your last name still Wilkins?" Spaz Wilkins sounded pretty lame to me.

"No, it's just Spaz. Like Bono or Prince."

I pressed my lips together to stifle the giggle that wanted to escape. "Well, good for you."

"Thanks," he said with a smile. "I tried calling you, but since I hadn't heard back I thought I'd stop by, see how you were doing."

"Yeah, I got your message."

He leaned across the counter. "The thing is, I miss you." He brushed his knuckles over my cheek.

I sighed and leaned away. "Kevin, we only went out for a few weeks."

"Those were the best three weeks of my life. Just give me a chance. Whatever I did wrong, I'll fix it."

"I'm sorry...Spaz, but I just think of you as a friend." I

hated break-ups. Especially prolonged ones.

"You introduced me to your family. Doesn't that mean something?"

Actually it didn't. I took him to my second cousin's wedding. If I hadn't been dating Kevin at the time, I would have taken Axton. I never knew Kevin—excuse me, Spaz—would read so much into it.

I stared at his pierced lip because I couldn't look him in the eye. "I'm really sorry," I said.

"I'm not giving up that easily." He reached out and took my hand in his. He kissed the back of it, stroked it. "I'm playing at The Carp this week. Will you come? Please?"

I snatched my hand out of his grasp and opened my mouth to decline, but Roxy chimed in.

"She'll be there." She stepped behind the counter and put the coffee pot back on the burner.

"You come too, Roxy." He stared into my eyes. "I'll see you soon, Rose."

After he left, I turned on her. "Why did you do that? I don't want to hear him play. I broke up with him."

"He's sweet. And he's crazy about you."

"I'm not interested in him and I don't want to lead him on."

"Well, if you go, you could introduce me to Turkey-Jerk's drummer."

"Oh, now I see. It's not about poor Kevin at all. It's about you."

"Um, I believe his name is Spaz, and yeah, it's always about me." With that she flounced back to the kitchen.

Chapter 11

We finally took a break at one when Ma flipped the closed sign. Roxie grabbed a doughnut from the cake stand and tore it in two, giving half to me.

"Boy, I need a cigarette," she said.

"You're doing fine, honey. Just keep up the good work." Ma reached out and patted her back.

"I'm very proud of you. You've gone five days this time." As I devoured my half of the doughnut, I described the hellacious dinner with my parents and Packard's assholiness. I was soon covered in glaze flakes. I wiped my hands on a towel and pulled out the envelope Dane had left. "And Dane found out that NorthStar Inc. owns a bunch of businesses around town."

Roxie finished licking the glaze from her fingers. "Let's have a look." I handed her the envelope, stood over her shoulder, and perused the list.

"Some of these places are in pretty rough neighborhoods." She lifted a shoulder. "But I've been to a couple."

"Wow, I'm shocked. Anyway, I'm going to skip my accounting class tonight and hit a few of those places. You in?"

"But you never skip class."

It was true. No matter how boring the subject—hello,

Statistics 101—I always went to class. And even though I had a test coming up, Axton beat spreadsheets, hands down.

My phone vibrated. I glanced at the number then used the phone next to the kitchen door.

"Hey, Jacks, what's up?"

"Hey there, favorite sister, how would you like to babysit tomorrow night? Our sitter just canceled."

There's nothing I'd rather do than spend time with Scotty. But I had this Axton situation on my hands and a list of businesses to check out. "Sorry, Jacks, I'm busy."

"I already told him you would. He's going to be just heartbroken if Aunt Rose doesn't come over."

Jacks didn't play fair. "What time?"

"Be here at six and we'll probably be home before ten."

"Fine." I glanced over at Roxy. She had another doughnut—chocolate with sprinkles this time—halfway to her mouth. "I'll probably bring Roxy. She seems to be in the middle a carb crisis right now." Plus, I figured we could check out some more NorthStar places on the way home.

"Is her hair still blue?" Jacks whispered, as if Roxy had radar hearing.

"Yeah. And you're starting to sound like Mom."

"That's a low blow, Rosalyn."

I grinned as I hung up. "Hey Rox, I have to babysit Scotty tomorrow night. You want to come with?"

"They'll leave you pizza money, right?"

"You're going to gain four hundred pounds if you keep at it."

She waved the doughnut at me. "It's either this or smoke. Pick one," she said. And by 'said,' I mean she growled and her head rotated like that girl in the Exorcist movie.

"Do we have anymore doughnuts in the back, Ma?" Roxie asked.

Behind her back I shook my head at Ma and made the throat cutting gesture with one hand.

Ma looked at me, then Roxy. "Sorry, hon. I think you ate the last of them."

"Okay, I'm off to the grocery store."

"No, Rox, you're coming with me. I'll even buy you a meatball sub." I had to keep her away from the baked goods.

She stuck out her lip. "Fine. But I have to go home and get some more gum."

"We'll take my car, okay?" I used the same placating tone of voice when Scotty got cranky. "You're doing great."

After we cleaned the diner, we drove to Roxy's apartment. She grabbed a pack of gum off the small dresser and tore into it. "I hate this gum," she mumbled.

"Are you supposed to be chewing that when you wear a nicotine patch?"

"Are you going to bug me all day or what?"

Smoking Roxy was a lot nicer than nicotine patch Roxy.

We stopped by the sub shop and I picked up three meatball sandwiches. Eric was going to have to suck it on the ham because meatball was the special of the day. I didn't buy one for myself, mainly because I wanted to keep a roof over my head and couldn't afford to do both.

We drove to the college and Roxy kept pushing the buttons on the radio. "All this music is shit. And you should get a better stereo."

"You're right."

"You're just humoring me."

I shifted my eyes from the road to her and back again, afraid to say much of anything at this point.

"I'm sorry I've been so bitchy. I just really, really, really, really want a cigarette."

"I know." I patted her knee.

I parked two blocks from campus. The day was cool and bright and a breeze teased my hair as we made our way to Blake Hall.

The guys stood up when we walked into the IT room. I introduced Roxy and handed out sandwiches.

Roxy and I each pulled a rolling chair up to one of the desks and the two men joined us. Steve sat so close his leg brushed mine. I subtly shifted away.

"Thanks, Rose," he said. "This was really nice of you."

"Sure. Please tell me you guys found something on Axton's computer."

"Not the computer," Eric said around a meatball, "the internal hard drive. I'll show you in a minute."

Roxy pushed her sandwich toward me. "I've eaten enough today. Besides, every time I eat, I want a cigarette."

"I'll split it with you." I tore the messy sandwich in half.

When we were done, Eric returned to his desk, wadding up his napkin and lobbing it in the trashcan. Then he tapped on the keyboard. "This is what I found. That hard drive came out of a laptop. Does Ax have a second one?"

"No." I leaned over his shoulder. "This must be what BJ has been looking for." I stared at the computer screen looking at...well, gibberish. "What is it?"

"It's encrypted. I haven't broken it yet." He raised his brows. "Who's BJ?"

"The Bossy Jackass who broke into Rose's apartment," Roxy said.

Eric stared at me for a second. "You didn't tell me he broke in. You just said some guy was asking about Axton."

"BJ wants this back and he's willing to hurt Axton to get it," I said.

He scratched his jaw. "I'll keep working on it."

"You should call the police if this guy shows up again," Steve said.

"Tell them about NorthStar," Roxy said.

"Right. I got something that may be nothing. Axton wrote down the name of this business that owns a bunch of other businesses. NorthStar Inc." I pulled out the pages and unfolded them.

Eric stood and he and Steve read through the list.

"Sports clubs? Country bars?" Eric looked up at me. "What does this have to do with Axton or his disappearance?"

"I'm not sure. But it's the only thing I have to go on at this point. Why did he write it down? Why did it matter to him? He sure didn't mention anything about NorthStar Inc. to me." Axton had been hiding quite a lot from me apparently, and if I wasn't so worried about him, I'd be pretty pissed.

"We're going to go check out some of those bars tonight," Roxy said. "Maybe we'll figure it out then."

"Where are these bars?" asked Steve.

Roxy popped another piece of gum in her mouth. "Downtown, mostly."

"Maybe you could use some backup." Steve adjusted his frames. "You don't know what you could be getting into."

She raised a brow. "I know exactly what I'm getting in-to."

"Well, I think it's a great idea," I said with a smile. If nothing else, it would keep Roxy's wrath away from me. "How about you, Eric? You in?"

"Sure," he said rubbing his eyes. "What the hell."

Roxy and I spent the rest of the afternoon checking out a few of NorthStar businesses. One store sold comic books. I thought Axton would have been there for sure, but when I showed the pimply-faced kid behind the register a picture of Axton from my phone, he just shook his head and stared at Roxy's boobs. And the antique store—and I use that term loosely, unless you consider a clock of Elvis and his swinging legs an antique—was likewise a waste of time.

We stopped by my place for a bite to eat, and it was seven when I parked in front of Eric's two-bedroom stucco cottage. By the glow of the porch light, the exterior looked dark yellow. Eric opened the screen door for us.

"Hey, guys." He stepped aside to let us in.

Most of the space in the tiny living room was taken up by a flat screen TV and two mossy green loveseats. The shiny hardwood floors stood out against unadorned white textured walls. And not a picture or knickknack in the place.

Steve smiled and stood when we entered. "Hi Rose, Roxy."

"Okay, are we ready to go?" Eric asked.

"Yep," I said. "Why don't you guys follow us?"

I'd Googled directions to the first place on my list, a small seedy bar called Chucky's. The freestanding building sat on the outer road of the highway. We weren't quite downtown, but the clientele was definitely downscale.

Chucky's was filled to capacity with people who took their drinking seriously, hunched around their glasses as if protecting them from booze bandits. The scattered tables were full and the two pool tables were in use. Nearly everyone looked up when we entered. Gazes lingered on Roxy and her Catholic-skirt-slash-goth-boots ensemble before returning to their treasured drinks.

"Okay," I said, "what's next? How do we find out if Axton was here?"

"Maybe we should ask the bartender," said Steve.

Roxy rolled her eyes. "Where's a picture of Axton?"

I pulled out the photo I stuck in my purse when we stopped at my place. It was much better than the one on my phone. Roxy took it on my birthday, and both Axton and I wore stupid party hats and had big margarita-fueled grins on our faces.

Roxy grabbed my arm and dragged me behind her as she walked toward the bar. "Hey," she said to the bartender, "what's your name?"

"Who wants to know?"

"She does." Roxy tipped her head in my direction.

He gave me a once over. "Brad." Brad reminded me of a squirrel. Bald with a severe overbite.

Roxy shoved the picture under his nose. "This guy. He look familiar, Brad?"

"What's in it for me?"

"I'm trying to quit smoking and you do not want to piss me off." She slammed the photo down on the bar. "Now look at the damn picture."

I nudged her aside. "Hi, Brad. Sorry about her. She's having nicotine withdrawal."

He filled an empty bowl with pretzels. "Uh-huh."

"The thing is, my friend here is missing. His name is Axton."

He popped a pretzel in his mouth and chewed it. With his mouth open. "Uh-huh."

"So does he look familiar?"

He picked up the photo. "Nope."

"You're sure?"

"Look lady, what do you want from me? I haven't seen this guy, okay?"

My shoulders slouched as Roxy and I walked back to the guys. "Nope, nothing."

"That guy was a jerk." Roxy gave him the stink eye.

"You know, there are over two dozen places on that list," Steve said. "It may take some time."

"You're right," I said. "Should we move on to the next one?"

Roxy flew out the door like a shot, then slowly strolled through the smokers out front who puffed away in the chilly air. She closed her eyes and took a deep breath. "Smell that, Rose. Doesn't that smell fantastic?"

"It smells like lung cancer. Come on." I grabbed her hand and pulled her toward the car.

We stopped at the next bar, which occupied the corner of a brick building in a scary part of town where shootings occurred with regularity. Steve parked behind me, but I didn't turn off the ignition.

"Are we getting out?" Roxy asked.

Before I could decide, Eric and Steve ran up to my car

and Steve tapped on my window.

"You guys, I really don't see Axton coming here," I said.

Everyone spoke at once.

"No you're right..."

"I don't either..."

"Not Axton's type of place..."

"Should we hit the next bar?"

I glanced at Roxy and she nodded. "Let's get out of here. This place scares me." I didn't know anything scared Roxy.

"Next place," I said to the boys.

They ran back to their car and followed me out of the lot. We backtracked and took a two lane highway just outside Huntingford city limits to a two-story steel building called Honky Tonk Heaven.

The large parking lot was packed, but I finally found a spot around back next to the dumpsters. The guys parked near us and we all made the long trek around the building to the front entrance. The music was loud. Even through the gravel I could feel the bass thumping beneath my feet.

The temperature had dropped about ten degrees and as I rubbed my arms against the cold, I wished I had worn something warmer than my black blazer. Steve noticed and took off his fleece jacket, settling it over my shoulders.

I looked up at him. "Thanks."

He smiled and continued walking.

There was a short line to get in. The girls in the queue dressed in either tight jeans and cowboy boots or tiny skirts and cowboy boots. The guys skipped the skirts. Roxy received her usual warm welcome. The girls eyed her suspiciously, then whispered about her amongst themselves while the guys seemed a little turned on and scared at the same time.

When we finally made our way to the front of the line, we had to pay a cover charge of ten bucks. If we didn't find Ax soon, I was going to have to get a second job.

I flashed Axton's picture at the bouncer. "Have you seen this man?" I asked.

He scratched his dark buzz cut and shrugged.

After curling my lip at him, I trudged inside.

Like most clubs, the lighting was low. A long wooden bar took up the left side of the building and two dance floors stretched out before us. On the upper floor, people were line dancing and the lower, larger dance floor held a mass of people moving in a circle.

I grabbed Roxy's hand and we jostled our way to the bar. I figured the guys would follow.

The wait at the bar was three people deep, but Roxy just shoved her way forward, edging people aside. She got several dirty looks and so did I. I think I was the only one bothered by it.

"Hey," the bartender, a woman in a Honky Tonk Heaven t-shirt, yelled over the music. "Wait your turn."

Roxy snapped her fingers in my face. "Picture."

I handed it over.

"Have you seen this guy?" she asked.

"You have to wait your turn," the bartender yelled again.

Taking over for Roxy, who was obviously at the end of her patience, I said, "This is my brother. He's been missing for over a week." I gave her a very sad, yet worried face that mainly involved furrowing my eyebrows. "He loves line dancing. It's his passion in life. Please, take a look at the picture. Have you seen him?"

That wiped the scowl off her face. "Oh, honey, you must be worried sick."

I nodded. At least that part was true.

She took the picture from me and held it closer to her face and squinted. Shaking her head, she frowned. "I'm sorry. I haven't seen him."

I nodded and mustered up a brave smile. "Thanks anyway."

We spent the next three hours winding our way around the place, flashing Axton's photo to waitresses, bouncers, and people in cowboy hats, but no one recognized him. "I think this place is a bust," I said. "I just want to go home."

"Me, too." She tugged at her skirt. "I've had enough of this shit for one night."

We made our way through the crowd and found the guys exactly where we had left them, standing against a wall by the door. Frankly, they'd been pretty useless.

We all headed out to the parking lot and I handed Steve his jacket, then climbed into my car. I dropped Roxy off at her apartment and even though it was only ten-thirty, I looked forward to crawling into bed. The past few sleepless nights had left me exhausted.

I made sure there were no strange cars in my parking lot, no menacing bad guys lurking in the shadows. When all was safe, I darted out of my car and ran to my building, sprinting up the stairs to my thankfully empty apartment. After washing my face and brushing my teeth, I grabbed my blanket and pillow, left the lamp on, and fell onto the futon.

I had just dozed off when something startled me and I bolted upright. I glanced around the room, my heart pounding. I didn't know what had awakened me.

Then I heard pounding on the door.

Chapter 12

"Open up, Rose."

It was BJ. I debated what to do. Open the door or ignore him? Open the door, and I'm an idiot. Ignore him, and he'll just break in. While I'm standing here in my underpants. I didn't like either option.

"Go away," I said in my sternest voice.

"Let me in."

"No."

"This is me, asking nicely," he said.

"Why should I? You threatened Axton."

I swear I heard him laugh. "Are you still holding that against me?"

"Not funny." I was tired and out of sorts and the last time I saw him I was all pressed up against him. It made me hot and cold and embarrassed at the same time. I threw on some sweats and opened the door. But kept the chain on.

He sighed. "Come on, Rose. I'm not going anywhere until we talk and I don't want to wake your neighbors."

Since most of my neighbors were barely functioning alcoholics who passed out before ten o'clock, I wasn't worried. "I'm listening."

He reached a finger through the crack of the door and

touched the bridge of my nose. "You get a crinkle right here when you frown."

I jerked out of reach and tried to slam the door on him. He anticipated my move, because he pulled back his finger and wedged his foot between the door and the jamb. His lips flattened into a straight line. "You have quite a temper. Have you thought about anger management?"

I just glared at him.

He sighed. "Open the door, Rose. This is getting tiresome."

I didn't want to let him into my apartment. I didn't trust him. Yet I still wondered if I could get information out of him. Maybe he would slip up and tell me something useful. Besides, his asking to come in was just a formality and we both knew it.

"Just a minute." I shoved at his foot, shut the door, and grabbed my cell phone. I dialed Roxy's number.

She picked up on the fourth ring. "This had better be good."

"BJ's at my door," I whispered. "If you hear me scream, call 911."

"What? No, don't be stupid."

"He might know something about Ax."

"Hang up and call the police right no—"

"Calm down and be quiet." I tucked my phone in the pouch of my sweatshirt, then unhooked the chain to let him in. "Five minutes or I scream the place down."

"Okay," he said. Putting his hands up in a placating gesture, he stepped into the apartment. He was dressed in an expensive suit with a red striped tie.

"I'm not crazy about that tie."

He looked down and fingered it. "Why not?"

"Did I say that out loud?" God, I *was* tired.

"Yes, you did." He walked toward the kitchen. "Got anything to drink?"

I trailed after him. "Not for you."

He stopped at the sink and turned, wagging his finger in my direction. "I thought you and I had come to an understanding."

"If that were the case, I think I'd remember it."

"I remember it quite clearly. You were going to mind your own business."

"I have."

"No, you haven't. You've been quite a busy little bee, dashing all over town looking for Axton."

How the hell was this guy tracking me? I'd checked my rearview mirror frequently all day. I hadn't seen anyone following me, hadn't seen Henry lurking about.

He moved toward me and even though I wanted to back up, I held my ground. "You have my property. Or you know where it is." He stood so close, the front of his chest skimmed my breasts. I stopped breathing for a second.

I craned my neck, looking up at him. "I already told you, I don't know what you're talking about."

"I think you're lying."

He was so close I could see his pupils contract. And that spicy, citrusy smell enveloped me.

"Tell me what you're looking for and maybe I can help you find it."

His eyes narrowed. "If you're lying to me, you'll regret it."

Yeah, he scared the hell out of me, but he also made

me angry and a feeling of helplessness got tossed into the emotional mix, too. All of it was boiling inside me. This was exactly how I felt when I tried to pummel him. I found myself wanting to do it again. "Listen, you bastard, this is my house. You can't just keep barging in here and bossing me around."

He took a step closer and leaned down until we were nose to nose. "Want to bet?" He smirked and his nose bumped mine. "Tell me, Rose, if you went missing, would anyone care?"

I flinched. "People would miss me. My family…" I clammed up when I realized what I'd almost revealed to him.

"You're a waitress. You live in this shithole. Except for your sister, Jacqueline, and her son," he paused, tapping his mouth with one finger, "what's his name?" His eyes hardened. "Oh, yes, Scotty. Except for Jacqueline and Scotty, you don't have much of a relationship with your family, do you? Would they even bother to look for you?"

I was suddenly freezing. I rubbed my arms, comforted that Roxy was only a phone line away.

He walked around me to the door and opened it, but turned back. "Why don't you like my tie?"

"Get out."

I snatched the phone from my pocket and assured Roxy I was all right. Apparently, my sweatshirt muffled the noise so much, she hadn't heard any particulars of the conversation, so I gave her the Cliffs notes version and hung up.

I turned on all the lights and huddled beneath my blanket. BJ knew everything about me. My dysfunctional family dynamic, my job, my house, probably even my favorite breakfast cereal. Who was this guy? Finding that out was at the top of my short list. If I could find out who he was, maybe I could get the upper hand. Divert him until I found Ax. Knowledge was power and I'd had precious little in this whole thing, that was for freaking sure. And the fact that every time BJ came near me my heart beat a little faster— well, I'd deal with that later.

The next morning I decided against drinking a tankard of coffee, even though I was exhausted. Last time I'd done that, it hadn't worked out so well.

When I got into work I greeted Jorge and Ray, who waved me at me with a spatula and mumbled a hello. Ma stood in the dining room filling salt shakers. "Good morning, Ma."

She stopped pouring and looked me up and down. "You look like ten miles of bad road, toots."

"Thanks."

"Didn't get much sleep again, huh?"

Roxy came out of the bathroom. She wore a short shepherdess dress and a schoolgirl tie. "Jeez, you look terrible."

"That's the general consensus."

She glanced at Ma. "She got another visit from BJ last night."

"He broke in again?" Ma asked. "Oh my God, honey, did he hurt you?"

"No, he just wanted to talk."

"Talk about what, for God's sake?" Ma asked, hands on her hips. "And why did he have to break in to do that? Hasn't he ever heard of a goddamn telephone?"

"Wait until you hear this," Roxy said between chomps.

My cheeks felt hot. "He didn't break in." My voice got

quieter as I went on. "I...let him in."

Ma's eyes widened. "You let him in? Did you offer him a beer, too?"

"No, I didn't offer him a beer. I just thought maybe I could get some information out of him."

"And did you?" she asked.

I took a deep breath. "No." I walked around the counter and began rolling silverware into paper napkins.

"Oh no you don't." Ma wrangled the fork out of my hand. "Finish the story, Rose. Why did he come to your apartment in the first place?"

"He still thinks I have his property." They waited for me to continue. "And he told me to mind my own business. That's all, I swear."

Roxy looked skeptical. "Did he say what would happen if you don't mind your business? Did he threaten you?"

Totally. "Not really," I lied. I hated keeping things from them, but the last thing I wanted to do was freak them out any more than they already were.

"Oh, if I could get my hands on that man—I'd have socked him in the mouth, too," Ma said.

By then we had a few early customers, so we quit talking and got down to business. Ma manned the counter while Roxy and I did our thing. I tried to concentrate on my job, rather than my problems.

When we hit our midmorning slow down, I checked my phone. Still no Axton. But I had texts from Eric, Sheila Graystone, Dane, and two from Kevin.

I used the diner phone and called Eric. He answered on the first ring. "I've got something. When can you get here?"

"What? Did you decrypt the hard drive?" I twisted the old, curly tan phone cord around my finger.

"Yeah, I decrypted it, but I still don't know what it is."

I wanted to leave work immediately, but I needed the money. Badly. "I'll be there a little after one." Ma and Roxy wouldn't mind if I skipped clean up for a good cause.

I read Sheila's text next. She wanted to meet at Starbucks. Maybe she heard from Axton or thought of something that might help me. I texted her back and then called Dane. I figured he'd be in court and was surprised when he answered.

"Have you heard from Axton?"

"No," I said. "He's still missing. But I checked out some bars from your list and filed a missing person report."

"I heard through the country club grapevine the police interviewed Packard."

Maybe that's why Sheila wanted to talk. Was she upset the police questioned Pack?

"...get together?"

My eyes watered as I stifled a yawn. "What was that?"

He laughed. "I said do you want to get together this weekend?"

"How about tonight? I was going to check out a few more places on that list after I babysit my nephew."

We discussed the details and I got back to work.

When one o'clock rolled around, I told Ma about Eric's phone call.

"Of course, toots. Roxy and I can handle clean up."

I thanked her and gathered my stuff together. Roxy followed me outside. When we reached my car, she stared out at the traffic squinting her blue eyes against sun. "Rose,

I'm worried about you. This guy who keeps showing up at your apartment, he could be dangerous."

"I know."

"I think you should stay with me. At least until you find Axton." Roxy valued her space and her privacy almost more than anything else. Growing up in foster care, she never had a real home of her own. Her apartment wasn't much, but it was hers, and the fact she offered to share it with me touched me deeply.

"Thanks," I said as I opened the car door, "but I'll be all right. Honest." I held up three fingers.

She snorted. "Like you were ever a Girl Scout. I'll meet you at Jacks' house at six?"

"Yeah, and Dane's going with us to the cigar bar."

She shook her head, her shiny blue hair gliding over her shoulders. "No cigar bar for me. I have plans later."

"What kind of plans?"

She shrugged and walked back into the diner.

Because I was so excited to see what Eric had found on that hard drive, I blew through two red lights and sped across Apple Tree Boulevard. I snagged a spot in the campus parking lot and practically ran to Blake Hall.

When I burst through the door of the IT office, Eric was alone. He glanced up from the laptop and blinked like an owl.

"What have you got?"

He waved me over. "Pull up a chair."

I sat next to him and he shifted the laptop toward me so I could see it better. "What am I looking at?"

"A spreadsheet. Although the information was encrypted, first I had—"

I completely tuned him out as I stared at a spreadsheet of one hundred twenty-seven names in alphabetical order. There were numbers and dates next to each. "Oh my God, Eric, do you know what this is?"

He frowned. "I told you. It's a spreadsheet. Don't you want to know how I broke the encryption?"

"No." I looked at him, my eyes wide. "This is a list of some of the most prominent people in Huntingford. The mayor, the chief of police... Holy freaking cow."

Chapter 13

Eric leaned over and stared at the screen. "Oh."

"What do we think the numbers mean? Forty-five thousand, eighty-three thousand. Packard Graystone's name is on this list and his numbers add up to one hundred ninety-six thousand."

"I have no idea."

"How does this tie in with Axton?" I asked, staring at the computer.

"I really don't know."

I rubbed my hands over my eyes. How did NorthStar Inc. come into play? Or did it? And where did BJ fit in?

Eric reached out and patted my back. "Hey, you okay?"

I shook my head. From the corner of my eye, I saw the door open. Steve popped his head into the office, his gaze darted from Eric to me.

"Hey, Rose, what are you doing here? Is everything all right?"

"I finally broke the code," Eric said.

"That's great. So what was it?" He pulled a chair over to Eric's desk and sat next to me.

"It's a list of prominent Huntingford citizens with

numbers and dates next to their names," I said.

He looked at the screen. "Hmm. Money?"

I shrugged. "Could be. These are wealthy people. Could be donations for all we know."

Minutes lapsed as we contemplated the list. With a sigh, I finally stood. "Eric, would you make a copy of this for me?"

"Sure." He punched a couple of keys and the printer next to him spit out a copy of the list.

I folded the paper and tucked it in my purse. "Thanks. And thanks for breaking the code."

"Anytime, kid."

"Oh, there's one other thing." I told them both about BJ's latest nocturnal visit. "And I'm about to meet with Sheila Graystone. Hopefully she'll have information that will help."

Steve had been pretty quiet until now. "Whatever you're doing, it's dangerous if it's getting the attention of this BJ character."

Eric nodded in agreement. "He's right. You have to let the police handle this."

"I can't. The police think Ax is just some stoner who's run off and I don't have any real evidence—about anything. I need to find Ax and I can't count on anybody else to do it for me."

Eric scrubbed at the stubble on his cheeks and sighed. "I'm worried about him, too. And I've been covering for him with the administration, but I don't know how much longer I can keep it up. Since he got busted last year, he's skating on thin ice."

"I'm going to find him." I wondered if my expression

was a fierce as my voice.

Eric nodded. "All right, kid, but let me help."

"You just told me how dangerous it was to keep looking."

"Yeah, well, I kind of miss him. But if you repeat that, I'll deny it."

I smiled. "I need to find out everything I can about NorthStar Inc. Not just a list of the businesses, but the owner. And how BJ fits in to all this."

"Okay, I'll get to work," Eric said.

Steve stood. "I'll walk you out."

"Thanks, but I'm fine."

He ignored me and placed his hand on my arm. "I'd like to talk to you for a minute."

We walked up the stairs and out of the building. The day was warm, the afternoon sun blazing low in the sky.

With his hand still on my arm, he turned to me. "I'll do anything I can to help you find Ax. But please, don't let this guy into your apartment again." His eyes, the color of dark chocolate, were filled with concern.

"You're really sweet, Steve. And I don't plan on letting him in again."

"Good. Look I know you're worried about Axton, but you have to eat. There's this Thai place off the Boulevard—"

"Maybe once I get Axton back?" I had too many men to deal with right now. I waved over my shoulder and jogged to my car.

When I walked into Starbucks, the sharp smell of coffee hit me. I loved that smell—comforting and mouthwatering at the same time. Sheila sat at a two-person table in the corner and waved when she saw me.

"Aren't you going to get some coffee?" she asked.

Unfortunately, I couldn't afford the Frappuccino I so richly deserved. I pulled out a chair and sat across from her. "No, I'm good."

"Thanks for meeting me."

"Has Packard heard from Axton again?"

"No, I'm sorry."

"Oh." I blinked at her. "If you don't have information on Ax, why did you call?"

She looked down at the table. "This is hard," she said, more to herself than to me. She glanced back up. "Pack has been acting strange since Axton's disappearance."

"How?"

"I don't know, really. He's been on edge, secretive."

"Secretive?"

She gestured with one hand. "He'll get phone calls and walk out of the room to take them. Even in the middle of dinner. He won't talk in front of me. I know my husband and something is wrong."

The thought crossed my mind that maybe Packard was having an affair. Call me Captain Obvious.

"Have you checked his phone history?"

"I don't feel right doing that."

"And you're sure it's about Axton? It's not work or…" I left the words hanging in the air.

She got what I was implying and sat up straighter, a haughty look on her face. "My husband is a good man. An honest man. He would never do anything to hurt me."

I nodded. "Okay."

"I just think Packard's weird behavior has something to

do with Axton, that's all."

"Did the police ever talk to Pack?" According to Dane they had, but I wanted to hear it from Sheila.

"An officer called him and asked a few questions. That was about it."

I sighed and looked out the window. "So, you think these phone calls have something to do with Ax?" I turned back to face her.

"I think so."

"Why don't you look at Packard's phone and get me a list of the incoming numbers?"

She nibbled her lip and ran her thumb over the rim of her cup lid. "I don't know."

If she didn't want to help me, why did she call this little meeting? "Look, Sheila, Axton is missing. The police don't care and your husband has been acting strange. You said yourself he's been on edge since Axton's disappearance." I looked directly into her brown eyes. "Please?"

She was silent for a few minutes. "My husband is ambitious. He wants to run for mayor. He sees it as a stepping stone for bigger things." She clutched her coffee cup. "He's probably just under a lot of stress at work."

I reached out and touched her wrist. "I don't care about your husband. I don't want to hurt him, I really don't. I don't care what Packard's done, as long as it doesn't involve Axton. Every time I've needed him, he's been there for me. He may be flaky in some areas, but as a friend, he's as steady as they come. I need to find him."

Finally, she looked up at me. "Okay. I'll check his phone tonight."

I pushed my chair back to leave.

"Rose, if he has been talking to another woman?"

I waited.

"I want to know."

I mulled over our conversation on the way to my apartment. I hoped the phone numbers would yield some results, but I wasn't holding my breath. Ax and Pack weren't close. I wasn't even sure why Ax called his brother the night he disappeared. It was odd.

As my mind wandered, I drove past a strip mall that housed a tanning salon. Something about it niggled at the corner of my mind. I had seen the name of that tanning salon before.

Making a U-turn, I drove back and parked in front of a row of small shops. I dug in my purse for the list of businesses owned by NorthStar Inc., then looked up at the Sun Kissed Tanning Salon with a big ass grin on my face. Shoving the list in my purse, I got out of the car and walked inside.

A girl in her early twenties stood at the counter, rows of tanning products lined the glass shelves behind her. She smiled when I walked in. "Hi," she said, "how are you today?" Her skin—the color of a radioactive carrot—clashed with her purple tie-dyed bikini.

"I'm great, thanks, and you?"

"I'm great, too." She flipped her bleached hair over her shoulder and continuously petted it with two hot pink-tipped hands. "You look like you're in the right place."

I raised my brows. "I do?"

"Definitely. You're really pale."

For some reason I thought she was going to blurt out

everything about NorthStar Inc. and how it was connected to Axton. All my questions would be answered. Instead she just wanted to orange me.

"Are you interested in a spray tan or the beds?" She scrunched her nose. "In your case, I would do both." Not having tan must be a bummer in her world.

"I'm not really here for the tanning."

And before I could whip out my picture of Axton, she nodded. "Oh, okay. You're here to see Manny."

My hand froze inside my purse. "Yep. I'm here to see Manny." My heart began to pound. Could this finally lead to a clue? God, I hoped so. I was so tired of chasing my own tail.

"Well, come on." She motioned for me to follow her down a short hallway behind the counter. Unused tanning beds stood in darkened rooms and posters of sunny beaches covered the light blue walls.

Skin Cancer Barbie opened the last door on the left and stood aside so I could walk through. "Someone to see you, Manny."

"Thanks, Tif." A round short man with a Benjamin Franklin hairdo and a green Hawaiian shirt sat behind a desk in the small office. The walls were bare and a computer monitor stood on his desk. He gestured to a folding chair. "Sit."

I smiled and did. "Thanks."

"What's your name?"

Oh, crap. I didn't know he was going to start with the hard questions. "Sue," I said.

"Pleased to meet you, Sue." He picked up a gold pen and began twirling it between his fingers. "Now, what can I do you for?"

I searched for a clue, but there was nothing here. No pictures, no decor, nothing. Maybe he thought I was here for a job. My pale body could be the 'before' to Tif's 'after.' "Oh, just the usual," I said.

"There is no usual, really."

"I'm just looking at the basics. I don't want to get too creative."

"Great. That's smart." He tapped his noggin with the pen. "You can screw yourself by getting too creative."

Kind of like what I was doing at this very moment. I nodded and smiled.

"I just need the name of your referral and we'll get started."

Shit. "I don't really remember. I'm so bad with names." I laughed and tossed my hair over my shoulder.

The smile dropped from his face faster than a drunken girl's bikini top on Spring break. "Well, that's a shame."

I smiled a real charmer. "Can't we just skip the referral?"

"No, we can't."

"Maybe you could make an exception?"

"We don't make exceptions." His voice was as cold as his pale blue eyes. Manny Ben Franklin wasn't buying what I was selling.

The vibe in the room shifted from benign to dangerous in a second. I didn't know what they were doing here, but I knew it wasn't kosher. Probably wasn't legal, either. I stood up and smoothed my leg with one hand as I hoisted my purse up my shoulder with the other. "Sorry to have wasted your time."

I moved to the door, but Manny jumped out of his

chair and blocked my exit. "You're not going anywhere. Who told you about me?"

My breath caught in my throat. I gulped and blurted out the first name that popped into my head. "Packard Graystone." My pulse hammered against my throat and I audibly heard my heartbeat.

"I don't believe you." He grabbed my wrist and pulled me closer. He wore strong aftershave that made my nose itch and little beads of sweat dotted his massive forehead.

I yanked my wrist back, but Manny's hand tightened and pain shot from my wrist down my hand. I struggled against his grip, but he didn't let go. So I screamed. One of those loud, shrill screams that hurts the ear drums. Then I belted him on the side of his head with my fist and brought my knee up at the same time. I didn't make contact with his crotch, because he brought up his own knee to block it, but he loosened his grasp.

I took advantage and pulled away, then shoved him as hard as I could with both hands. When he stumbled against the file cabinet, I yanked open the door and ran.

Halfway down the hall, Tiff stood in my way with wide eyes. "What's going—"

Not slowing down, I slammed my shoulder into her arm.

"Ow, that hurt." She spun to the side as I ran past her and out of the building.

I jumped into my car, jammed the key into the ignition, and without turning to look behind me, I thrust the car into reverse and hauled ass out of the parking lot.

Chapter 14

I pulled up to Jacks' house just before six. After my run-in with Manny, I'd taken a long winding way home, checking the rearview mirror more than the road in front of me. My hands shook so badly, I gripped the wheel until my fingers hurt. I replayed the conversation with him over and over. I'd found out two things: the tanning salon was a cover for something shady—no pun intended—and Manny knew Packard Graystone. But I didn't know how either of these facts tied into Axton's disappearance.

I was still a nervous mess as I got ready for the evening. After babysitting Scotty, I was meeting Dane and wanted to look nice. Not that this was a date or anything. We were just trying to find Axton. Together. At a bar. An un-date, that's what it was.

As I got out of the car, I adjusted my dress—the nicest one I owned actually. Black, not too short, showing a little boobage, but not enough to be slutty. I thought I looked pretty spiffy.

Then I saw Roxy.

She wore a ruffled blouse with a short black skirt over layers of stiff white petticoats. She topped it off with an enormous black bow attached to her blue sausage curls.

"You look very pretty," I said.

We walked up to the door and stood on the lighted porch. She glanced at me. "What happened? You run into that BJ guy again?" Her gaze moved over my face. "You look as tense as shit."

I had been going for casual hot. Apparently I had the holy-hell-I-got-the-crap-scared-out-of-me-by-a-Ben-Franklin-impersonator look instead. "I'll tell you later."

The door flew open and I peered down, saw Scotty, and grinned. "Hey Sport."

"Aunt Rose! We're having pizza tonight. No salmon."

"Yay! I love pizza."

He stepped back to let us in. His blue eyes widened as he took in Roxy from head to toe. "You look like a Bubble Guppy."

She smiled. "Thanks."

My sister walked down the stairs fixing her earring as she came. She glanced over at Roxy and froze in place. "The two of you are too dressed up to spend the night babysitting."

"I'm going out afterward," I said.

"Me, too."

"Won't it be kind of late?"

"It's not a school night, Mom," I said. Roxy snorted. "Quit worrying about us, just go and have a good time."

Allen walked into the foyer in a suit and tie. "Hey, Rose," he said, not looking at me but at Roxy. His brows made a trip north. "Hello." He held out his hand. "I don't believe we've met. I'm Allen Smythe."

"Roxy Block," she said, shaking his hand.

"That's a very…unique outfit you have on, Roxy."

She smacked her gum and nodded. "Like I know, right?"

Jacks slipped a lightweight coat out of the hall closet. "We've already ordered the pizza, and the money is on the kitchen counter with a coupon. Scotty will try to talk you into letting him stay up until nine, but bedtime's eight-thirty." Allen helped her into her coat. "Don't let him have sugar. And we should be home between nine and nine-thirty."

"Scotty," she called. "Come kiss me goodbye."

He flew into the foyer and slid across the marble floor. "Bye Mommy. Bye Daddy." He hugged my sister's leg and she leaned down to kiss him on the cheek.

Allen ruffled his hair. "Be good for Aunt Rose, okay?"

"Kay," he said before running off.

"Where are you guys going anyway?" I asked.

Allen frowned. "To your parents' house, of course."

I looked at Jacks, but she wouldn't meet my gaze. "It's a hospital thing. You'd be so bored."

Realization flitted across Allen's face as he stood next to Jacks with his mouth hanging open. "Oh yes, bored. God, these things are so boring. Wouldn't be there unless we had to, right Jacqueline?"

I forced a smile on my face. "Sure." I waved one hand. "You two go on."

My smile left as soon as they did. Fact is, I'd rather have my tooth drilled without anesthetic than go to my parents' house. What did I have in common with a room full of doctors? Still, I knew I hadn't been invited, not because I didn't find talk of gallbladders and golf games fascinating, but because my parents were ashamed of me.

"Wow," Roxy said. "That was harsh."

"No, it's fine. It's all fine. Let's go find Scotty."

He was in the den watching *Sponge Bob Square Pants*. I found it annoying, but Roxy laughed just as hard as Scotty did.

When the pizza came, I turned off the TV and we ate in the kitchen. After he was done eating, Scotty begged me for candy.

"We have a whole new bag of Snickers for the trick-or-treaters." He pointed to the cabinet above the refrigerator. "That's where Mommy hides it."

"How do you know where she hides it, Sport?" I asked.

"Duh, because that's where she hides the cookies."

"Well, maybe you can have a piece after lunch tomorrow, because your mom said no sugar tonight."

"Ah man." He pounded his little fist on the table. "That sucks!"

Roxy nodded. "That does suck." She pulled out a piece of gum and stuck it in her mouth.

"Can I have a piece of gum?"

"No, this is special gum. I'm trying to quit smoking because it's a bad habit, so I chew the gum instead."

He paused for second, his blue eyes narrowed. "Maybe if I quit picking my nose, I could eat candy."

I grinned. "It doesn't hurt to have dreams."

We played Old Maid and Go Fish until it was time for Scotty to go to bed. Normally we'd play Candy Land, but since sugar was a forbidden substance, I didn't want to rub it in.

At eight-fifteen, I watched him brush his teeth, listened to his prayers, and together, we read his favorite book. By that time, he'd just about conked out. When I kissed his forehead and left the room, I felt a pang in my chest. Sometimes I envied my sister.

Back downstairs I flopped onto the sofa next to Roxy.

"Okay," she said, "spill."

I filled her in on the decrypted list—'Names, dates, and numbers? WTF?'—my conversation with Sheila—'Packard's totally getting some on the side'—and my run in with Manny—'Maybe he's a pimp in charge of a secret prostitution ring.'

"A prostitution ring in Huntingford?"

She lifted a shoulder. "Stranger shit has happened."

"I just want Axton back."

"You'll find him. In the meantime, if you want to know what's going on in that tanning salon, we could always break in."

"Who are we, Charlie's Angels? With my luck, I'd get caught."

"I never get caught. Well, not since I was twelve."

"Is that why you spent time in juvie?" I knew Roxy had a tough childhood. She'd mentioned her stay in Juvenile Hall over the years, but never told me why.

She shrugged. "I put syrup of Ipecac in my foster father's beer."

"Oh."

She played with a flounce on her skirt. "He deserved it, trust me."

"I do."

"Seriously, though, if you want to break in after hours, I'm your girl."

"I will keep it in mind."

Roxy and I watched TV until Jacks and Allen came home an hour later. I gave them an update as Roxy pulled on her cardigan and I grabbed my purse and dug out my keys.

"Okay sis, I'll call you next week."

"Rose, I'm sorry about tonight. I should have told you we were going to Mom and Dad's house. It's just after the salmon incident the other day—"

"It's okay. Really." I gave her a quick hug.

She kissed my cheek and said goodnight.

Roxy and I were walking toward our cars when she glanced over at me. "Sorry you didn't get invited to the hospital thing."

"No biggie."

"Yeah, well, if you were my daughter, I'd be really proud of you." She grabbed a piece of my hair and gave it a tug. "Even though you still don't have your degree, you loser."

I drove out of my sister's neighborhood and hooked a left on Crabtree Lane. When I pulled up to the cigar bar, Dane was waiting for me out front, looking handsome in a dark jacket and slacks. He smiled when he saw me pull into the lot and headed over, opening my door after I parked.

His blue eyes sparkled as his glance took me in from head to toe. "You look beautiful."

I pushed a lock of hair behind one ear. "Thanks. You look nice, too."

He leaned down and kissed my cheek. When he pulled back, his hand lingered on my shoulder. "Still no word from Ax?"

"No."

"Let's have a drink and you can fill me in on the latest." He slipped his hand around to my lower back and escorted me inside.

Penn's Cigar and Fine Tobacco was a one story mellow brick building near my parents' country club. Arched leaded glass windows looked out onto the street and the golf course beyond. The warm lighting inside made the club chairs and round mahogany tables seem rich and inviting. Expensive-smelling smoke hung thick in the air.

Dane helped me out of my coat and handed it to the check girl. Then he cupped my elbow and guided me to the bar.

I gracefully slipped onto a tall barstool and arranged my dress so I didn't flash my official sexy panties to the world. I smiled at Dane as he slid an arm along the back of my seat.

"Mind if I smoke?"

I shook my head.

"Order me a Hennessy? I'll be right back." He slid off the stool and walked toward the humidor.

The bartender made his way over. I ordered for Dane and ordered myself a glass of wine, feeling like I was in over my head. I knew my parents would have felt at home here, but I didn't know anything about cigars or cognac. Most of the wine I drank came out of a box.

I took out the picture of Axton from my purse. The bartender placed our drinks in front of me and set a cigar cutter next to Dane's snifter.

"Have you seen this man in here?" I asked, handing him the picture.

"Sorry. Why are you looking for him?"

"He's missing."

He handed back the photo. "I haven't seen him."

I tucked the picture in my purse. "Thanks, anyway."

I swiveled on my stool and checked out the place. The room was full, and I saw at least four of my parents' friends. I swiftly turned back toward the bar so I wouldn't inadvertently make eye contact and have to participate in small talk about my career choice. Or lack of one.

Fifteen minutes later, Dane returned a little flushed and out of breath. "Sorry about that, I ran into a client and everybody wants free advice."

"No problem." With my elbow propped up on the bar, my chin in my hand, I watched Dane grab the cutter.

He held up the cigar. "You have to snip the end off like this," he said demonstrating. "Then you light the edges." He proceeded to rotate the cigar, charring the edges he'd snipped.

"Seems like a lot of work."

"It's worth the effort." With narrowed eyes he put it in his mouth and gently puffed. I got a little turned on, watching it.

We started chatting and Dane was good at drawing information out of me. I found myself telling him everything, from the decrypted list, which I pulled out of my purse and handed to him, to BJ, to the tanning salon visit, but leaving out the bitch slap I gave Manny. He glanced through the pages, then looked over at me.

"I don't understand. What does this have to do with Axton? And why the hell didn't you call the police when those two men broke into your apartment?"

Good questions. "BJ made it sound like going to the

police was a really bad idea. And I have no proof he was even there. He may have broken in the first time, but there wasn't any damage."

"And you still don't know what he wants?"

"I'm pretty sure he's after the hard drive."

"This guy means business or he wouldn't keep showing up. You have to go to the police with this, Rose. Please. I know some cops, good men. They'll be discreet, I promise."

"I don't know..."

"Maybe they'll take Axton's disappearance more seriously if you report this."

What if that was true? Time was getting away from me. Axton had been missing for five days and I wasn't any closer to finding him now than I had been on day one. Besides, he needed to show up for that drug test on Monday or he'd be out of a job. Then how would he pay his mortgage, his car payment, or keep Stoner Joe in chips and ganja? I missed him so much I ached with it. But the police? I wasn't convinced it was the right move.

"Trust me. Please," Dane said, taking my hand.

Tears stung the backs of my eyes. I was so tired, so weary, and I missed my friend. I cleared my throat. "I need to use the restroom."

As I made my way toward the ladies lounge, a door on my right opened and a server stepped into the hall. I peeked in before the door closed. Through the thick gray haze, I made out a group of men gathered around a table, playing cards. I wondered how they could breathe through all that dense smoke.

After making use of the facilities, which turned out to be larger than my apartment and much, much nicer, I checked myself in the mirror, making sure my mascara hadn't smudged and touched up my lipstick before heading back to the bar.

I sipped my wine and Dane swirled his cognac and smoked. While he was occupied I turned things over in my mind. Where did this whole NorthStar thing fit in? Just because Axton wrote it down didn't mean it was connected to all this. Axton would no more have been at home in this place than he would have at Honky Tonk Heaven or Chucky's or a pseudo-antique store.

"You know, I can't help but wonder if this is a waste of time," I said. "Axton doesn't hang out in places like this. He doesn't even go to bars much, except The Carp. The thing at the tanning salon could just be a coincidence."

"The man who broke into your apartment, how did he know you'd been looking for Axton? Have you noticed anyone following you?"

"No, and I've been checking, believe me. Unless they're ninjas, no one has been tailing me."

"Do you think someone from one of the businesses tipped this guy off?"

"It's a possibility."

"What about Packard or Axton's roommate? Could either of them be working for BJ?"

"Stoner Joe? He can't remember what day it is. Packard?" I thought about Manny's reaction to hearing Packard's name. But Pack knew Eric had the hard drive. He would have passed that info on to BJ, so no need to harass me.

"I don't know what to think. I just know that I have to find Ax. And wherever he is, I hope he's safe."

Dane slipped a hand down my back. "You're a good

friend." He looked into my eyes and leaned in. Our lips almost touched when my purse vibrated.

"Sorry," I whispered. I dug my phone out and glanced at the ID. It was Roxy.

Chapter 15

Joe Carpino, also known as The Carp, opened his bar when avocado green was all the rage, burnt orange counter tops seemed like a good idea, and fake wood paneling was somehow more attractive than real wood paneling. But he featured live music and had cheap—albeit watered down—booze.

Roxy waited for us outside the bar, where smokers huddled in circles and people drifted in and out of the building. Each time the door opened a wave of music and a roar of chatter spilled out onto the sidewalk, where Roxy paced, chewing a wad of gum as if her life depended on it. She kept smoothing her hands down the black ruffled skirt and her large hair bow was a little cockeyed.

"Jeez, Rose, what took you so long?" She didn't even glance in Dane's direction.

"Dane," I said, "this is Roxy."

He seemed stunned, but he recovered quickly. "Hello, Roxy, it's nice to meet you."

"Yeah," she said, smacking her gum. She grabbed me by the shoulders, her mouth tilted down at the corners. "I am so sorry. I mean, I had no idea this would happen."

"Okay Rox, just calm down and tell me."

"I came to The Carp tonight because TurkeyJerk was playing." She glanced at Dane and angled her head toward my ear. "And I didn't want to drag you along because of *you know who*. But I wanted to meet Spork, the drummer."

"Okay…"

"But then I saw *you know who*," she said in a low voice, "and he went ballistic. He was all 'Where's Rose? I know she was with someone. Some guy answered her phone the other night. Who was he?' And I was all, 'What the hell does it matter to you? She dumped your lame ass.' And then Spork was all 'Hey man, don't talk to Spaz that way.' I'm really sorry."

I guessed Kevin—let's face it, I was never going to call him Spaz—was upset because BJ answered my phone. Why the hell had he answered my phone? And what else had he done while he was waiting with Henry in my apartment?

Roxy squeezed my shoulder and I filed BJ away for now. "Okay, that doesn't sound too bad."

"Here's the bad part. Kevin is all 'I'm going over to Rose's right now' and Spork is all 'Don't let that bitch get you worked up' and I'm all 'Don't you call my friend a bitch' then Kevin is all 'Yeah, don't talk about Rose that way' and then Kevin punched Spork."

I looked up at the night sky and sighed. This was my life. I couldn't believe this was my life.

"Is everything all right?" Dane asked.

I turned and looked at him. He was so handsome. And normal. "It's fine. There's a guy inside that I broke up with. We barely even dated. But he's harmless. I think I just need to go talk to him. I'll be firm, make him understand it's over."

"I'll go with," Roxy said.

"Rose," Dane said. "I've dealt with men like him. You shouldn't confront him, you should get a restraining order."

I scrubbed my hands over my face. Before I could make a decision, the door opened and Kevin stormed out, followed by Spork, who had spiked blond hair, a dog collar around his neck, and toilet paper shoved up his nose.

Kevin's chest heaved and he pointed at Dane. "Is this the guy who was in your apartment the other night?"

"Let's go, Rose." Dane slipped his arm around my shoulders.

"Don't touch her," Kevin said. "I will kick your ass, man." Spork made a move to hold him back.

Roxy swung her head around, making her curls bounce. "Control him, Spork."

I'd had enough of the adolescent drama for one night. Actually, I'd had enough drama to last me a freaking lifetime. I stepped away from Dane.

"Shut. Up." I clapped my hands with each word, like an elementary school teacher. "I have had it. Kevin, you and I went out for exactly three weeks. Get over it. Don't call. Don't text. Don't come see me. Do you understand?"

"You and I have something special," he said, sounding like a little boy. "I wrote a song for you."

"I don't want to hear it. I don't love you. And changing your name to Spaz was a stupid idea."

He looked so hurt I almost relented.

"Baby." He reached out to me, but I stepped back and bumped into Dane.

"I mean it, Kevin. I want you to leave me alone." I turned my attention to Roxy. "Rox, why don't we follow you home?"

She cast a glance at Spork. Did I mention he had toilet paper in his nostrils? And his name was Spork? That's not a name, it's barely even a utensil.

"Come on," I said. I placed my hand on her back as I guided her to the side parking lot.

Dane didn't say much as we followed Roxy home, or when he dropped me off to pick up my car at the cigar bar. He was the most normal man I had dated in years—not that this was a date—and he must think I was crazy. Bar fights with people named Spaz and Spork. My best friend was a punked out Shirley Temple. *I* would think I was crazy.

After he parked the car, Dane turned toward me and brushed a finger down my cheek. "I'll follow you home, Rose." He stepped out and walked around the car, opening the door for me.

When we reached the parking lot of my apartment, Dane insisted on coming inside. "I want to make sure you don't have any more unexpected visitors."

I felt a little self-conscious about Dane seeing my shabby apartment. With my orange futon, small bistro table, and secondhand dresser, it wasn't much to look at.

I shut the door with my back. "See? Safe as houses."

But Dane wasn't looking at my apartment, he was looking at me. "I had a very interesting time tonight, Rose."

"That's one word to describe it, I guess."

"Things are never dull around you, that's for sure. Axton's lucky to have you as a friend." He leaned forward and kissed me. Softly. His lips teased and nibbled. He rested his hands on my shoulders and pulled me close as the kiss deepened. When his tongue stroked mine, my fingers found their way into his short hair. After several pleasant minutes he slowly pulled away. "I should probably go."

Feeling a little dizzy, I nodded. "Yeah."

"You want to meet at the police station tomorrow or do you want me to pick you up?" His thumb brushed the side of my neck.

"I'll meet you after I get off work."

His forehead wrinkled. I was quickly learning this was a sign that he wasn't pleased. "We should go first thing in the morning. You've already waited too long as it is."

I stepped out of his hold, a little stung by his comment. "I did what I thought was right, Dane."

He sighed. "I know, I didn't mean to criticize. I'll see you after you get off of work." He kissed my forehead and left.

As soon as Dane was out the door, I blocked it with my dresser. It was a flimsy piece of pressboard crap, but it made me feel marginally safer. I actually got some sleep that night.

The next morning I looked out my window to make sure there were no strange cars in the lot before I left my apartment. I peeked out entrance door before venturing outside. I was becoming terrified of my own shadow and I hated it.

It was foggy and cold and as I jogged with my keys in my hand, I noticed glass on the ground, but my brain didn't register what it was. But once I reached the front of my car, I realized the glass used to be my passenger side window. Small shards littered the interior of the car. I spun around, looking for the guilty party, but I was completely alone.

My shoulders slumped. What else could go wrong, for God's sake? I kicked at the broken glass, then stomped back to my apartment and locked the door. I called Ma's and Ray answered. He told me not to worry about coming in, just call the police. Which I did. And they were as helpful as they had been when I reported Axton's disappearance. They took a report over the phone, told me to take pictures and call my insurance company. Since my car was barely worth a couple thousand dollars and I only had liability, I didn't bother.

Using my bathroom trash can and a small broom, I cleaned up all the glass I could manage and got to the diner a couple of minutes before six. Because I *no longer had a passenger window*, my hair looked as if I had been caught in a cyclone. Ma and Roxy were sympathetic to my latest drama and Jorge duct taped a plastic trash bag to my door until I could afford to get it fixed.

But I didn't have time to whine because Saturdays were so busy. Ray put pumpkin pancakes on the menu and I won't say they sold like hotcakes, but…well.

I checked my phone at closing. I had a text message from Sheila Graystone. She was actually waiting for me by the dumpsters behind the diner.

When I poked my head out the door, I saw her sitting behind the wheel of her running SUV. She waved me over and rolled down her window. "Rose," she whispered.

"Hey, Sheila. Did you get the numb—"

"Shhh, get in." She jerked her head to the passenger seat.

The fog had dissipated, but it was still a gray chilly afternoon, and the rotten smell of garbage carried on the wind. I was happy to hop inside.

"Sorry Rose, I can't be seen talking to you," she said as she ducked down in her seat.

"There's no one else here." I was surprised she hadn't shown up in a fedora and trench coat.

Sheila shoved a piece of notebook paper in my hand. "I had to wait until Pack went to bed last night to look at his phone."

There were four numbers on the list. "These are incoming numbers you don't recognize?"

She nodded. "That last number called nine times. And the calls ranged from two to five minutes each."

I folded the note and stuck it in my purse. "Thanks. I'll let you know what I find out."

"I feel like such a coward going behind his back like this." She rubbed her finger across her forehead. "I should be calling those numbers myself. But I really don't think it's another woman."

"You still think this is about Axton?"

"Packard knows more than he's telling. I asked him what he told the police and he got so angry. In ten years of marriage, he's never screamed at me. Raised his voice, yes. But when I asked about Axton, he went nuts."

I put my hand on her shoulder, not knowing how to comfort her. "Thanks, Sheila. I really appreciate it."

Before I met Dane at the police station, I ran home to change clothes. I pulled my hair out of its ponytail, giving it a quick brush, then threw on a navy sweater, jeans, and a pair of brown leather boots I'd bought last July.

Dane was already there when I pulled into a parking

spot in front of the building. He leaned against the brick wall next to the entrance and it was the first time I'd seen him without a suit. He wore faded jeans, a long-sleeved shirt, and tennis shoes. He smiled as he watched me walk toward him. "Hi."

"Hi, yourself." We looked at each other for a moment. His gaze drifted to my lips but moved past me to the passenger door of my car. He walked over to it, and reaching out, flicked the plastic bag. "What happened?"

"Vandalism."

"Is this related to everything else?"

"I don't know. Maybe."

He moved back to my side. "You're going to get this fixed soon, right?"

"Yeah."

"If it's a matter of money—"

"It isn't. I'll get it fixed soon." I gave him a bright smile.

He nodded. "Okay, let's go make that report." He took me by the hand led me into the building. As we walked through the twisting corridors, I felt like a rat in a maze.

We finally stopped at a small cubicle in the back corner with gray padded walls and a gunmetal gray desk. Andre Thomas, his uniform crisp and starched, took down my story about Henry and BJ and I threw in my vandalized car for good measure.

"How did you say they got in?" he asked, for what seemed like the millionth time.

I sighed. Loudly. "I told you, I don't know. They were already in my apartment when I got home."

Officer Thomas had café au lait skin and was handsome in a drill sergeant kind of way. His light hazel eyes stared at me through rectangular glasses. "You'd been to a couple of bars? How much did you have to drink?"

I threw my hands in the air and glared at him. We'd been at this for over an hour. "I didn't have anything to drink and I'm not on trial. I didn't do anything wrong."

"I'm just curious why you didn't report this sooner, Miss Strickland. Seems odd to me. If two men broke into my house, I'd have called the police immediately."

"I told you, I didn't think the police could help me and BJ was pretty specific about not messing with him."

He drummed his fingers on the desk. "So why are you reporting it now?"

Dane leaned forward. "What's the problem, Andre? She's telling you what happened."

The officer scrutinized me with laser-like intensity. "I'm just trying to get an accurate picture of what occurred."

I stood up. "Here's an accurate picture for you. My friend, Axton Graystone, is missing." I pointed at him. "I report that and you police people have done nothing about it. I report two men broke into my apartment and they seem to know my every move. I report someone vandalizes my car, but there's nothing you can do about that, either. And now you're treating me like the criminal?"

"Sounds like trouble follows you around, Miss Strickland. Now, sit down, and we'll go over this again." He nodded at the chair I'd vacated.

I shifted my gaze to Dane. "I told you this was a mistake." I grabbed my purse, haphazardly finding my way out of the labyrinth, wishing I'd left a trail of breadcrumbs to make it easier.

When I made it outside, I closed my eyes, tilted my face to dark clouds overhead. I took a deep cleansing breath. Sitting in that gray box being interrogated like a career criminal left me a little shaky. Dane came out a minute later. He placed his hand on the small of my back. "Hey," he said, "I know he's a hard ass, but he was just doing his job."

I opened my eyes and faced him. "I don't have much faith in the police anymore, Dane." I gestured toward the building. "This was pointless." I pulled my keys out of my purse and headed toward my car.

"Where are you going? We need to go back in there and finish up."

"I'm going to find Axton."

Chapter 16

I pulled into the nearest gas station, sat in my car, and scanned through the NorthStar list. I was determined to hit at least one more place today. I wasn't sure it would lead me to Ax, but it made me feel like I was doing something.

I had just picked out my next target when my phone rang. It was Jacks. "Yeah?" I was still hurt she lied about going to my parents' house last night. I knew Jacks hated to be stuck in the middle between my mother and me, but I wish she'd take my side occasionally.

"Do you want to come over for dinner? I'm making lasagna."

My stomach gurgled at the thought. This was her peace offering. And it was a yummy one. "Sure. What time?"

"Around six. Although you might want to get here early because someone got his Halloween costume."

"I did, Aunt Rose," I heard Scotty yell in the background.

"Tell him I can't wait to see him." I hung up and drove the five miles to Pour Femme, a chichi boutique close to the salon where my mother and Jacks got their hair done. It was full of beautiful dresses and gowns that cost more than I made in six months.

I walked in and probably still smelled of eau de bacon judging by the wrinkled nose of the woman who approached me. In her early forties, tall and painfully thin, she looked like a chic vampire in her tight black sheath.

"Yes?" she asked with one brow artfully raised.

Flashing Axton's picture around and telling my missing friend sob story had so far gotten me nowhere. Besides, this woman would have tossed Axton's pot-loving ass out of here in two seconds flat.

"Hello," I said with a smile, "I'm here from NorthStar." I waited for her to either toss me out on my ass or start spilling information.

She did neither. She inspected me from head to toe, and from her world-weary sigh, I didn't come up to snuff. "I wish they would send me taller girls."

Say what, now?

"What size are you? Eight?"

"I'm a four."

She propped her chin on the back of her hand and pursed her dark red lips. "Up top you're maybe a two, but that ass is definitely an eight."

"Excuse me?" I puffed out my size-two chest daring her to say more.

"Come," she said with a disdainful look on her face and slinked across the store. "Do you need a cocktail dress or a gown?"

"Cocktail," I said with confidence.

"When do you need it?" she asked, thumbing through a rack of short dresses.

"Now." Wow, I liked this new brazen me.

She sighed. "Of course, you need it now. They give

me short girls with big asses and they want me to work miracles yesterday."

I put my hands on my hips. "That's enough big ass talk, sister."

She didn't even respond. She pulled three dresses from the rack and shoved them at me. "Try these on." She stretched out her arm and pointed toward the back of the shop. "In there. Go."

I walked to a dressing room and hung up the three dresses she'd given me. In my old life, I took dresses like these for granted. My dad handed me his AmEx card and I bought what I wanted without ever looking at the price. Those days were long gone. I glanced at the tags and almost passed out.

I took a deep breath. I wasn't going to have to buy anything, I reminded myself, I was just on a fact finding trip. I'd try them on, ask a few questions, and get the heck out.

The first was a black halter dress with a lacy bodice and a full skirt. The V-neckline exposed half my chest.

The saleswoman knocked on my door. "Let me see."

I stepped out into the store. She walked around me, like a shark circling its prey. "Not bad," she said. "It camouflages that bottom and minimizes your lack of breasts. Next."

She was full of encouragement, that one. I walked back into the room and took off the dress. After carefully hanging it up, I tried on the next. This one was royal blue with an asymmetrical neckline. I walked out on my own this time.

"It does not hide that big bum of yours, but the color is flattering."

"Hey, big butts are in, you know. JLo, Kim Kardashian, ever heard of them?" Why was I defending myself? I did not have a wide ass.

"Go try the next."

I trudged back into the dressing room. This was worse than shopping with my mother.

The last dress was dark red with a sweetheart neckline and a full and rather short skirt. I felt like I was ready to skate in the Olympics.

I stepped out of the dressing room and stood there, bracing myself for another blow to my ego. She shook her head. "Awful. Go change." She turned and walked to the front of the store.

Before I could make my way back, a familiar voice stopped me.

"Rosalyn Strickland?"

Oh no. Tatum Hopkins. Could my life possibly suck any harder?

Tatum and I attended Huntingford Prep together. Tatum had been a cheerleader, student class rep, Winter Court Queen, and valedictorian. Yeah, I thought she was overcompensating, too. Tatum's mom, Stella was in my mom's bridge club, so I knew the news of my shopping in the ritziest boutique in town would find its way to my mother sooner rather than later.

Tatum kissed the airspace near my cheek. "Oh my gosh, look at you. You look fantastic." She tossed her shiny dark hair and smiled. She wore a leather Burberry jacket, skinny jeans, Manolo ankle boots, and clutched a Gucci purse.

"You too, Tatum. How are you?" *You big label whore.* All right, I used to be one, too.

"I'm home from med school for the weekend. I'm trying to decide where to do my residency. It's so hard."

I tried to smile through the pain. Tatum had her life all mapped out. I didn't even know what useless class I was going to take next semester. "I'm sure. Well, it's been just swell seeing you. Take care now." I spun toward my dressing room.

"Wait, what have you been up to?"

I turned back, with a phony smile on my face. "I've been taking classes at the city college. It's just great."

"You must be doing well to shop in here. Last I heard you were slumming it as a waitress."

She did not just say that. With narrowed eyes, I straightened my spine. "Oh, I still am. I work at Ma's Diner. You should come in sometime and try the pancakes. If you don't eat carbs, you could always purge them later, like you used to do in high school."

The smile slowly faded from her face.

"Tell your mom hello for me." I returned to the dressing room and quickly changed into my own clothes, then stood there for a few minutes, leaning against the wall. The Tatums of the world made me feel like crap. All that "only you can make yourself feel inferior" blah, blah, blah was bullshit. I felt just fine about myself before she showed up. Mostly. I hated running into people from my old life. Axton of course, being the exception. He was an oddball, like me. And he loved me just the way I was.

When I came out of the dressing room, Tatum was gone and I sighed with relief. It would have been too humiliating to put the dresses back with her standing there, knowing I couldn't afford them.

The saleswoman took the them out of my hands, then hung the blue and red on the rack. Still holding the black one, she walked to a small desk with gilt accents and removed the price tag. When she put the dress in a garment bag with the Pour Femme logo on it, I started to panic. Even if I sold a kidney, I couldn't afford that dress.

"I'm not really sure about the black one. I need to think about it." I began edging toward the door.

She wrote out a ticket. "Don't be ridiculous. It's the best looking of the three and flatters you the most."

She held out the bag to me. "Here you go. Do you have shoes to go with that?"

I stared at her for a moment. "Um...yes?"

"Good. Tell them next time to give a few days' notice. You would have had more of a selection if I had time for alterations."

"You bet." I grabbed the bag and made a run for it.

It wasn't until I was sitting in my car that I realized I hadn't asked her anything about NorthStar. I dropped my head on the steering wheel. I was so freaked out at seeing Tatum Hopkins and the thought of having to pay for the dress, that I forgot my first objective.

I reached over to the passenger seat and ran my hand along the side of the bag. A little thrill shot through me. At least I got something out of it.

As I drove to Jacks' house, the wind made a horrible *thwap-thwap-thwap* sound against the clear plastic bag affixed to my passenger door. It was loud and annoying, but I didn't feel like I was in the middle of a tornado anymore.

Scotty answered the door in a Spiderman costume. I peered down at him, a confused expression on my face. "Excuse me, Spiderman, do I have the wrong house? I'm looking for my nephew, Scotty."

He started laughing like a little maniac and pulled up his mask. "It's me, Aunt Rose. I fooled you."

I gasped. "You sure did. I thought I was at Spiderman's place by mistake."

He turned and ran toward living room, leaving me to step in and close the door. The savory smell of oregano and tomato filled the house and made my mouth water.

Although I was alone in the foyer, all of the sudden every hair on the back of my neck stood on end. Only one person caused that reaction.

I swung around, my hand on the door knob, ready to make a run for it.

"Hello, Rosalyn."

The theme from *Jaws* started to play in my head. I glanced back at her. "Hello, Mother."

"I see you're as surprised as I am." She didn't look surprised. She looked like she'd stepped on a turd.

"I guess so."

Her posture was as stiff as always. She wore silky golden pants and a flowing tunic. She took in my appearance as well, her gaze landing on my jeans.

"I talked to Stella Hopkins today. She said Tatum ran into you at Pour Femme."

I leaned against the door and shoved my hands into my jacket pockets. Here we go. "Yep."

"First of all, what were you doing there?" She lifted her nose in the air. "I know for a fact you can't afford it."

"Hey, have you been hacking into my bank account again?"

"I know you like to think you're amusing, Rosalyn, but Tatum was traumatized by your rude behavior."

Really? Traumatized? How does the woman expect to become a doctor if she can't handle one little conversation? With a waitress, no less? Still, I said nothing. I was in Jacks' home and the last thing I wanted was another incident with my mother.

"She's gotten treatment for her eating disorder. You were rude and hateful. And while you sneer at people like Tatum, at least she's doing something with her life."

I was getting a weird sense of déjà vu, like I'd had this conversation before. Like a thousand times. And she was wrong—I didn't sneer, I'd derided. Totally different.

Before Barbara could speak again, my sister stepped into the foyer. "Hey, you two. Isn't this nice?"

We both gaped at her as if she'd escaped from a mental health facility and was still wearing the straight jacket. Her smile looked more like a grimace and her wide eyes reminded me of a frightened horse, all wild, with the whites showing. "How about a glass of wine? Does anyone want a glass of wine?" she asked before fleeing.

A glass? How about the whole freaking bottle?

My mother and I eyeballed one another as we walked from the foyer into the living room. Scotty was telling my dad important Spiderman facts and Allen sipped a glass of whiskey. He looked up when we entered the room.

"Hey, Rose," he said. He put his glass on the coffee table and reached forward to kiss my cheek, something he'd never done.

I pulled back before his lips could make contact. "Hey, Allen. What are you doing?"

He threw out a nervous laugh. "Oh, sorry. How about a drink? Barb, glass of wine?"

Just then my sister walked into the living room with a tray of cheese and crackers, a bottle, and three glasses. "Here we go," she said a little too loudly. She poured and handed each of us a glass.

I stood by the fireplace, sipped the wine and nibbled a piece of cheese. My mom refused any food and sat down, her spine never touching the back of the sofa.

Jacqueline sent Scotty off to change out of his costume before dinner. Once he left she turned to the rest of us. "All right," she said and cleared her throat. "I know you might be a bit upset that I did all this without telling you. But I decided this unfortunate situation has gone on long enough." Her shoulders sagged with relief, like she'd been screwing up all of her courage to say her little sentence and now she could relax. My poor, deluded sister. She had no idea what hell she'd unleashed.

"Pardon me?" Barbara asked. Her face was expressionless, her eyes cold. "To what situation do you refer, Jacqueline?"

Pity, fascination, and a little schadenfreude had me riveted to my sister's reaction. Rarely was she a victim of my mother's displeasure. That was almost always reserved for me, thank you very much.

Jacks' gaze flew around. If she was looking for help, she wasn't going to find it in this room. "Um," Jacqueline said and cleared her throat again. "The situation between you and Rose."

"And what situation is that?" my mother asked.

At this point my father shifted in his chair and attempted to calm the tension. "All right, let's all just relax."

My mother's gaze shifted to him. "I'm perfectly relaxed, John. Do I not look relaxed to you?"

My father, being a man of reasonable intelligence, shut up and sipped his whiskey.

Jacks' eyes were shiny with unshed tears. I decided to take pity on her. After all, she tried to do a nice thing, brokering peace between my mom and me. She didn't realize it would never happen.

"That's enough, Mom. She was just trying to help." My mother sucked in a breath. "Thank you for trying, Jacks." I set my glass down. "Now, I'm going to go find Scotty." I left the room and climbed the stairs.

I stepped into his bedroom with its race car wallpaper. Scotty, still in his costume, attempted to climb on top of his dresser. His Spidey sense must not have been working because he never heard me enter. I wrangled him off the dresser, made him put on his jeans, sweater, and tennis shoes then chased him down the stairs.

Dinner was awkward and quiet. So pretty much business as usual. Scotty talked about school, my dad and Allen talked about work, and my mother ate miniscule bites of food, refusing to speak to anyone except my gap-toothed nephew.

I helped Jacks clear the table while the men went to the den to watch Sports Center and Barbara went to the living room with Scotty.

"What were you thinking, Jacks?"

"I don't know." She twisted the napkins in her hands.

"I just wanted the two of you to get along. Now Mom's mad at me."

"She'll get over it. If you want to make her get over it even faster, grovel." I loaded the flatware into the dishwasher.

"Seriously, Rose, how do you stand it? It makes me crazy when she freezes me out like that."

"I got used to it. It was preferable to kissing her ass."

Jacks winced.

"Sorry," I said, "I didn't mean it like that."

"No, you're right." She leaned against the fridge. "I'm a people pleaser. Always have been."

I hugged her tight. "You're a good person and a great mom."

"Thanks."

We finished the dishes and I left the kitchen and headed downstairs where Allen and my dad watched TV. I said goodbye and my dad gave me a distracted pat on the arm. Then I went upstairs and found my mother sitting alone in the living room, her laptop open on the sofa next to her. She looked up when I walked in.

"I'm taking off."

"Oh." She shifted slightly. "Any word on Axton?"

"Why do you want to know?"

She sighed heavily. "Honestly, can't I even ask a simple question?" She shook her head and took off her reading glasses.

I decided to be honest for once. "No, Mom, not really. I feel like I need a lawyer before I answer anything or you may use it against me later."

"Fine." She turned her attention to her computer.

But I wasn't quite finished with her. Normally, I let things slide off my back. It's so pointless to argue with her, that I don't bother. Sure I get pissed at her more aggressive than passive digs, and stew about it later, but rarely do I give her the satisfaction of getting a rise out of me. Tonight though, I was worried about Jacks.

"Listen." I waited until she looked up before continuing. "I know you're pissed—"

"Language."

"Fine," I conceded, "I know you're *angry* at Jacks for arranging all this." I wiggled my finger between the two of us. "And for interfering." I paused to see if she would respond. If you could call an icy stare a response, then I guess I got one. "She meant well. And I don't want you to be mean to her."

"I'm sure I don't know what you mean, Rosalyn."

"Huh, I'm sure you do, Mom."

I found Scotty in his room, playing with his little racecars. "Play cars with me, Aunt Rose."

"Sorry Sport, not tonight. How about a hug goodbye?"

He hopped up and ran to me, reaching out his arms. I caught him and swung him high before pulling him into a tight hug.

Back downstairs I kissed my sister on the cheek and thanked her for dinner before leaving.

"What did you say to Mom?" she asked.

"What makes you think I said anything?"

"She looks mad enough to spit nails and you're the only one who inspires that look."

"Good." Hopefully she would be so angry with me for calling her out she'd forget all about Jacks' interference.

It started to drizzle, so I flipped on the windshield wipers and hoped my plastic bag window was strong enough to keep the inside of my car dry.

As I drove home, the drizzle became a full blown storm. The temperature dropped and the heater in my car blew out lukewarm air. But so far, the plastic held up.

I pulled into my parking lot, and as I got out of my car, I covered my head with my purse and made a run for it. But before I taken more than a few steps, a large, black SUV with tinted windows slammed to a stop in front of me.

Chapter 17

Henry jumped out of the passenger seat and grabbed my arm, then yanked me toward the car.

I dropped my purse and tried to break away from him as cold rain stung my face. I screamed and pulled and slapped at him. It didn't do me a bit of good. Henry simply scooped me up and tossed me into the back seat next to a bald giant dressed in black.

He looked at me with pale, expressionless eyes. "Boss wants to see you." He didn't blink. It was creepy.

"Well, I don't want to see him." I tried to open the door, but they must have engaged the child locks because it wouldn't budge.

Henry climbed into the front seat.

I glanced out the window at my purse lying on the wet pavement and hoped they didn't notice it. If Henry or his henchmen looked inside, they would find all my clues. The list of names Eric decrypted, the numbers from Packard's phone, the list of businesses owned by NorthStar. Also, if they weren't planning on letting me go, finding my purse might convince the police I had been kidnapped. Always a long shot with Huntingford's finest, but a shot just the same.

"Let's go," Henry said to the driver, who looked like

his doppelganger.

My seatmate leaned toward me. I instinctively pulled away, but he jerked me to him. He blindfolded me with a black cloth from his pocket, then grabbed my wrists and bound them in front of me.

Terror slowly crept up my chest and I thought I might hyperventilate. Getting shoved into a car by Henry was frightening. But not being able to see where I was going or what they might do to me? That took my fear to a whole different level. I had never felt so helpless. I shivered in spite of the vent blowing warm air directly on me.

No one said anything during the ride and they didn't turn on the radio. Rain lashed against the car. That and the engine were the only sounds I heard. It felt like we were moving pretty fast, so I assumed we were on the highway. When we stopped, I tried to gauge how long we'd been on the road. Maybe thirty minutes at the most. I desperately tried to keep my brain engaged so fear wouldn't take over. If I could keep a level head, I might get out of this.

The door next to me opened and Henry hauled me out, slinging me over his shoulder. I thought it was Henry. It certainly smelled like Henry. Rain pelted me, and for a crazy second I thought about what I must look like with my butt bouncing next to Henry's head. My size eight butt. I stifled a giggle, realizing I was close to hysteria. I swallowed the inappropriate laugh and reached up with my bound hands to tug at my blindfold.

"Don't do that." It was the guy who'd been sitting next to me. He followed behind us.

I dropped my hands and continued to flop against Henry's back. I knew we'd walked into a building when the rain stopped hitting me. I heard a door open and Henry lowered me to my feet. I swayed a little and felt his hand on my arm steady me. He removed my blindfold, but left my wrists tied.

I blinked at the light and looked around. I was in a study. A personal library, really. Two tall windows flanked a stone fireplace along one wall. Shelves and shelves of hardback books lined the other three. An enormous wood desk stood in front of me, empty except for a laptop computer.

Henry pushed me toward a tufted leather chair in front of the desk. "Sit."

I dripped a trail of water on a red Persian rug until I reached the chair and sat down. Henry stood sentinel behind me and it made my stomach clench.

Crossing my legs, I bounced my foot up and down. Exactly how Axton had acted the last time I'd seen him. I forced myself to stop fidgeting, but my stomach was still doing back flips and my heart raced.

After several minutes the door behind me opened. I twisted my head and watched BJ enter the room.

"Thank you, Henry. You can wait outside." The Boss wore black today. Black jacket, black shirt, black pants. He just needed a villainous mustache to twirl and his ensemble would be complete.

He sat in the chair next to mine. He stared at me with those gold eyes as he worked the thin rope at my wrists. When my hands were free, he rubbed them, his long elegant fingers using just the right amount of pressure from my fingertips to my pulse point. The contact of his skin against mine made me shiver.

"Are they sore?"

"What the hell do you care?"

He stood and moved behind the desk and sat down. Placing his elbows on the desktop, he steepled his fingers against his lips. We sat in silence. He stared at me with no expression on his face, and I fought the urge to squirm like a naughty school girl brought before the principal.

"What am I going to do with you, Rose?"

I didn't think he really expected an answer, so I said nothing.

"I've warned you to mind your own business. Several times. I've never done that before."

Guess he was a little pissed I went to the police station. I chewed my bottom lip as my gaze travelled around the room. "Have you read any of these?"

"Pardon?"

"The books, have you read them?"

He glanced around at the books lining the walls. "No. I hired a decorator."

"Oh." For some reason I was disappointed. I could sort of picture him here, in a smoking jacket and slippers, reading a book with a snifter of brandy at his elbow. Does anyone actually own a smoking jacket? Where do you buy a smoking jacket? I almost did that inappropriate laugh thing again, but took a deep breath to calm myself.

"I like you, Rose, I really do. But not enough to let you fuck up what's taken me years to build."

"I don't want to fuck up anything, I just want to find Ax. Then you can keep doing whatever criminal bullshit you do and leave me alone."

"Unfortunately, I can't do that."

I wasn't exactly sure what that meant. Was he going to

kill me, torture me, lock me up?

He reached into the top desk drawer and pulled out a manila folder. He hesitated just a second before laying it on the desk in front of me.

I stared down at it, shaking my head. I didn't want to see its contents. I knew it couldn't be good news.

"Go ahead. I know you're curious."

With trembling fingers I flipped open the cover. Inside were eight by ten color photos. I snatched them up and thumbed through them. Scotty on a swing at school, my sister in her car, my mother and father eating in a restaurant, Ma pouring coffee at the diner, Roxy standing outside The Carp. The last picture was of Axton. He had a gag in his mouth, his eyes wide with fear. My gaze flew from the photo to BJ.

The pictures wobbled in my shaky grip. My skin grew clammy, a wave of nausea swept over me.

His cold eyes studied me, like I was a lab specimen he couldn't quite figure out. I think I started to blackout because he calmly stood up from behind the desk and came to stand beside me. He plucked the photos from my hand and gently pushed my head forward until it rested between my knees.

"Take deep breaths," he said. "In and out. That's it."

I did as he said and bright dots sparked behind my eyes. I sat like that, breathing in and out, his hand rubbing circles along my damp back, until the dizziness passed. I took one last deep breath before lifting my head back up.

"Slowly, now," he said, his fingers still caressing me.

I raised my arm and tried to twist away from him. "Don't."

Our gazes met as he slid his hand up to the back of my

neck, through the tangle of wet hair. He squeezed my nape gently before he stood and walked to his desk. Behind it sat a crystal decanter filled with liquor. He poured a small amount into a matching crystal glass and brought it to me. "Drink this."

"No, I don't want to." I sounded childish, but I didn't care.

"Drink it."

I took the glass from his hand, making sure my skin didn't brush against his, and sipped. Whiskey. I never liked whiskey.

"Drink some more." He retreated to his chair.

Without taking another drink, I reached forward and set the glass on the edge of his desk.

"My God, you're stubborn." He wore a grim expression, the brackets around his mouth seemed deeper. "I have Axton. I know where your friends and family live. I can get to them at any time. Keep your mouth shut and stop asking questions."

My short nails dug into the padded armrests. "You really are an asshole."

"I didn't want to do this, but you forced my hand. And I will do whatever it takes to protect my interests."

"What interests?"

He barked out a laugh and shook his head, staring up at the ceiling. "You are unbelievable."

As we continued to sit there, a sense of calm detachment stole over me, as if all this was happening to someone else, like I was watching a movie. "There's something you need to know."

"What's that?"

I pointed toward the file, which now lay on his closed laptop. "If anything happens to my friends or family, if anything happens to Axton, I'll kill you."

His gaze flickered over my face. "I believe you, Rose." He clapped his hands. "Now we know where we stand, don't we?" He stood up, walked to the door, and opening it, spoke to Henry. "Take her home." BJ left the room and didn't look back.

I was hauled out and blindfolded, then shoved into the SUV once again.

Worst. Field trip. Ever.

Chapter 18

Henry all but pushed me out of the SUV and it spun off into the night. I stood there in the rain, watching the red tail lights disappear from view.

BJ had Axton.

When did he take Axton? Where did BJ find him and was he okay?

I picked up my drenched imitation leather purse and my keys still lying next to it on the rain-soaked pavement. I brushed at a wet strand of hair as I made my way to my apartment.

I stripped off my clothes and stood in the shower stall, letting the warm water flow over me as I mulled over my night with BJ. Kidnapping me, showing me he had Ax, those were pretty desperate moves. His threats meant I was on the right track. I was making him nervous. I thought over what I had done the last couple of days. I'd gone to Penn's Cigar Bar and shown Axton's picture to the bartender. Went to the tanning salon and tussled with Manny. Saw Sheila Graystone a couple of times. Filed a police report—which I assumed set BJ off, but maybe I was wrong on that score—and ended up with a swanky cocktail dress from Pour Femme courtesy of NorthStar.

That was the key, NorthStar. Had to be. Between Manny and Pour Femme, I was onto something. I smiled at the thought.

This jerk had my Axton, and one way or another, I was going to get him back.

I hopped out of the shower, dried off, and pulled on a pair of sweats. I made myself a pot of coffee. There was absolutely no way I was going to get any sleep. Not after my day. I decided to look up the numbers Sheila gave me.

I booted up my laptop, and using the reverse address, I found the first number. Huntingford Bank and Trust. According to Sheila, the bank called Packard six times in two days. Seemed excessive, but what did I know? My banking needs were small, just like the balance in my account.

The next number belonged to Charles and Willa Beaumont. These two were unfamiliar to me, so I did a little research. Turns out both Willa and her husband Charles were civic-minded citizens. Willa worked with the Historical Preservation Society and Charles sat on the city council with Packard. Seemed legitimate.

The next number was for the Sun Kissed Tanning Salon. Someone—Manny—called Pack once. I gasped in excitement. Finally a tangible link between NorthStar and at least one Graystone brother. I had no idea what it meant, but it wasn't a dead end, and that had me doing a happy dance. Literally. I got up and danced around my apartment. I may have even pumped a fist once or twice.

After I calmed down, I looked up the final number, the one that popped up nine times. That number, of course, was unlisted.

Although it was close to midnight, I decided to call it. I

pressed star sixty-seven before dialing to block my number from Caller ID. Axton taught me that.

A smooth voice answered on the second ring. "Sullivan."

I froze for a beat in shock before I quickly pushed the end button on my phone. I knew that voice. The Bossy Jackass.

I stared at my phone as if it might reach out and bite me. Sullivan. That was his name. First or last?

I immediately took to the computer and looked up several combinations. Sullivan and NorthStar Inc., Sullivan and Sun Kissed Tanning, Sullivan and Packard Graystone, and every other pairing I could think of. Nothing.

I called Eric and woke him up. "What," he grumbled.

"I found out who BJ is. I found him, Eric."

"Who is this?"

"It's Rose. And I have a link between NorthStar and Packard Graystone."

"Hang on, give me a minute."

I continued to punch the word Sullivan into the search engine as I waited for Eric to become coherent.

"All right, tell me again. Slowly."

I told him about Packard's call from Sun Kissed Tanning. "And I think I have a name for The Bossy Jackass."

"How did you find out his name?"

I explained how I had made this amazing discovery, then sat back, feeling pretty darn pleased with myself.

"You rock, Rose."

I grinned. "I do rock. I rock hard."

"Let me do a little digging and see if I can turn up anything."

There wasn't any more I could do to find Axton tonight. I suppose I could have studied. Instead I watched infomercials until it was time to go to work.

"I'm going to saw my wrists, I swear." I walked from the kitchen into the dining room the next morning and saw Roxy holding a butter knife in the air. Ma grabbed it out of her hand.

Pounding her fists on the counter, Roxy glared at her. "I need a cigarette."

"You're doing fine, honey," Ma said, rubbing her back.

I plucked an apron from the hook and forced a smile. "Hey."

They both looked up when I entered.

"Hey, toots, any news on Axton?" Ma asked.

I debated whether to tell them about Henry's abduction and Sullivan's latest threat. It would upset Ma, and Roxy would insist I stay with her. I decided to do some creative editing. "I went to Pour Femme yesterday and told them I was from NorthStar. They gave me a dress. Then I found out BJ's name and he admitted he has Axton."

"What?" Ma slammed the knife on the counter. "He has Axton? What does that mean?"

"Sheila gave me that list of numbers. When I called he answered 'Sullivan.' He told me to quit asking questions and said he had Axton." That was creative and no one would worry, right? "Also, Pack and Sun Kissed Manny know each other."

"What's the dress look like?" Roxy asked.

Ma lightly smacked her arm. "Is Axton all right?"

I thought about that horrible picture of Ax bound and gagged. He looked terrified. "I'm not sure."

She came around the counter and pulled me into a hug. "I miss him so much, Ma. I just want him to be okay."

"Maybe you should go to the police, Rose. I know this Bossy Jackass—"

"Sullivan," I mumbled against her shoulder.

"I know he said not to, but maybe it's time."

"I already went yesterday with Dane. They don't care. The cop treated me like I was the criminal. He didn't believe me."

"Dick," Roxy said.

"He kind of was."

"I wish I knew what to tell you, toots."

"Me too, Ma."

I went to the bathroom and splashed some cool water on my face. Had I done the right thing not telling them Henry kidnapped me and took me to a Godfather-style sit down with Sullivan? I didn't know what the right thing was anymore. I was putting everyone around me in jeopardy. Would it be better if I warned them? Or would it just make them as paranoid and jittery as I was?

Sundays were usually our busiest day with people waiting up to thirty minutes for a table. But because the heavy rain continued throughout the morning, we were pretty slow.

Dane showed up at eight. He shrugged out of a wet all-weather jacket and hung it on the peg by the door. Running a hand over his hair, his gaze moved around the diner until it found me in the corner pouring coffee.

I smiled and made my way over to him. I felt pretty guilty for leaving him in front of the police station yesterday, but I'm not sure I wouldn't do it again. I didn't appreciate Officer Thomas or his piss-poor attitude.

"Hey," I said.

He smiled. "Hey." He brushed his thumb along my cheek. "You look tired."

I raised my brows. "Oh stop, you're making me blush. About yesterday, I'm sor—"

"No," he said, "I'm sorry. Andre Thomas may be a good cop, but he acted like an ass and I told him so."

"I found a name for BJ." Before I could explain further, Ma walked up.

"Hello, young man."

"Ma Ferguson, this is Dane Harker."

She held out her hand. "Dane, it's a pleasure."

"Nice to officially meet you. Do I call you Ma?"

"Everyone else does. Rose, we're not busy right now. Go sit down with this handsome young man and take as much time as you need."

Dane smiled a little at the compliment.

I grabbed him a cup of coffee and led him to the table.

Dane snapped his fingers. "Oh, before I forget, I have something for you." He reached into the back pocket of his jeans and pulled out a folded piece of paper, then handed it to me. It was a copy of a webpage for NorthStar.

"What's this?"

"All the information I could find about NorthStar. And that," he nodded at the paper, "was not a quick Google search."

"This is it?" There was a logo and an address for a PO

Box in Florida.

"Afraid so. Looks like a dummy corporation."

"And that is?"

"A shell company that's a front for another company, and that company is just a dummy for yet another company."

I sighed and looked up from the paper. "So can we find the dummy who's in charge?"

"Easier said than done. These things are usually set up as tax shelters. There are often many, many knots to unravel. Think of it as the Russian nesting dolls of corporations. Could take years to figure it all out. And that isn't my area of expertise."

One step forward, two steps back.

"Now what is this about finding out BJ's real name?"

I told him the creative version of my conversation with BJ and finished up with Sullivan having Axton.

"How do you know it's true? Maybe he's just telling you that to make you back off." He sipped his coffee and glanced at me over the rim of the cup.

I shrugged. "He sounded pretty convincing. But I also found at least one NorthStar business has a link to Packard Graystone." I told him the link I found between Packard and Sun Kissed Manny.

Dane rubbed one finger along his temple. "None of this makes sense."

"I want to know more about that list of people I showed you, the one with dates and numbers. How do they fit in?"

"You can't seriously think the people on that list have anything to do with Axton's disappearance? I know those people. Mayor Briggs was on that list. And Martin Mathers, the Chief of Police? You think he's involved?"

"Why else would Axton give it to me for safekeeping? What else could Sullivan want?"

"I don't know, but the idea of these people being involved with..." he trailed off.

"Kidnapping a pothead?"

"Come on, even you have to admit this is a little crazy. Do you think Michael Dayton, one of the partners at my firm, and my boss by the way, even knows Axton?"

"What do you mean even I have to admit this is crazy? Axton had this hard drive for a reason, Dane. He gave it to me for a reason. This is connected to his kidnapping whether you want to believe it or not."

He leaned forward, a look of pity crossed his face. "I know you want to believe that, but there's no evidence to support it. Axton doesn't move in these circles. It doesn't make sense."

"Axton doesn't, but his brother does."

He leaned back. "Right. A well respected doctor, a member of the city council, somehow ties into Axton's disappearance? How? Why? It's probably a donor list for a charity."

It bothered me how Dane kept referring to Axton's kidnapping as a disappearance. It stopped being a disappearance when I saw that chilling photo. But I couldn't tell Dane that. "Thanks for the info about NorthStar. I need to get back to work."

Dane grabbed my wrist. "Come on, don't be like this."

I pulled away. "It's fine. I'll talk to you later." I stepped into the kitchen to take a deep breath.

Dane totally dismissed me.

Why would Axton have an encrypted list on a hard drive if it wasn't important? I was convinced I was right. If Dane didn't want to help, fine. I'd keep going on my own.

Even after Sullivan's latest threat, it never crossed my mind to quit looking for Ax. I missed him so much. His goofy grin, his *Star Wars* t-shirts, the way he'd drop by the diner for breakfast or bring me a pizza and a horrible sci-fi movie. Axton had the sweetest spirit of anyone I'd ever met.

Sullivan certainly made it clear he wanted me to quit looking. I had a good reason to let this go, the safety of my family and friends. But my heart had an Axton-shaped hole right now. I would keep going.

An hour after Dane left, Steve Gunderson walked through the door and propped his umbrella against the wall. He smiled and waved at me before taking off his glasses and rubbing them against his white button-down.

"Hey." He slid onto a stool and leaned his elbows on the counter. "Haven't heard from you in a couple of days, so I thought I'd check in."

"That's nice of you." I poured him a cup of coffee, introduced him to Ma.

"Now which one are you?" she asked.

"Steve works with Axton."

Roxy walked up, her jaw in constant motion. "Hey, what are you doing here?"

Steve's cheeks turned pink. "I just wanted to see if Rose had any news."

I gave Roxy a death stare. "Steve's worried about Axton, too."

"Wanted to see you is more like it," she muttered as she moved behind me.

"What can I get you, Steve?" I asked.

He ordered another cup to go and only stayed ten minutes. Long enough for him to ask me out. "Do you like Indian food? The Taj Mahal over on Blossom Avenue makes this curry—"

"Steve." I touched his arm. "You're a really nice guy—"

He glanced down at my hand. "Hey, no problem." His crooked grin tilted to one side. "I'll talk to you later."

I felt a little bad for him, but it was better to cut these things off at the pass. Cruel to be kind and all that.

Customers were few and far between as the cold rain continued, so I didn't feel guilty about calling Sheila Graystone during my shift. She didn't waste time on pleasantries.

"What have you found out?" she asked as soon as she heard my voice.

"The first number belonged to Huntingford Bank and Trust."

She paused for a long moment. "Go on."

"One call from Charles Beaumont."

"That makes sense. He and Charles are both on the city council. What else?"

"One call from the Sun Kissed Tanning Salon."

"What?" she asked, surprise in her voice. "That must have been a wrong number or something."

"Maybe. And the last number belongs to a man named Sullivan." If I had been waiting for a big revelation, I was in for a disappointment.

"Is that it? That's all? I mean, there wasn't...?"

"No women."

"Of course not. I told you." In spite of her words, I heard the relief in her voice.

"So, who is this Sullivan guy?" I tried to make the question sound casual. "He and Packard spoke nine times."

"Who knows? Probably something to do with the city council. Pack even has a committee meeting tonight and that almost never happens on a Sunday. I guess I was worried for nothing," she said with a little laugh.

Uh huh. "Take care, Sheila."

Roxy stood next to me chomping her gum as she filled the coffee pot with water.

"I'm going to follow Packard tonight, want to come?"

She shrugged. "Sure."

"Where are you going?" Ma sat at the counter, sipping her coffee.

Ray came out of the kitchen with my omelet in one hand, Roxy's cinnamon roll in the other. "Thanks, Ray."

"Son, the biscuits were too salty this morning," Ma said to Ray's retreating back. She looked at me. "What's going on tonight?"

"We're going to follow Packard. He told Sheila he's going to a city council meeting, but I think he's lying."

"Ooooh, that sounds like fun. Just like a television show." She looked at me expectantly. When I said nothing, her face dropped. "Well. You girls have a good time." I knew she wanted to come, but I wasn't sure if that was such a good idea. It could be dangerous. And the woman was almost eighty, for crying out loud.

"Don't you have bingo or dominoes or bridge club tonight?" I asked.

"No, bunko got canceled. The woman hosting it had a stroke."

"Oh Ma, I'm sorry."

"Is she going to be okay?" Roxy asked.

"Oh, sure, it was a mild one. Hey, at our age, stuff like that happens."

That's what I was afraid of. "Well," I said, frowning, "you probably don't want to go with—"

"I'd love to." She giggled like a schoolgirl. "This is going to be such a kick."

I wished I shared her enthusiasm.

Chapter 19

When I got to Roxy's apartment later that night, I was surprised to see her dressed in normal clothes. Well, normal for her. True, the crotch of her black slacks hung to her knees and the hood of her furry coat had bear ears, but the t-shirt and ballet flats were perfectly normal.

The rain had finally stopped, but the air was still damp and cold. I parked in front of Ma's blue and white Victorian house. I still thought Ma coming had bad idea written all over it, but I didn't want to disappoint her.

I hopped out of the car, ran up the front stairs, and knocked. Ma stepped onto the porch, handing me a thermos and a plastic grocery sack. "I'm so excited. Do we need a camera, because I've got one in my purse, just in case."

"I don't think so." I followed her down the steps. "In fact, I think it's going to be pretty boring."

She brushed me off as she walked to the car. "Don't be such a downer, Rose."

Roxy climbed into the back seat so Ma could sit shotgun. "I brought snacks," Ma said. "And hot chocolate."

We drove to Packard's subdivision and I parked at the end of the cul-de-sac. I cut the headlights, but left the car running.

Ma skillfully poured hot chocolate into cups she'd pilfered from the diner, the ones with a lid and sleeve around it so we wouldn't burn our hands. She reached back into the plastic bag and pulled out a container. "Who wants Chex mix?"

We waited about forty-five minutes before Packard came out of the house and got into his SUV. I followed him from a discreet distance keeping my headlights off until we turned onto a main thoroughfare. He led us through town before taking the highway.

"Where do you think he's going?" Ma yelled. She had to if she wanted to be heard over the *thwapping* noise of the plastic bag window.

"It's not City Hall, that's for sure," I said.

"Crap," Roxy said from the backseat.

"What's wrong?"

"I only have two pieces of gum left."

Ma twisted in her seat to look at Roxy. "What about that patch? How's that working?"

"I hate that stupid patch. And I hate this sucky gum. I want a cigarette. Argh!" She sounded like a pirate.

"Feel better?" My gaze met hers in the rearview mirror. She shrugged. "A little."

Packard pulled onto the Crabtree Avenue exit. We were officially out of Huntingford and into country territory. He drove another fifteen minutes to a deserted highway. When he turned right, I turned left, then doubled back and cut my headlights once again, letting him get far ahead of me. We pulled into a long gravel drive that led to a two-story brick building.

"This used to be a school, I think," said Ma. "The

country kids went here."

"I'm assuming this is a bar, right? What else would be out here?" I asked.

"Well, there's only one way to find out." Ma put the snacks back in the plastic sack at her feet.

Packard parked in front of the building with about seventy-five other cars. Every light in the place was on.

When he walked in, I drove the rest of the way down the long drive and parked in the last row, as far from Pack's car as I could get. I switched off the ignition and turned in my seat. "What are we going to do? We can't just march in there."

"Pull around back," Roxy said.

I restarted the engine and did as she asked. There were cars parked behind the building as well, but I found a space near the back entrance. "Now what?"

"Now we do reconnaissance." She shrugged out of her jacket. "Will you be all right here, Ma?"

"Of course."

"I'll leave the car running," I said. "It's extra chilly because of the busted window."

"Go on, girls. Call if you get into trouble." She waved her phone at us.

I shrugged out of my coat and left it with Ma, just in case she needed it. Roxy and I walked toward the building. "Okay, Rox, what's your big plan?"

"This is it. Reconnaissance."

I stopped and stared at her. "You don't have a plan?"

"I can't do everything, Rose." She huffed and stomped toward the building.

Good God.

When she got to the door, she waited for me to do the honors. With a deep breath I twisted the knob and opened it. Clinking plates and noisy chatter filled a professional stainless steel kitchen. Steam smacked me in the face and the briny smell of shrimp made my stomach growl. I glanced back at her. "At least we're in familiar territory."

I walked in with Roxy behind me. Men and women dressed in black slacks, white dress shirts, and black bow ties hustled around the kitchen. Now this I could do.

A woman with oversized black eyeglasses and a clipboard strode toward us. "Who are you? What are you doing in my kitchen?"

I smiled. "We're new. NorthStar sent us." I held my smile as she looked from me to Roxy, taking in her blue hair and baggy pants.

"I wasn't told about this. Where are your uniforms?"

Roxy smacked her gum. "They said you had 'em."

The woman put her palm up to Roxy's mouth. "Spit."

"Huh?"

"Gum is not allowed. Now spit."

Roxy looked slightly panicked, but spit the gum into the woman's hand.

Alice, as marked on a very large nametag pinned to her shirt, looked disgusted as she marched to the other side of the room and threw the gum in the trash. She briskly walked back to us. "That blue hair has got to go. It's not regulation. You can work in the kitchen tonight." She turned toward me. "You, come with me."

I glanced over as Roxy flipped off Alice behind her back.

"I have a few extra uniforms. What's your name?"

"Uh, Sue." Damn, why didn't I ever have a good answer for that question?

In a little cloak room off the kitchen, several uniforms hung on a rolling rack. She grabbed one and thrust it at me. "I have very strict standards. Follow them and we'll get along just fine. Get dressed. Then grab a tray of shrimp puffs and take it out." She left the room and I locked the door behind her.

As I changed clothes, I wondered what we had stumbled into. And I wondered if I could snag some of those shrimp puffs. I was hungry.

I adjusted the bow tie, then grabbed the phone out of my jeans, and shoved it into the pocket of my new uniform. I walked back to the kitchen and glanced over at Roxy. She slapped doilies on a tray, and by the look she gave me, she wasn't happy about it.

I grabbed a tray on my way out of the kitchen and walked down an empty hall. The worn hardwood floors were dull in the dim light. There hadn't been much updating in the place. It looked exactly like what it was—an old school.

Quiet voices came from a room on the left. I poked my head inside but didn't see Packard. Pretty young women in dressy gowns with glasses of champagne in their hands stood close to three round baize tables. Men sat at the tables, cards in their hands, drinks at their elbows. Poker. Just like at the cigar bar. The air was thick with smoke in here as well.

I smiled and tried to be unobtrusive as I moved around with my tray. Only one woman took a shrimp puff. She sniffed it and placed it back. I gave Miss Manners a disapproving look and moved on. The men were involved with their cards, and the dealers didn't even notice me.

I stepped out of the room and peeked into the one across the hall. Jackpot. Poker, pretty women, and Packard Graystone.

Packard sat at the table, his body contorted to look up at a dapper man in a tuxedo. I walked into the room and slipped behind a tall brunette in a stunning evening gown. I peeked around her and listened as Pack yelled at the older man.

"Don't fuck with me, Robert. Don't you know who I am?"

Robert spoke in a low, calm tone. I had no idea what he said, but it nearly gave Packard an aneurism.

"Like hell I will. You don't fucking tell me that. You know I'm good for it." Packard's face was almost purple and a big vein throbbed in the middle of his forehead.

Robert glanced over Packard's head and beckoned to a large bald man on the other side of the room. The bald man looked as if he used to bench press European cars for a living. His massive arms strained the material of his tux. If I'd been Packard, I'd have crapped myself if I saw that guy coming for me.

But Packard wasn't scared, he was pissed. "I need more credit!"

The big guy simply lifted Pack's arm and dragged his ass out of the room.

"What are you doing?"

The tall woman I'd been hiding behind glared down at me. She was very pretty, but had on way too much eyeliner. Sometimes less is more, ladies.

"That's a great dress," I said. "Where'd you get it?"

"Pour Femme, of course."

A piece just clicked into place. I smiled and held up my tray. "Shrimp?"

"No," she sniffed and walked away.

I meandered around offering my puffs to people who didn't want them. These women were eye candy for the men who gambled. That's what the saleswoman at Pour Femme thought I was. I wondered if the Pour Femmes did more than stand around drinking champagne. Might make things interesting.

I waited until I was sure Packard had left the building, then I booked it down the hall toward the kitchen. I got halfway there when Alice came out of nowhere and grabbed my arm.

"You're very slow, Sue. Get in and out of the rooms at a much quicker pace."

"Sorry. Where's the restroom?"

"You don't have a break for another two hours. Go upstairs. And remember, in and out." With her clipboard pressed to her chest, she glared at me while I climbed the stairs.

Roxy was going to kill me or perhaps everyone in the building, if I didn't get her out of here and shove a piece of gum in her mouth.

They layout was similar to downstairs with four rooms on either side of the hall, only these rooms hosted blackjack and roulette. I carted my tray from room to room and actually had a few takers. As I made my way down the stairs, my eyes locked on Manny, who was on his way up.

"You." He pointed at me and ran on sandaled feet up the steps.

I panicked as he came toward me and nearly fell face

first into the banister. He kept coming. I lifted the tray, tossed the shrimp over my shoulder, and slammed it into Manny's face as hard as I could.

He staggered then tumbled backward, landing on his ass. I threw the tray at him and ran down the stairs. I almost made it past him, but he grabbed my ankle and brought me down.

My knee slammed into the corner of the hard wooden step and I grabbed the railing. I tried to shake my foot free from his grasp, but couldn't. I reached back and slapped the top of his bald pate. "Let go, asshole."

Alice looked up from the bottom step and gasped so hard I thought she was choking. "What is going on here?"

"Ben Franklin…tried to…cop a feel," I said between slaps to his head.

"She's lying. She's not who she says she is."

I kicked out with my other foot and made contact with his nose. He finally let me go to grab his face with both hands. Blood poured through his fingers.

"You bitch," he said, sounding like he had a cold.

I ran down the stairs, flying past Alice. Her wide eyes and gaping mouth said she couldn't quite believe what was happening.

I ran to the kitchen and saw Roxy out of the corner of my eye. "Run," I yelled, not slowing down as I fled the kitchen and sped out into the cold night.

Footsteps pounded on the gravel behind me. I looked back to make sure it was Roxy. To my relief it was.

I ripped open the driver's side door and flung myself into the car. Roxy hopped in the back.

Ma, who had been dozing, sat up. "Bingo." She

looked around as I put the car in gear and stomped on the gas. Rocks flung from my tires as I sped out of the lot.

"What the hell is going on?" Ma asked.

I told them about Manny between ragged breaths. My knee throbbed as I drove back to the deserted old highway, glancing in the rearview mirror every few seconds. Once we made it back into Huntingford, I pulled into a McDonald's parking lot so I could calm down and catch my breath. "Just give me a minute, guys." I laid my forehead on the steering wheel. Pulled off the bow tie and unbuttoned the top button on the white blouse. It occurred to me I left behind my gray hoodie and my second best pair of jeans. Damn.

"So Manny's the guy who called Packard and they were both in the old school tonight. That can't be a coincidence, can it?" Ma asked.

I raised my head and looked at her. "No. And we told the woman in charge that NorthStar hired us." Just then my phone buzzed. I dug it out of my pocket with trembling hands and glanced at the text.

"Eric wants me to come over. He has something on Sullivan."

Chapter 20

Ma yawned and stretched in her seat. "Tell me again who this Eric person is. You're not dating him, too, are you?"

"He works with Axton. He's helping me find information on Sullivan and NorthStar," I said as I pulled back on the road.

When we got to Eric's, I introduced him to Ma. "Nice to meet you," he said.

"I need to use the little girls' room. Would you like some Chex Mix?" She held up the plastic container.

"Yeah, I love this stuff." After setting down the beer he'd been holding, he lifted the lid, grabbed a handful of cereal, and popped it in his mouth.

Ma walked down the hall and Roxy flopped onto the loveseat in front of the TV and began flipping through the channels. While Eric munched, I felt amped up and antsy.

When Ma stepped back in the room he asked, "You guys want a beer or something?"

"I'll take one," Ma said, settling down next to Roxy.

Eric scooted off to the kitchen and came back with a long neck, handing it to her.

"Thanks. What are all those for?" She pointed to a

pile of controllers on the floor in front of the TV.
"This is a wireless control. I play these," he pointed to
a shelf full of video games, "on this." He pointed to a con-
sole.

"Can I try one?" she asked.

Eric looked a little pleased. "Sure. First-person shoot-
ers are good. Let's start with..." He studied the games and
plucked one from the shelf. "This one. Do you guys want to
play, too?"

"I will," Roxy said.

I shook my head. "No thanks." I'd been playing
enough games lately.

Eric showed the controller to Ma and Roxy. "This one
is to shoot. You move like this. If you need help, let me
know."

He picked up his bottle and pulled me aside. His dining room—more of a dining area really—was separated from
the living room by an arched wall. Desks and card tables
were cluttered with computers, laptops, and motherboards.
"Are you ready to see what I found out about your Sullivan?"

"He's not my Sullivan, and yes, more than ready." I
sank down on a desk chair, sore and weary.

"I dug through the county records for personal property taxes. I figured that would be the best place to start."

I held up a hand. "Wait, can you do that?"

"Of course."

"No, I mean, isn't that illegal?"

"Nope, it's a matter of public record. I found tax records for one Thomas Malcolm Sullivan, thirty-four years of
age. He was the most likely candidate, and after doing a deed
and title search, I found out he owns a ton of property.

Mostly office buildings and strip malls." He handed me a stack of papers. "Here you go."

I scanned the pages. "He owns the old school." I slapped the paper with one hand. "We followed Packard tonight and he went to this old school building out in the country. It's on the list."

"What was in an old school?"

"A gambling club. Pack was losing and they wouldn't extend him credit."

"How did you find this out?"

I wagged my thumb over my shoulder. "Rox and I went undercover."

I continued to read the long list of properties. Sullivan owned the strip mall that housed Sun Kissed Tanning and the Pour Femme boutique building. Like Ma said—bingo. "Oh my God, this is amazing. Evidence, Eric. Real evidence."

My enthusiasm was intoxicating. "Okay, let's walk through this," I said. "Axton gives me his backpack. I see Sullivan in the park and he's looking for Axton. He finds Axton—"

"Kidnaps him," Eric said.

"Yep, Sullivan kidnaps Axton to get his hands on the hard drive. But I have the hard drive. On that hard drive is a list of people with a number next to their name. I think we can safely assume it's money—"

"Money they lost gambling," he said.

"We know Sullivan has Axton, we know Packard has a gambling problem. I saw a poker game in the back room at the cigar bar and Manny's running something in the back of that tanning salon. And I saw Manny tonight. He and I had a little smackdown."

"Are you all right?" Eric sat on his haunches and touched my knee.

I winced and jerked my leg to the side. "I fell. I'm okay. Anyway, I don't think it's a coincidence that Sullivan leases his property to NorthStar businesses."

Rubbing his head, Eric narrowed his eyes. "And Axton went to a club the night before he was taken. It was a NorthStar club, wasn't it? And Axton took the hard drive?"

"Probably stole it from Sullivan. We know there's gambling in some of these places, and Sullivan must be in charge, right?" Oh God. It finally dawned on me, if that was the case, I'd put Eric in a very dangerous situation. I clutched his arm with my free hand. "What if they figure out you have the hard drive? What if they come for you next?"

"Hey, Rose." He took the papers from me and laid them down on a keyboard. Then he took both my hands in his. "You have enough on your plate, kid. The last thing you need to worry about is me, okay? I can take care of myself. Let's concentrate on rescuing Axton."

"Okay." I nodded and took a deep breath. "Sullivan told me he would do anything to protect his interests. The gambling, the people on this list, the properties—he's in charge of it all." Sullivan was the big cheese, the head honcho, the Kaiser Soze. I didn't call him the Bossy Jackass for nothing.

I dug the list of NorthStar businesses out of my purse and compared it to the sheaf of papers Eric gave me. "Not all the businesses Sullivan leases to are NorthStar businesses. There's a barbershop in the same strip mall as the tanning salon. It's not owned by NorthStar."

"Maybe he rents to other businesses to make it seem

legit."

"Packard got a call from the tanning salon and he was gambling in one of Sullivan's properties tonight. We have a real connection. Yes!" I threw my fist in the air, jumped out of my seat, and did my little happy dance. Eric laughed, but I was too excited to care. We finally had a real trail to follow. Eric smiled and high-fived me.

I reached out and hugged him. "Thank you so much.

He planted a big smacker on my cheek. "You're welcome." He gestured to the stacks of papers. "Can you take this to the police?"

My happy fled the scene. "All I have are theories. And NorthStar is a shell company. Dane says it could take years to unravel, and I can't prove Sullivan is in charge of anything. And besides, the Chief of Police, Martin Mathers, was on the decrypted list."

He scratched his stubble. "You can't really prove anything."

I flopped down in the chair. I went from elated to deflated in under thirty seconds. "I guess not."

A growl sounded from the living room. I glanced over at Ma. She sat on the edge of the sofa, her wrinkled face scrunched up, her teeth bared. "Die, zombie bastard."

Roxy moved her whole body as she punched the buttons on the controller, leaning left then lurching to the right. "Take that, you undead asshole."

I looked back up at Eric, my lips a thin line. "What did you do?"

Eric tipped his head back to finish off the last of his beer. "It's fun." He gestured toward the TV with the empty bottle. "You should try it."

Nibbling on my thumb, I glanced back over the list of properties and compared it once again with the NorthStar businesses. I finally had a few pieces of the puzzle, but I didn't know what to do with them.

Feeling more frustrated than ever, I finally went to the living room and sank to the floor to watch Ma and Roxy try to defeat brain-eating zombies. It was after midnight and they showed no signs of stopping the carnage.

"Hey, ladies, we need to go."

They completely ignored me.

"Get the rock, pick up the rock," Roxy said.

"I'm trying, but that damn zombie keeps blocking me." Ma had a fierce look of concentration on her face.

"Hey, zombie slayers, we need to leave."

Still no response.

Eric wrestled the controller from Roxy and paused the game. They grumbled at him.

"Just a few minutes longer," Ma said. She sounded just like Scotty when he was in the middle of a game.

Roxy frowned and tried to get the controller back from Eric. "We were just getting some decent weapons, Rose."

Eric looked at me and grinned. "I could take them home."

"See," Ma said. "You go on, hon. We'll be fine."

"Yeah, see you tomorrow," Roxy said, grabbing the controller from Eric's hand.

I shrugged. "Okay."

Eric showed Roxy how to resume the game. I grabbed my bag and the information Eric had found on Sullivan. Thomas Malcolm Sullivan.

"Sorry about them." I flicked my finger toward Ma and

Roxy.

"They're fine. Let me walk you to your car."

Eric waved as I started the engine and drove off.

I actually accomplished something tonight. I'd been so sick of hitting dead end after dead end. But now I had something tangible to link Sullivan and NorthStar and Packard Graystone. Officially I couldn't prove anything, and I didn't know what my next move should be, but I was determined to figure it out. One way or another, I was getting Axton back.

I parked in my lot and scoured the area before I got out of the car, then hustled inside. As I entered the building, my neighbor opened her door and poked her head out. A slim woman in her fifties, Wanda's fried, bleached hair had a Bride of Frankenstein thing going on. She held a glass of red wine in one hand. "Hey, blondie, want to keep it down up there? I got work in the morning." She worked at The Gutter Ball, and by the way she slurred her words, I could tell that wasn't her first glass of red this evening.

"Hey, Wanda, I just got home. I've been out for hours."

"Well it sounded like balls being thrown down the alley." She slammed the door in my face.

My heart began beating like a bad techno song. I knocked on Wanda's door. She answered it with a scowl. "What now?"

"When did you hear the noise?"

"'Bout an hour ago." She slammed the door again.

Could be nothing, I told myself. But myself knew I was lying. Bowling alley sounds coming from my apartment—not a good thing. I pulled out my cell phone and punched in 911, my finger hovering over the send key.

I slowly climbed the stairs to my apartment and tiptoed to the door. It stood half open, the new lock busted. The overhead light was on. I knew that whoever had been here was probably long gone, but I didn't want to take any chances. I pushed the door open farther with my toe.

My apartment looked like it had been swept up in a tornado. The futon was hacked up and chunks of blue foam dotted the room like enormous confetti. My laptop had been thrown to the floor, the hinge broken. The small TV overturned, the screen shattered, but the cord was still plugged into the outlet. The framed pictures from my dresser lay scattered on the floor along with textbooks, their pages ripped out and crumpled into balls.

Trembling, I couldn't breathe, couldn't think. In silence, I scanned the room, threw my hand over my mouth and sobbed.

Clothes were pulled from the closet, slashed to ribbons. Including the new dress from Pour Femme. And every single item from my dresser drawers. Underwear and bras were ripped and torn. I glanced down and saw a decapitated flamingo.

The small amount of food from my fridge was splattered all over my kitchenette. Milk and orange juice mixed together in a puddle and spilled onto the cracked linoleum.

The bathroom hadn't faired any better. My makeup and toiletries smashed and dumped in the toilet.

Even my little bistro table and chairs were demolished.

Shit. Who would do something like this? Sullivan? Why now? Revenge for crashing his gambling club? He must know about my fight with Manny on the main staircase. But even for him, this was some kind of fucked up.

I pressed the send button on my phone and went back downstairs to wait for the police.

It took them forty-five minutes to arrive. The longest forty-five minutes of my life. They dusted for prints, talked to the neighbors—who by then had stumbled out into the hall to see what all the commotion was about—and took my statement. One of the officers told me to come down to the station the next day and get a copy of the report.

After the police left, I just stood in the doorway of my apartment staring at the damage. Everything I owned had been destroyed.

Chapter 21

It was just after three a.m. when I called Roxy and explained what happened. Fifteen minutes later she walked through my door carrying a broom, cleaning supplies, and a box of garbage bags. She laid everything on the ground, then enfolded me in her arms.

Roxy's not big on displays of affection, I think because she had so little of it growing up. But she hugged me like she wouldn't let go. I clung to her and cried.

When I finally pulled away, my gaze swept over the room. "Who would do this?"

"Sullivan, of course. We can't rule out Dane, either."

"Dane?" I frowned at her. "What are you talking about?"

"Did it ever occur to you that Dane might not be helping you out of the goodness of his heart?"

I gave a little humorless laugh. "Yeah, I think he's doing it to get into my pants."

"Maybe." She shrugged. "Or he could be working with Sullivan. Dane popped up out of nowhere at the exact same time your bud, Ax, disappeared. That's quite a coinkadink."

"That's crazy talk. He went to Penn's Cigar Bar with

me. Why would he do that? And why would he give me a list of NorthStar businesses in the first place? That doesn't make sense."

"He never thought you'd find any real evidence? Maybe Sullivan wants Dane to keep tabs on you."

My gut clenched in a knot. "No, I can't believe Dane would do that."

"He didn't seem real excited after you showed him the list from the hard drive."

True. He'd pooh-poohed. Was that because he just didn't want to mess with the bigwigs of Huntingford or because he was trying to throw me off track? Maybe Dane was setting me up.

Roxy snapped open a trash bag. "All I'm saying is, be careful what info you share with him. He may be working for the enemy."

She was absolutely right and it had never occurred to me. It should have. What did I even know about Dane? He was cute and dimply? And very eager to help me. Because he sat behind me in sixth grade? I automatically assumed he was attracted to me. He kissed like he was attracted.

"You know, even Kevin could have done this," Roxy added.

"I hadn't even thought about Kevin."

"Jealous ex." Roxy picked up a broom and began sweeping. "He was all shades of pissed when I saw him the other night. Kept going on about how you two were meant for each other and wanted to know who you were dating." She stopped mid-sweep. "He's cute and all, but he's not that smart."

"He wouldn't think about consequences, that's for sure.

He did change his name to Spaz."

"What about Packard?"

I ripped a wad of paper towels off the roll and started mopping up the milk/juice combo. "I told him I didn't have the hard drive, but maybe he didn't believe me."

"Anybody else not in your fan club?"

"Officer Hardass wasn't too fond of me." I threw the sopping towels into a trash bag. "But he wasn't on the spreadsheet."

"Chief of Police was though," Roxy said. "Or maybe Manny figured out who you were and decided on a little payback."

"Well crap. I shouldn't have such a long list of enemies. I'm a likeable person, right?"

She glanced up at me. "I like you. But I have low standards."

I actually laughed. "Thanks, Rox." I grabbed a trash bag and began stuffing it with the remnants of my clothes.

It took over two hours, but eventually we put everything into bags. We dragged them, along with the remains of my futon mattress and the busted bistro table and chairs, out to the dumpster—it took several trips.

"I still can't believe no one called the cops," I said as we walked back inside. "This is such a small building and no one heard or saw anything?"

"People pay attention to their own shit," she said. Putting her hands on her hips, she leaned back, stretching her muscles.

"No kidding. See if I give wino Wanda a bottle of red this Christmas."

I tried to boot up my computer, but wasn't having

much success. "I'll take this to Eric today. Maybe he can fix it."

"What are you going to do, Rose?" She sat on the floor with one knee pulled up to her chest.

"I'll replace what I can. Mainly a few clothes and food right now."

"I mean about this Sullivan guy. He's the most likely person to have done this, right?"

I put the laptop on the kitchen counter and sat down next to her. "I thought we decided Sullivan was just one of many."

She shrugged. "I don't think you can rule the rest of them out, but Sullivan's my number one suspect."

"There's something I didn't tell you." I slid her a sideways glance. "Henry tossed me in the back of a car the other night. He took me to see Sullivan."

I've seen Roxy in a pissy mood. Plenty of times. And pissy was her only mood since she quit smoking. But I'd never seen her truly angry before. She jumped up, her fists clenched, the muscles in her jaw working. "What? He kidnapped you? Did he hurt you?"

I shook my head.

"Answer me, Rose. Did he hurt you? Because if he did..." She pounded her fist into the wall.

I got to my feet, trying to ignore the ache in my knee. "Roxy, stop. He didn't hurt me."

"They why did he take you? And why didn't you tell me?" I heard the pain in her voice.

"He told me to quit asking questions. Quit looking for Axton. Then showed me pictures of all my friends and family. Like surveillance pictures." I bit my lip and stared at my empty futon frame. "There was one of you. You were standing outside of The Carp. There was one of Scotty, Jacqueline, my parents, Ma, and one of Axton, bound and gagged." I glanced at her. The look of betrayal on her face was almost more than I could stand.

"What the hell? Why did you keep this from me? Don't you trust me?"

"Of course I do. I didn't want to tell you because I didn't want to worry you."

"Bullshit, Rose." She poked a finger in my sternum. It hurt. "You didn't want to stop looking for Axton. You were afraid I'd tell you to quit."

Was that the truth? My head hurt and my eyes felt grainy. I covered my face with my hands. I stood that way for some time, just breathing, blocking out Roxy, blocking out my empty apartment. Finally, I dropped my hands and looked at her. "I'm sorry."

She glared at me for what seemed like an hour, then finally said, "It's okay." She pointed at me, and I backed up a step in case she wanted to poke me again. "But you're on my shit list once this is over."

"Fair enough."

Then she scuffed the floor with the toe of her shoe. "I thought we were best friends."

"We are. I was wrong to keep it from you. From now on, full disclosure. I promise."

"Okay." She knocked her shoulder against mine. "You are such a dumbass. I wouldn't have told you to stop looking for Axton."

"I'm sorry." Tears pricked my eyes. I thought I was all cried out, but I was wrong. I slid to the floor and covered my head with my arms, sobbing.

Roxy sat next to me and patted my arm. "Please don't cry." She handed me paper towel.

When the tears slowed down, I mopped up my face. The paper towel was rough on my cheeks and even rougher when I blew my nose.

"Gross," Roxy said with a chuckle.

I laughed a little, too and then looked down at borrowed catering uniform. "I guess I'm going to have to wear this to work, huh?"

"You need to skip work and replace all your shit."

"Unless I go to work, I can't afford to replace any of my shit."

Chapter 22

My first stop at the diner was to pour an enormous cup of boiling hot coffee from the fresh pot. Roxy had gone home to change, and walked in a few minutes later. Two blue braids dangled on either side of her face and she wore a dress with blue birds embroidered on the hem. She looked like a strung out Heidi on crank.

Ma stared at us. "What in the world happened to the pair of you? You look like you've been to hell and back. And Rose, why are you wearing that outfit from last night?"

Ma's face lost its color as I described the apocalypse that was my apartment. "What is going on? First Axton, then your car, and now this? What did the police say?"

"Not a whole lot. They took prints, questioned my neighbors. They don't know why I was targeted."

"It must have been that Sullivan," she said.

"I don't know. Maybe. Probably." I rubbed my bleary eyes with both hands.

"Take the morning off, honey, and go get a new bed. She pointed a finger, wagging it between Roxy and me. "I want both of you to come to dinner tonight. You girls need a good meal."

"Thank you, Ma, but I can't. And I don't want the day

off."

She pursed her lips. "I don't like this. Not one little bit. I don't want anyone to hurt my girls." She pulled Roxy and me into a hug.

I hugged her back and Roxy patted Ma's shoulder.

"Now," she said, briskly, releasing us, "Ray will put new locks on your door. They're on me." When I opened my mouth to protest, she cut me off. "Ah, ah, ah, no arguing."

"Thanks, Ma, but I left a message with the super this morning. He'll take care of it. The doorjamb was busted, too, so he needs to fix it."

"You won't let me do anything for you. You're too independent for your own good, you know that?"

"So I've been told."

I canceled my study date with Janelle. Too much drama, I tapped out on my phone's tiny keyboard. Then I busied myself with customers and coffee, trying not to dwell on the mountain of problems crashing down on me. Apparently I didn't do so hot. Said customers weren't impressed with my disposition and my tips sucked.

Janelle walked in a half hour before closing. She'd never been here before and she surveyed the room as she walked up to the counter and took a seat. "So this is where the magic happens, huh?"

I smiled, happy to see her, and poured her a cup of coffee. "This is it."

"It could use a little freshening up." She glanced at the photo of a younger Ma, Frank, and little boy Ray hanging next to the cash register.

"Nah. I think it's perfect like this."

She took a sip of coffee and appraised me. "You look

like shit on a shingle, girl, and you're paler than usual. What have you been up to?"

"You wouldn't believe me if I told you."

She rolled her eyes. "Try me. Any news on Axton?"

In between taking care of my last customer and introducing her to Ma, I filled Janelle in on the shit storm my life had become.

She nodded at my now lukewarm cup of Joe. "You may need something stronger than that after the week you've had."

"I hear you."

Ma came up and patted my butt. "Take it easy, toots. Roxy and I will clean up."

Roxy stuck her tongue out at me. I was going to have to make it up to them at some point. They'd been shouldering the load for a week now.

Janelle brushed a braid over her shoulder. "So, let me get this straight. You've got a missing friend, a crazy ex, a cute lawyer, a hot guy busting down your door, you beat the shit out of Ben Franklin, and everything you own, except that trashy car, has been destroyed? That's what you're telling me?"

"Yep," I said, "that about covers it."

"Sounds to me like you need some personal protection and I am not talking about a love glove. What if this asshole breaks in again? Or that guy who was with him?"

"Henry?"

"Yeah, Henry. What if Henry comes back? You need to be able to protect your shit, girl."

"Are you talking about a gun?" I think my voice went up an octave. "Because I don't know about that."

"Hell yes, I'm talking about a gun." She poked me in the arm with a blue-tipped nail. "You pull a gun on his ass, he'll think twice about fucking with you."

I imagined toting a big honking six-shooter in my backpack. "I'd probably wind up shooting myself in the elbow. Lose my good texting arm."

Roxy glanced up from the table she was wiping. "I think it's a good idea."

I pressed my lips together and shook my head. "No way."

"Fine," Janelle said. "How about a stun gun? Zap him right in the balls, see how he likes that."

Now we're talking. The thought of zapping Henry in the balls filled me with delight. "Where do I get one of those?"

"My cousin sells them. He'll give you a deal."

Ma put her hands on her hips. "I think we all need some kind of protection. Get me some of that pepper spray." She walked behind the counter and scrounged around in her purse, pulling out two twenties. "And see if they have a rape whistle. A girl can't be too careful."

I shoved the bills in my pocket. "Roxy, you in?"

"Hell yes."

So I'd eat ramen noodles for the next two weeks. Feeling protected would be worth it. "Where's his store?"

"He doesn't have a store so much as a full trunk. I'll have him meet us at school in an hour. Bring cash."

Roxy and I drove out to the college the second we locked up the diner. We found Janelle and her cousin waiting for us in the parking lot. Tariq wore jeans and a striped polo that looked four sizes too big. Dozens of little braids covered his head and large diamond adorned his right earlobe. He shook our hands when we met, his gaze lingering on Roxy.

"Blue's a good color on you," he said.

Twisting a braid around her finger, she smiled. "Thanks."

"Come on, Tariq," Janelle said. "I don't have all damn day. I've got a class to get to." Unlike me, Janelle was a full time student.

Tariq held up his hands. "All right, cuz, calm down." He turned back to Roxy and me. "I hear you ladies are in the market for a little personal protection."

"First I want a can of pepper spray and a rape whistle for my boss," I said.

He opened the trunk of his silver Ford sedan to a large display of miscellaneous self-defense items. "I don't have a rape whistle," he said. He handed me a can of pepper spray, then reached back into the trunk and came out with a black leather pouch. He pulled a shiny four-sided weapon out of it. "I got a Chinese throwing star, though."

"Aren't those illegal?" I asked.

Tariq shrugged.

It seemed like something Ma would like. "Okay, I'll take it."

"Fifty."

"All I have is twenty."

"Since you're a friend of Janelle's, I'm willing to work with you."

For myself, I bought a can of pepper spray I could hang from my key chain, then Tariq handed me a stun gun. "You got to be careful with this."

I pressed the trigger, jumping as a current shot between

the two points. "I'll take it." I forked over forty dollars—mostly in ones from my tip money.

"Now," he focused on Roxy, "what do you need, baby?" I could tell by the way his eyes swept over her, he wasn't just talking about the stuff in his trunk, he was talking about the junk in hers.

"A cigarette," she said in a husky voice.

Tariq smiled. "I can get you one of those."

Oh boy. "No," I said. "She's quitting."

She blew out a breath. "All right, I'll take some pepper spray."

"For you, my blue-haired beauty, ten dollars." She handed it to him with a smile.

Janelle rolled her eyes. "I've got to go. Rose, I'll see you at class tomorrow night?"

I sighed. "Probably not."

She said she'd take notes for me and walked off.

"Thanks a lot, Tariq." I tucked everything in my purse.

He shut the trunk lid, his eyes never leaving Roxy. "My pleasure, ladies."

Roxy grinned as I pulled her away from Tariq's car. With her love of breaking and entering, and his love of selling possibly—okay totally— stolen goods, this was not a relationship I wanted to encourage.

I needed to stop by the IT office while I was here to see if Eric could fix my computer. We walked toward Blake Hall and ran in to Steve near the entrance.

"Hey, Rose," he said, adjusting his messenger bag. "Roxy. Any news on Axton?"

"We're still working on it," I said.

He reached out and touched my shoulder. "I meant

what I said the other day. Anything I can do to help."

"I appreciate that."

He gave me a squeeze and with a crooked grin walked off.

As soon as he was out of earshot, Roxy nudged me. "Someone has a little crush on my Rose."

"He's a nice guy."

She wrapped her hands around her throat. "The kiss of death."

In the IT office, Eric sat at his desk, rubbing his head. He looked up and smiled when I entered. "Hey, Rose, you're becoming quite a regular around here."

"Actually, today I have a different favor to ask you."

"I don't know. This might cost you another sandwich." When I handed him my computer his smile changed to a look of horror. "What the hell did you do, hurl it off a building?"

"My apartment was ransacked last night. Everything I own was broken, smashed or shredded." I ran my fingers over my ponytail.

Eric jumped out of his seat and rounded the desk. "My God, Rose, are you all right?" Placing his hands on my arms, gave me a once over.

"I'm fine. I was at your place when it happened. Really, I'm fine."

"You think Sullivan did this?" Eric asked.

Roxy propped her hip on the edge of his desk. "Yes."

I stepped out of Eric's hold, pulled up a chair, and dropped into it, rubbing a hand over my eyes. I was tired beyond belief. "I don't know for sure. Probably."

"Why?" he asked.

I shrugged. "Another warning? Quit looking for Axton, quit asking questions, blah blah blah. Anyway, I can't afford a new laptop. Is this one fixable?"

Eric glanced down at the broken hinge and hit the power button. "I'll do what I can."

"Thanks. I get paid next week, so let me know how much—"

"Rose, stop. I'm not charging you. This will be a test of my skills. I welcome it." He stepped back to the desk and dismissed me, focusing instead on the laptop.

"Thanks, Eric, I'll see you later."

I dropped Roxy off at Ma's and headed to Walmart, where I bought makeup, toiletries, two pillows, two bras, two packages of underwear and socks, a phone charger, and the largest coffee pot on the shelf. I swung by the grocery store and stocked up on generic pop tarts and ramen noodles, then I stopped by a mattress store and bought a new firm futon, which the salesman promised, would be delivered the next day. My last pit stop was Goodwill where I scoured the racks for a limited amount of jeans, t-shirts, and sweats. With my depleted bank account, I was lucky the volunteer at the counter took pity on me and tossed in two blankets.

Back at my apartment, the super left the new keys in my mailbox as promised. I hauled all the bags up the stairs. I didn't even hesitate at the door. I was operating on fifteen cups of high octane coffee and zero sleep. If there was a destructive maniac waiting for me, I'd whack him over the head with my Walmart bags, then tase the crap out of him with my new stun gun for good measure.

It took less than twenty minutes to unpack my worldly goods. Wasn't too hard since I didn't even have a dresser to unpack things into. As I looked around my barren apartment and the empty futon frame, my anger grew. It was a craptastic futon, but it was mine. My futon, my clothes, my milk. Someone invaded my privacy and not only destroyed my stuff, but my peace of mind. Not someone. Sullivan. He followed me, kidnapped me, threatened my friends and family.

I whipped out my cell and the notebook paper Sheila gave and punched in the number I'd dialed just two days ago.

He didn't answer, went straight to voice mail. Which pissed me off even more.

"Hey asshole," I yelled into the phone. I paced from my bathroom door to my kitchenette and back again, my phone hand shaking with agitation. "I just want to know one thing. Did you get your rocks off when you slashed my panties, you perv?" I jabbed the end button and paced back to the living room. I was fired up and needed to get out of there.

I jumped in my car and drove to Roxy's. She answered the door wearing a traditional, but super short pink and white kimono. "I'm going to talk to Sheila. You in?"

"Yep." She slipped her feet into wooden sandals.

"Don't you want to change?

"No, why?"

When we got to Sheila's house, I parked on the street. Roxy whistled as we walked up to the front door. "Nice digs, huh? And you grew up in a place like this?"

"Not exactly, but close enough."

"Do you miss it?"

I thought back to the house where I'd been raised with my mother's coldness and my dad's apathy. I'd never felt at home there. "No."

"Well, I'd miss it."

Sheila answered the door and she didn't look good. Instead of the pulled together, suburban mom outfit she usually sported, she wore dirty jeans and a faded green t-shirt. Her hair looked limp and there were dark circles under her eyes.

"Hi, Sheila. This is my friend Roxy. We need to talk."

Sheila's gaze flicked from Roxy's bright blue hair, down to her kimono, her bare legs, to the sandals on her feet. She paused a beat before her ingrained manners kicked in. "Hello, Roxy. Nice to meet you. Come in."

Roxy openly looked around the foyer, taking in the marble tile and the crystal chandelier. "This is really nice," she said, her voice a little hushed.

"Thanks. Would you like some tea or coffee?"

"Coffee would be great," I said.

"This way." She turned and walked toward the kitchen.

I spotted a pile of mail on a small table in the foyer. On top was a letter from Huntingford Bank and Trust.

"Roxy." I pulled her next to me. "Keep her busy for a second."

Roxy nodded and followed Sheila.

I quickly rifled through the mail. There were several bills from different credit card companies. I held the letter from the bank up to the light, but couldn't see a thing.

I desperately wanted to know what was inside. If Packard had a gambling problem, a bank statement would reflect that. If he owed one hundred ninety-six thousand dollars to someone—cough, Sullivan, cough—he must be in real financial trouble.

"Rose," Sheila called from the kitchen.

I jammed the letter in my purse, my heart beating so fast I thought I might have a heart attack there on the spot.

"Sorry," I said, hustling into the kitchen, "I have to keep retying these stupid shoelaces."

"I keep telling you to get new laces. Ones that aren't so long," Roxy said. She pointed to me and shook her head. "Every day we go through this."

Sheila poured two cups of coffee and set them on the counter in front of us. She grabbed a bowl of sugar and a carton of creamer from the fridge and placed them with a couple of spoons next to the coffee. "Any news on Axton?"

"We're making progress," I said. "Are you okay, Sheila? You look tired."

She ran a shaky hand through her hair and tried to smile. She failed. "I don't know what's going on with Pack."

"I came to tell you we followed him last night."

"He said he had a city council meeting."

"Yeah, well he lied," Roxy said.

I dug my elbow into her side and frowned.

"What'd I say?" she asked.

"He lied to me?" Sheila placed a hand over her heart. "If he didn't go to the meeting, where did he go?"

"There's an old school out in the country," I said. "They have illegal gambling there."

"I know Pack likes to gamble a little. Why would he lie to me about it?"

"I think he likes to gamble more than a little, Sheila. I think Packard has a problem." I felt like crap springing this on her, but I knew that somehow it was all tied up with Axton's kidnapping.

"You don't know what you're talking about. You don't

know my husband." She grabbed a hand towel from the counter and refolded it. "He likes to play a little poker. He likes to go to Vegas a couple of times a year. That's not a problem."

"Then why did he lie about it?" I asked.

She threw her hands in the air. "I don't know. Maybe he just wanted to have a few hours to himself. He deserves it, you know. He works really hard."

"Why wouldn't he just go to a casino then?" Roxy asked.

Sheila put her hands on her hips. "How do I know you're not lying? You could be making all this up. And Axton's probably not even missing, he's probably out somewhere living it up while Packard's getting questioned by the police."

"Why would we lie about this, Sheila?" I asked. "What would we have to gain from it?"

"I don't know. But following my husband is…intrusive."

I shook my head in disbelief. "You came to me."

"Well, that was a mistake. He wasn't doing anything wrong. He's just stressed from work."

"Sheila—"

She crossed her arms over her chest and jutted her chin toward the door. "You need to leave."

I shot Roxy a look. We hopped off the barstools and headed for the door. As we walked to the car, I glanced back. "That woman is in deep denial."

"Yep. She's also in deep shit," Roxy said.

I nodded in agreement. "By the way, I stole her bank statement."

Chapter 23

"You, Rose Strickland, are turning into a criminal. And I'd like to take a little credit for that."

I laughed and started the car. "I need to stop by the police station."

Roxy snorted. "Gonna turn yourself in?"

"I have to get a copy of the police report from last night. My landlord needs it."

Ten minutes later, I parked across from the police station and pulled Sheila Graystone's bank statement from my purse. I held it in my hands and stared at it. I felt weird about taking it, but I had to know what kind of trouble Pack was in.

Roxy tapped her finger on the plastic bag window. "You hoping the information will jump into your head or are you going to open the damn thing?"

"I suppose I should, since I went to the trouble of stealing it." I squared my shoulders and ripped the flap, pulling out the piece of paper inside. "Wow."

She leaned over and peeked at it. "What? What's it say?"

"They're overdrafted to the tune of fourteen thousand dollars. That's a lot of money."

"No shit," Roxy said.

"And the rest of their mail? All credit card bills."

"He makes a butt-load of cash though, right? I mean he's a doctor, and all."

"A doctor who is in debt up to his eyeballs." I shoved the statement back in the envelope, and stuck the whole thing in my glove box. Although I felt guilty for stealing Sheila's mail, getting Axton back was more important than mail theft. Well, maybe not to the postal service.

Roxy and I walked into the police station and up to the reception desk. I was beginning to know my way around here and that probably wasn't a good thing.

Officer Delany, whom I spoke to on my first visit, was on duty. Her gaze swept over me, then moved to Roxy. Her bored expression didn't change. "Can I help you?"

"I'm here for a police report. Someone broke into my apartment last night."

"What was the name of the officer who responded to your call?"

"I don't remember. I wasn't paying attention." I think I was in shock the night before. Watching the police, my neighbors, seeing my things broken and scattered, had left me numb. It wasn't until Roxy arrived with her cleaning supplies that I woke up from what seemed like a really bad dream.

Officer Delany sighed. "Wait over there and someone will be with you shortly." She gestured to a small room across the hall. It had a vending machine and four black padded chairs.

Roxy sat and texted while I wandered around. Cops may not care about Axton or all of my worldly possessions being trashed, but apparently they loved softball. Years' worth of team photos covered the walls. My gaze drifted over last year's picture. Police Chief, Martin Mathers, held a trophy in one hand. His other arm was thrown around the shoulder of a grinning Officer Andre Thomas. The two looked very chummy. Roxy was right. Officer Thomas might not be on the hard drive list, but he could be doing dirty work for his softball buddy.

Speak of the hardass, five minutes later he walked into the room. My life just kept getting better and better.

He hooked his thumbs in his belt. "Well, Miss Strickland. Seems you can't stay out of trouble." He gazed briefly at Roxy before staring me down, like if he looked at me hard enough, I'd confess all my sins.

Roxy lowered her phone and snorted. "Yeah, like it was her fault."

"Have any ideas on who would do that, Miss Strickland?"

Yeah, I could come up with a few names, and his just leaped to the top of the queue. "No. I don't."

He raised one brow and continued to stare.

"You know what?" I said. "I don't have the energy to argue with you today, so can I just get the report?"

"Come with me."

Roxy rolled her eyes and went back to texting, while I followed him to his corner cubicle.

He typed something into the computer and grabbed a piece of paper from his copier. "Read this over, make sure all the information is correct."

I read through everything I had told the police the night before. "It is." I hitched my bag up on my shoulder and turned to leave.

"Miss Strickland."

I faced him.

"It seems like large pieces are missing from your story. Is there anything you'd like to tell me?"

I peered at the ceiling, my brow furrowed as I pretended to think. Then I looked back at him with a blank expression. "Nope." My eyes lowered and snagged on a gold pen sitting on his desk blotter. I'd been seeing a lot of those lately.

I marched forward and grabbed it. "Where did you get this?"

He frowned. "Why?"

I rolled the pen in my fingers. Dane and Manny. They both had pens just like this one.

"Miss Strickland?"

He stared at me like I'd lost my shit. Maybe I had, because I was starting to think everything was a conspiracy. I dropped the pen on the desk and left his cubicle. I couldn't even think straight. I was a paranoid, frazzled mess.

I made it to the front of the building without getting lost this time. Roxy saw me and hopped up, following me outside.

Before I could cross the street to my car, someone called my name. I turned around and saw Dane in front of the City Hall. With a briefcase in one hand and a phone in the other, he jogged toward us.

"My God, Rose, I just got a call from Andre. He says someone broke into your apartment."

I hadn't seen Dane since the other morning in the diner. And my conversation with Roxy had me second guessing his motives about helping me. Was he one of Sullivan's lackeys sent to spy on me?

"Yeah," Roxy said, "*someone* trashed everything she owns."

"Are you all right?" Dane frowned, little lines creased his forehead.

"Yeah. I was out when it happened."

His blue gaze scanned me. Then he suddenly dropped his briefcase pulled me to him, buried his face in my hair. "What if you had been home? You could have been hurt. God, you could have been killed."

"I'm going to go sit in the car, now," Roxy said.

He pulled back and cupped my cheek with his palm. "Rose."

My heart skipped two beats. I wanted to believe he was genuinely concerned for me, and not there because of Sullivan. "I'm fine." I bit my lip as he continued to scrutinize me. "Really, Dane, I'm okay."

He hugged me again. My arms crept around his waist and hugged back. He tucked my head under his chin, stroking my hair. It felt foreign to be comforted by someone. It felt…good.

When we pulled away, I wiped at my eyes, and did that little not-a-real-laugh-just-an-awkward-pseudo-laugh. "So," I said, staring at the white gazebo in the park across the street. The afternoon light was fading, leaving orange and pink streaks across the sky.

Dane cleared his throat and shoved his hands in his pockets. "Who do you think did this?"

My eyes met his. "I think it may have been Sullivan."

"Who the hell is Sullivan?" His look of angry confusion seemed real. If Dane was in collusion with Sullivan, then

I was my parents' favorite daughter. Or he was an amazing actor. In that moment, a weight lifted off my shoulders and I believed Dane was for real.

"Who is Sullivan?" His mouth twisted into a frown, and there wasn't a hint of dimple in sight.

"Oh, um, the guy who broke into my apartment. You know, BJ."

"You know his real name?"

"Yeah."

"Have you seen him again?"

Should I lie and have a guilty conscience or tell the truth and let Dane drag me back to see Officer Hardass? "No, I just figured it out." I waved my hand like it was no big deal. But Dane was a better lawyer than I was a liar.

"Like hell. You have seen him again. When? Where?"

"Calm down. I found his phone number, okay? That's how I know his name." I looked him right in the eye as I said it. It was the truth. Just not all of it.

"Where did you find his phone number?"

I huffed in exaggerated annoyance. "I'm not on the witness stand here. I've been through a horrible experience and you're questioning me like Officer Thomas did. What the hell?"

He pinched the bridge of his nose. "I'm sorry, I'm just worried."

"Okay."

"Look at me," he said. "Things are getting dangerous. You can't go around asking any more questions. This Sullivan guy did this because you identified him. Think of yourself, of your own safety. Let the police find Axton."

He looked so concerned, so sincere. "You may be right,

but the police aren't as interested in Axton as they should be."

"They'll find him." He rubbed my arm with one hand. "Try not to worry."

"Sure." I nodded, absently. I wanted to believe him, I just didn't.

Dane smiled. "Good. Now until the police find Axton, maybe you should stay with your parents or your sister."

"That's an idea."

He leaned forward and kissed my forehead. "Let me take you out to dinner tonight, hmm?"

I put my hand on his chest. "I can't."

"I'll call you tomorrow?"

I realized Dane was the type of person who heard what he wanted to hear. And he wanted to hear I would stop searching for Ax so he didn't have to worry about me.

I felt a twinge of sadness as I made my way to the car.

When I got home, I went to the bathroom, and after washing my hands, realized I didn't have any towels to wipe my hands on. I held up my dripping fingers and heard a ping at my window. Then another. I pulled the curtains aside and saw Kevin standing in the side yard beneath my window. A yellow halo from streetlight bathed him in a florescent glow and he held a toaster-sized CD player above his head.

"Oh, dear Lord, why me?"

"Rose," Kevin called.

I unlocked and opened the window. "What are you do-ing?"

He pushed a button on the CD player. A TurkeyJerk

song blared. "Hang on. That's the wrong song." He fiddled with the buttons some more.

I grabbed a brand new used sweatshirt and pulled it on as I hustled out of my apartment and down the stairs, wiping my hands on the seat of my pants. By the time I made it outside, Kevin had another song going. Once again, he raised the CD player over his head.

"This is just like the movies and this song represents how I feel about you." Bret Michaels sang about roses and thorns. I rolled my eyes so hard it actually hurt.

"Turn it off," I yelled over the music.

"Huh?"

Kevin was much taller than me, but nevertheless, after a little scuffling, I pried the player out of his hands and pushed the power button. "What is wrong with you?" I asked.

"I'm crazy in love with you. I got a new tattoo to prove it." He lifted up his t-shirt. He'd gotten a rose inked over his left pec. Blood dripped from the thorn.

"Kevin." I took a deep, deep breath, and tried really hard to be patient. "I don't love you. We only went out for three short weeks. For the last time, leave me alone. If you contact me again, I'm going to call the police." Even though I didn't think the police would do anything, it was a good threat.

He looked at me with sad blue eyes. "But we're destined to be together, you and me."

I rubbed a hand over my face as I moaned. "Did you break into my apartment and trash my stuff?"

He gasped. "God no." Either Kevin was a great liar—which I doubted—or he was genuinely shocked. Or maybe I was a crappy judge of facial expressions. Seemed like I believed everyone's shock.

He reached out to touch me. "I would never do anything to hurt you. Did you call the police?"

"Yeah."

"You need a bodyguard." He stepped closer. "I will guard your body twenty-four seven. You can count on me."

I stepped back and almost tripped. "No, I don't want you guarding me. I want you out of my life. I don't know how to make that any clearer."

"Hey." A voice called. Dane walked around the corner from the parking lot, his gaze flitting between Kevin and me. "What's he doing here, Rose?"

I shoved Kevin's CD player at him. "He was just leaving."

"I will always love you," he whispered. "Always."

I hated to be derisive of Kevin's feelings, but we only had a handful of dates. We had nothing in common. We were sparkless, sizzle-free, flat. His attachment to me was odd and a little disturbing.

"If you love me, then you'll respect my wishes and leave me alone."

"Is it because of him?" He gestured at Dane with his chin. "You can't want this guy. He's a suit. You'll never be happy with him. I can make you happy if you'll let me."

Dane's face was a tight mask. "She wants you to leave her alone. Now get the hell out of here. If you bother her again, we're going to file an injunction. Understand?"

Kevin gave Dane a nasty look. "Whatever you need, Rose. I'll always be there for you." With his CD player in one hand, he flipped Dane off with the other and left.

Dane thrust his hands in the pockets of his trousers. "Tell me again why you dated him."

"He had on tight pants and I had too many margaritas."

He shook his head. "I've been trying to call you for the last two hours."

"I haven't had a chance to charge my phone."

"I thought you were going to go stay with your parents, or Jacqueline. They haven't seen or heard from you and they had no idea your apartment had been vandalized."

"Excuse me?" I stood there, glaring at him with my jaw on my chest. "You called them?"

"Let's go inside and discuss this." He put his hand under my elbow to lead me away.

I jerked my arm out of his grasp. "You had no right to call my family or tell them my business. Why did you do that?"

He bent toward me, his brows knit, his lips thinned into a straight line. "I had every right. I'm concerned about you. Why didn't you tell them about the break in?"

"Because I didn't want to worry them," I said. "And it wasn't your place to say anything. You didn't want to help me when I needed it. Too afraid of people like the Chief of Police and your boss. You can't get involved when it's convenient and blow me off when it's not."

"Is that what you think I'm doing? Because none of this has been convenient. I care about you and I'm worried about your safety." He continued to glare at me. "You said you'd let the police look for Axton. Was that a lie?"

I scoffed. "Of course it was. And if you knew me at all, you'd have known that. You just heard what you wanted to hear."

Dane turned away, watched a few cars drive by, their headlights whizzing past in the dark. He inhaled before glancing back at me. "I think you're being self-destructive. You're diving into danger head first and you don't even care. This Sullivan character could hurt you."

"Then I better get to Axton before that can happen."

"I can't do this anymore. You're on your own." He held up his hands.

"Fine."

"Fine."

He turned around and left.

I stood there next to my shabby little apartment building and felt more alone than ever.

Chapter 24

I trudged back inside and made myself a pallet on the floor using one of my new blankets and pillow. I tucked my stun gun under said pillow, pulled another blanket over me, and leaving the light on, instantly fell asleep.

A loud knock at the door woke me. The blankets tangled around my legs as I scrambled up. I was groggy and shaky, but still I grabbed the stun gun, my finger on the trigger.

The knock sounded again. "Who is it?" I yelled.

"Open the door, Rose."

Sullivan.

I pulled on the catering pants and the sweatshirt I'd worn earlier, and with stun gun in hand I unhooked the chain, unlocked the door, and opened it. Sullivan leaned one shoulder against the doorjamb. He slowly appraised me from head to toe, casting a glance at the weapon pointed at his face.

"Are you going to use that on me?"

"I'm definitely thinking about it. If you threaten me or my family one more time, you can count on it."

He thrust his hand into his pocket. "You called me, remember? Something about your panties? I found it intriguing."

I glared. "Why didn't you just break down the door again?"

"Because we're friends now and breaking in would be rude." He gave me a charming smile.

I wasn't charmed.

"You going to invite me inside?"

"Oh yes, by all means." I stood back, opened the door wider, my right hand tightening around the stun gun. Sullivan walked in and I shut the door behind him, never taking my eyes off him, never turning my back on him.

He glanced around the apartment. "Redecorating?" He looked at the futon shell with a frown and then pointed to the corner where I stood. "Where's your table?"

"You and your evil minions wrecked it, remember? You know, along with my underwear, my food, my clothes, etc."

His gold eyes darkened. "You think I did this?"

I actually laughed. "Oh, you are priceless. 'You think I did this?'" I imitated his deep voice.

"You think I destroyed your things?"

"Oh God, no." I waved him off with my hand. "You would *never*."

He looked me dead in the eye. "I did not do this."

"Well, not you personally. I wouldn't expect Thomas Malcolm Sullivan to get his hands dirty. But Henry, on the other hand…"

He narrowed his eyes. "How do you know my name?"

"Well, Rumpelstiltskin, I could tell you…but then I'd have to stun the hell out of you." I pushed the trigger. A blue current of electricity sizzled, filling the air with the metallic scent of ozone. "Oh, wait, I might enjoy that."

"You're welcome to try." The way he said it was mildly pleasant, but the way his nostrils flared slightly, his jaw clenched and unclenched, told me he was getting pissed.

"I may take you up on that."

He studied me and I could almost see the wheels turn. "You got my number from Packard Graystone. You called my cell and blocked your ID the other day."

"And you broke into my apartment and trashed all my possessions. This game of state the obvious is so not fun."

"I. Did not. Do. This." He spoke slowly as he advanced toward me.

"So you ordered Henry to do it. It's still on you."

"Not true."

Seemed we were at a stalemate. I wasn't going to get into an argument of 'did not' 'did too.' "Why should I believe you?"

Standing in front of me, his chest touching mine, he gave me a wolfish smile and flashed his teeth, completely unconcerned I could zap the crap out of him. "Because if I did it, Rose, I would take credit for it."

I blinked. Of course he would. He would rub my nose in it and tell me it was another warning, and something worse would happen if I didn't shape up. Oh my God, I actually believed him.

"What about Henry? He's capable of this."

"Henry wouldn't take a piss unless I told him to."

"Nice imagery."

"Who else have you ticked off besides me?"

This could take all night. "I have an ex who's not happy with me."

Sullivan walked around the room until he realized there was no place to sit. "Yes, Kevin Wilkins. Your taste in men is terrible."

"It is beyond creepy that you know so much about my ex-boyfriend." I tossed the stun gun onto my pallet. It seemed stupid to keep clutching it. I wasn't going to use it on Sullivan and he knew it. "And what do you know about my taste in men?"

"You've been dating Dane Harker." He made it sound like an accusation.

"That's none of your business. My life is none of your business."

"Right now, everything you do is my business. You're a wild card. Unpredictable. Anyway, Dane Harker is another mistake." He flicked his hand like he was shooing a fly.

"You don't know what the hell you're talking about."

He walked toward me, stopping just six inches away. "Dane Harker follows the rules. He likes things nice and neat. He plays golf on Saturdays, has Chinese takeout every Wednesday. Orders the same thing every time, by the way."

"He's nice."

"He's boring."

"Well, Kevin's not boring. Kevin's not predictable."

"Kevin is a moron. He legally changed his name to Spaz."

Yeah, okay, there was that. Kevin was a moron. But if Sullivan thought I was going to agree with him, he was cuckoo in the cabeza. Wait. Why was I arguing about my love life with this crime boss, in the middle of the night no less?

"Why are you here? To apologize for wrecking my apartment?"

His lips thinned. "I told you. I didn't do it."

I lifted my palms up, my fingertips brushing his chest. "Let's pretend that's true." I echoed his words from the first night he broke into my apartment. "You still have Axton."

"Yes, and I'm keeping him." Clasping my hands in his, he looked around the room. "You can't stay here. If whoever did this comes back—"

"I can take care of myself, thank you." I tried to pull my hands out of his grasp, but he tightened his hold on me. A little shiver zinged through me. Sullivan was the bad guy. Not the guy I should be zinging for.

"Yes, you've done an amazing job so far," he said, as his thumbs made little circles on my palms.

I glared at him, trying again to pull away. This time he let me go. I clenched my fists against the tingles.

"You don't even have a bed to sleep in, Rose." He nodded his head toward my pallet.

I raised a brow. "And that's your concern, why?"

His face, so full of emotion a moment before, became expressionless. "You're right. It's not."

He slammed the door when he left.

Ma looked me over. "Rose, you don't look too good."

What else was new? I had dark purple splotches under my eyes and no amount of cheap makeup could hide them. "I can't seem to get enough sleep."

Roxy walked out of the kitchen and tied an apron around her waist. She wore a short pink and white dress that looked like a flouncy birthday cake. "I swear, Rose, you look worse every day."

I glared at her and bared my teeth. I may have growled.

"Jeez, just saying."

"Sullivan came by last night. He says he didn't trash my apartment."

Ma slapped her hands on the counter. "What is wrong with that man? He's got a lot of gall, I'll tell you that for free."

"Or maybe he has the hots for Rose," Roxy said. "So, do we believe him?"

I nodded and refilled my coffee cup. "Yep. I do. But I also believed Dane and Kevin when they denied it. I'm too tired to think about it anymore. All I want is to rescue Axton and get a good night's sleep."

"Come and stay with me, Rose," Ma said. "You can have the spare bedroom."

Someone vandalized my car and my apartment. No way I'd put her in that kind of danger. "Thanks Ma, but my futon mattress is coming today. I'm hoping I can get to bed early tonight, with no uninvited guests."

We got to work and the morning passed quickly. Until ten-thirty when my mother walked in the diner.

She was awash in beige. Beige coat, beige slacks, beige sweater. Her hair was perfect, her brown leather handbag expensive, and her shoes probably cost more than I made in a month.

"Hello, Rosalyn." She looked around the diner, her lips puckered in contempt. "Is there somewhere we can speak privately?"

Ma came out from behind the counter. "You must be Rose's mother. I can see the resemblance."

Barbara tilted her lips into a fake smile. "Yes."

"Mom, this is Ma. Ma this is my mother, Barbara Strickland."

Ma wiped her hand on a dish towel and extended it to my mother. "Nice to meet you, Barbara."

My mother had that half handshake, where she just gave you her fingertips as if she were Queen Elizabeth greeting the little people. "It's nice to meet you. Ma."

Roxy finished refilling a cup of coffee at the table in the far corner. She walked up to us. "Hello," she said, chomping her gum.

Barbara quickly scanned Roxy's blue hair and pink confection of a dress. "Rosalyn, somewhere private?"

"You can use my office," Ma said.

Ma's office consisted of a small desk covered in fake wood and a rolling chair with yellow foam spilling out of its ripped seat. Metal shelves filled with cleaning supplies, toilet paper, and liquid soap in gallon bottles lined the walls.

"Make yourself at home," Ma said, closing the door behind her.

"With every advantage we gave you, this is where you ended up."

I was so tired and the stress of the past several days started catching up with me. My nerves were jumpy and jittery from too much coffee and the last thing I needed was my mother dispensing lectures.

"Why are you here, Mom?"

Her disgusted gaze turned from the shelves to me. Too bad the expression on her face never changed. I guess I ranked up there with the single ply.

"I have heard from several sources that you were seen in front of the police station making a spectacle of yourself."

I didn't say anything.

"Well?"

"Well, what?"

She took a deep breath through her nose. Good, she was having a hard time with the whole patience thing, too.

"What exactly were you doing with Dane Harker?"

I gave her my wide-eyed, confused look. "Making a spectacle of myself?"

"You know," she said through thinned lips, "we have put up with your nonsense for a long time. We've had to defend you to all of our friends. You work in a diner. As a waitress." She practically hissed the last word. "You befriend people like Axton Graystone and that blue-haired freak out there." She pointed toward the dining area. "And now I hear that you were getting 'physical'," she used air quotes, "with Dane Harker.

"Well I'm tired of having to tell people you're 'trying to find yourself'." She did the air quote thing again. "It's high time you grow up and act like a responsible adult. Really. Groping the man in the middle of the street. It's humiliating."

"I wasn't groping him, Mother. He hugged me. It wasn't a big deal."

She threw back her head. "Nothing is a big deal to you. Drop of out of college, waste your life in this dump, bring that boy with the big holes in his ears to your cousin's wedding, never caring about how mortified your father and I would be. You still haven't apologized to Tatum Hopkins. She was distraught. But no, nothing's ever a big deal for Rosalyn."

For years I'd been trying desperately to keep the peace

with my mother for Jacks' sake. I wanted to see Scotty, and I didn't want to put Jacks in the middle of it, so I sucked up whatever my mother had dished out, telling myself that between the two of us, I was the bigger, better person. But today, I'd had enough. Jacks was going to have to make her own decisions, because I had made mine.

"Sorry I'm such an embarrassment. But I am a responsible adult, Mom. I pay my own way because you cut me off five years ago. I was barely nineteen and you threw me out like a sack of trash."

She rolled her eyes. "Don't be dramatic."

"What would you call it? All I wanted to do was go to a different college. Why was that such a terrible thing?"

"You've never appreciated anything we did for you. We spent a fortune on that school, but of course, that wasn't good enough." She stood a little straighter. "And now you're paying us back. That's what all this 'acting out' is about, isn't it? Punishing your father and me?"

"You got me. It's all about you." I put my hands on my hips. "You may not like what I do or who my friends are. But that is just too damn bad. If I want to dry hump Dane Harker in the middle of the Apple Tree Boulevard, that's none of your business." I had lifted the lid off the pot of my boiling emotions and now they were bubbling over.

"Guess what? I don't care that you don't approve of me. And I could care even less about your snotty tight-assed friends. My life is just that. Mine. I've made it on my own, no thanks to you. And I will not have you waltz into my place of employment again with your little tirades and lectures, treating me like I am a child. Is that clear?"

She stared at me through slitted eyes. "Crystal." She

flung open the door and walked out of the office, her head held high.

"And by the way," I called after her, "air quotes are pretentious."

I sagged against the desk and gulped down the stale air. I felt a little dizzy and relieved and sick to my stomach all at the same time.

I didn't know what the fallout would be, but it wouldn't be good. Jacks might have to sneak around to see me. As far as my dad went, he just tried to keep my mom happy. It still stung that I didn't have her love and support, but it was time I got over it.

I walked back into the dining area. Ma looked concerned. Jorge looked curious. And Roxy looked at me with mixture of both.

"Your mom was really pissed," Roxy said.

"Yeah," said Jorge, wiping his hands on his apron. "She almost knocked me down as she left. Like she didn't even see me."

"Are you okay, toots?" asked Ma.

"I am," I said, nodding. "I just got some things off my chest."

"Do you need anything?" Jorge asked.

I smiled and shook my head.

"Okay, I'm going to help Ray with the kitchen, then." He turned and left.

"Start talking," Roxy said. "I want to know every detail."

Just then my phone vibrated. It was Sheila Graystone, so I answered.

"Rose! Some guy just towed my effing car."

Chapter 25

"Why did someone tow your car?"

"They said they were repossessing it. They repossessed my effing car. How the eff am I supposed to get home?"

"Um, do you want me to give you a ride?"

"Yes, I'm at the mall in front of Jamba Juice." She hung up.

I turned to Ma. "Sheila needs a ride. You mind if I go right now?" I hated to skip out on work, but I didn't want to leave Sheila stranded.

Ma patted my head. "Rose, honey, you go do what you need to do."

I drove to the mall, snagged a parking place near Macy's, and found Sheila in the food court sitting at a table between Jamba Juice and Panda Express.

"Sorry, Rose, but I didn't know who else to call. I was too embarrassed to call my friends, and Pack isn't answering his cell."

I didn't know if I should be flattered or insulted. "No problem. What happened?"

We walked toward the main entrance. "First I tried to buy some sheets," she said, her arms flapping in the air, "sheets. But two of my cards were declined. In fact, they cut them up." Her voice got higher with every word. "I thought it must be a mistake. But then I go out to the parking lot and find this fat man with tattoos hooking my car to a tow truck. He had paperwork and everything. Said we were four months late with the payments. Four months!"

I guided her to my car and opened the passenger door for her before sliding into my seat and starting the engine. The temperature had been dropping all day and the sky was overcast. I flipped the heater on and hoped it worked.

"Why don't you have a window?"

"Long story. Does Packard handle all the money?"

She looked at me with her mouth open. "Of course."

"Sheila, I told you, Packard has a gambling addiction. The night we followed him, he was losing. Big time. When he asked for more credit, he was thrown out."

I glanced over at her. Her skin was ghostly white. She held a shaking hand to her mouth. "Oh my gosh. What am I going to do?"

"I don't know."

She was quiet as I pulled out of the parking lot and drove toward her house. Then she suddenly sat up straighter than my mother in the Episcopalian church on Easter morning. "No, not home. Take me to his office. That son-of-a-bee has some explaining to do."

"I don't think that is such a good idea right now. Maybe you need to wait until you've calmed down a little."

Her light brown eyes sparkled with anger. "Take me to his office. Now."

I didn't argue any further but drove to a tall office building next to the highway. The mirrored windows reflected the stormy gray clouds overhead. If Sheila was going to confront Packard, now might be a good time for me to do the same.

I had barely pulled into a parking spot before Sheila leaped out of the car. I quickly shut off the ignition and ran to catch up to her.

Marching into the office building, she made her way to the elevator and punched the button. Tension and anger made her petite frame stiff, and as we stepped into the elevator and waited for it to slowly climb to the fifth floor, she crossed her arms and tapped her foot. Phil Collins sang a tune as we made our journey upward.

As soon as the doors slid open, she stalked toward the glass office door that bore Packard's name and threw it open. The receptionist looked up, startled. "Mrs. Graystone?"

The waiting room was full. Two teenagers with bad skin, their mothers, an elderly man, and a woman in a business suit. All eyes were riveted on Sheila.

"Where is he?" she asked the receptionist.

"He's...he's with a patient."

Sheila stormed through the waiting room door that led to the back.

"Packard," Sheila called out. She began opening doors, one after the other. I heard the startled voices. I followed along and kept quiet. "Where are you, Packard?" She was definitely using her outside voice.

The door to the fourth room on the right opened and Packard stepped out, holding one of those long Q-tips in his hand. "Sheila? What are you doing here?"

"I want some answers," she said.

Packard glanced at me, before looking around. All of the patients had come out of their rooms and stared at us.

"Sheila," Packard whispered, "I'm with a patient. Go home and I'll call you as soon as I can."

"No," she said, loudly, "either we talk right here in this hallway or we go to your office."

An elderly man stood next to me. He had on a hospital gown and a pair of dark socks. "What the hell is all the shouting for?" he asked.

"Right now, Packard. Choose," Sheila said.

Packard's ears turned red. "Everything's fine, everyone. Go back into your rooms and I'll be with you in a few minutes. Just a small family emergency."

A nurse in pink scrubs covered with cartoon kittens rushed down the hall and began ushering patients back into their rooms. The elderly man next to me turned around and I saw his ass. His bare, wrinkly, saggy ass. I shuddered thinking about why he was pants down in a dermatologist's office.

Packard and Sheila were already at the far end of the hall, so I hurried to catch up. Packard opened the door for Sheila, but glowered at me. "You," he pointed a finger in my face, "stay out."

Sheila grabbed my hand. "Oh no. She's coming, too." She pulled me into his office.

A large picture window looked out over the parking lot. The walls were painted hunter green and covered with framed diplomas and pictures of Packard with various political leaders, including Mayor Briggs and the governor.

Packard retreated behind his desk. Sheila plopped into one of the chairs in front of it and yanked me down into the other.

Photos of Sheila and Jordan, their mysteriously gendered child, sat on the desktop. There was also a picture of

Mary Graystone and a man I figured was her current husband, because he wasn't Axton's dad. And no pictures of Axton at all.

"What is so important that it couldn't wait until I got home, Sheila? And what is she doing here?" He stabbed a finger in my direction.

She sat on the edge of her chair, leaning forward. "Two of my credit cards were declined today."

"Is that all? It was probably a misunderstanding." He pushed away from his desk and started to rise.

"No, that is not all. They cut them up. And then, I went to the parking lot, the car was being towed. Repossessed, Packard. What the h-e-double-l is going on?"

He sank back into his chair, distracted and pale as all the color drained from his face. "I just needed a little more time. I could have paid them if they gave me a little more time."

Sheila jabbed a thumb at me. "She saw you the other night. Gambling. You didn't have a committee meeting, did you?"

He started to bluster, his eyes fixed on me. "You followed me? How dare you? Who do you think you are?"

I glared back at him. "The only one who cares about Axton. And you know exactly why he was kidnapped."

"Who said he was kidnapped? He's probably just done a runner."

"Cut the crap. I know about Sullivan."

All the bluster went out of him like a deflated balloon. His eyes skittered between me and the door, as if he was thinking about making a run for it.

"Wait," Sheila turned to me, "who is Sullivan?" She

glanced back at Packard. "That's the guy who called nine times, right?"

"You checked my phone? My God, Sheila—"

"Oh, shut the eff up, Pack, and answer the question."

Since I wanted to know more about Sullivan, too, I sat back in my seat and crossed my legs. "Yes, Pack, tell her who Sullivan is."

"He's a guy I owe money to," he choked out.

"That's not the whole story, though, is it?"

"Someone tell me what is going on. Who is this Sullivan? And how much do you owe him?"

"Almost two hundred thousand," he said. He rubbed his eyes and sighed. One hundred ninety-six thousand to be exact, but I didn't correct him.

"But why did he take Axton?" I asked.

He lowered his hands and tears welled up in his eyes. "I didn't know they would kidnap him. I needed Ax to do me a favor. I didn't know it would go so wrong."

Finally, I was getting somewhere. "What favor?"

"There's a rumor Sullivan keeps a list of all the people who owe him money. Prominent people. Sometimes he takes favors in lieu of payments. I thought if I had the list, I'd have leverage over Sullivan. So I asked Axton to get me the list."

"Is that what's on the hard drive in Axton's backpack?" I knew it was, but I was playing dumb. Sadly, it wasn't that much of a stretch.

"Yeah. Axton was supposed to make a copy of Sullivan's drive, not take the whole thing. Idiot. He ruined a perfectly good plan."

Sheila looked back and forth between us. "I don't understand. This is why Axton is missing?"

I glanced at Sheila. "Axton stole a hard drive from Sullivan's computer so Sullivan kidnapped him to get it back." I shook my head at Packard. "Ax even called you for help."

He shrugged. "How was I supposed to help him? If he'd followed my instructions, he'd be fine."

"You knew I had the hard drive," I said. "But you broke into my apartment and destroyed everything."

Packard eyed me like I was crazy. "What are you talking about? I never broke into your apartment."

Damn. He sounded sincere. I now officially believed in the innocence of all my suspects. But someone sure as shit broke in and spilled my milk. Who did that leave? Manny?

"By the way, was anything on the hard drive?" Packard asked.

"No." The last thing I needed was Packard getting his hands on that list. I didn't trust him with even the smallest amount of information. He was a screw-up and he'd gotten Ax kidnapped.

Packard ran a hand through his hair.

There was a knock at the door. We all turned to stare at it. The nurse with the cartoon cats poked her head in. "Doctor Graystone? The patients are getting restless."

Packard sighed and slumped in his chair, rubbing his forehead. He appeared tired and drawn.

Sheila didn't look much better. Her skin was ashen and her eyes glimmered with unshed tears. Poor Sheila. This son-of-a-bee just crushed her whole world.

"I'll get there when I can, Jean." He held his hand up and gestured, like he was trying to push her out of the office. "Give me a minute, okay?"

She withdrew her head and shut the door.

"Exactly how damaging is this list supposed to be?" I said.

"It gives details about everyone who owes Sullivan money. I was hoping it had the favors people had done for Sullivan, too."

I knew it didn't. "Go on."

"I know for a fact that Charles Beaumont rammed through a development deal for the Crab Apple apartment complex. There's been debate about that complex for the last year, but all of the sudden Charles has the votes to make it happen. And he was against it in the first place. I can't prove it, but I think Sullivan owns it.

"And a new construction company nobody's ever heard of got a contracting bid to renovate the country club. They weren't the lowest bid, either. I can't prove the construction company is owned by Sullivan, but I do know that two of the board members who pushed for approval spent a lot of time losing money at Sullivan's tables."

I agreed with Packard. Sullivan probably did own that construction company, and he probably was behind the apartment complex approval. But the man was too damn wily to leave an evidence trail.

"So Sullivan just wants the hard drive back?" I asked. "Then he'll let Axton go?"

"And a quarter of a million dollars," he said bitterly.

My jaw dropped. "Wait, you said you owed two hundred thousand."

"Sullivan says I owe more for all the aggravation I've caused."

Yeah, I could see Sullivan saying that. For some reason

it almost made me smile.

"Well, I can get the hard drive."

Sheila finally piped in. "We need to go to the police." It was as if someone had flipped her "on" switch.

"No." Packard pointed a finger at his wife. "We are absolutely not going to the police. Don't even think about it, do you hear me?"

Sheila stared at him defiantly, lifting her chin in the air. "Why not?"

"Shit, Sheila, he has all sorts of people in his pocket. Powerful people. We do not want to piss this guy off."

"Maybe you should have thought about that before you lost so much money," I said. "What else do you know about Sullivan?"

Packard frowned at me. "What the hell does it matter? He's the kind of guy you don't want to be indebted to."

"Answer the question, Packard," Sheila said.

"He runs floating poker games. I don't really know him, okay?"

She jumped up, pounded her hands on the desk, and leaned forward. "You don't really know him? You don't really know a man you owe hundreds of thousands of dollars to? A man you gambled our son's future on?"

Okay then. Jordan was a boy. Good to know.

"A man who kidnapped your brother? Who could have kidnapped our son?" Sheila's voice rose to practically a screech. "All this for a man you don't even effing know?"

Packard rolled his chair back a few inches. "Honey, I can make this right. I know I can. I just need a little time."

She lowered her voice. "You've had time. You've had time to tell me we're in debt up to here." She put a hand over her head. "You've had time to go to the police and tell them about Axton. You've had time to do the right thing. You don't get any more time. Just tell her what she wants to know." Breathing hard, she fell back into her chair and glared at her husband.

Sliding a finger inside his collar, he pulled it away from his throat. "Okay, sweetheart. Just calm down, okay?"

Oh boy. For a doctor, Packard was really, really stupid.

Sheila uncrossed herself and scooted to the edge of her seat. "Do not tell me to calm down. Do you hear me? You do not tell me to calm down." Her finger punched the air with each word.

"Okay." He bobbed his head up and down. I'm guessing this was a side to Sheila he'd never seen.

"Now tell her about Sullivan," she said through clenched teeth.

Packard rotated his shoulders, cleared his throat. "Sullivan started running poker games out of Penn's, you know the cigar bar?" I nodded. "That was about three years ago. Before that, I'd never heard of him. Bernard Penn owned it. His grandfather was a founding member of the Huntingford Golf and Country Club."

I made a circular motion with my finger. "Move it along. I don't need a Huntingford history lesson here."

"One day, three years ago, Penn up and sells. Never said why, but he moved to Florida soon after. Then this Sullivan comes in. Starts holding these friendly little poker games. Low stakes, no big deal. Not much different from playing at the club.

"But the new manager let it be known to a few people, myself included, when a game with higher stakes was being played. Usually in these out-of-the-way bars.

"Except for that place you followed me to the other night, the games always rotated. One week it might be in the city, the next week it might be a country bar, the next a sports bar in a strip mall. They would always advance you credit when you were down."

"But do you know anything about Sullivan himself?"

"Not really." His gaze shifted quickly to Sheila before resting on me. "He's always around, but no one ever really talks to him. And he'd never called me directly for money before. This guy who works for him, Henry, he always acted as a go-between. Until Axton took the hard drive, that is. Then Sullivan himself called me."

Now I knew more about Sullivan's business, but I still didn't know anything about him personally. "What about Sun Kissed Tanning? What do they have to do with all this?"

"Manny takes bets on the games, football, basketball," he made a motion with his hand, "standard stuff."

"I still say we should go to the police," Sheila said.

"It could ruin me. What about my city council seat? What about running for mayor?"

I raised my brows at Packard's level of denial. I wanted to tell him that ship had already sailed. But politicians were slippery little bastards, so who knew? Maybe he would become president after all this.

"I'm not worried about your political career, Packard. I'm worried about Axton and our family."

"Right, of course, sweetheart," he said in a placating, condescending tone that made me want to pick up the wooden mallard sitting on his desk and throw it at him. "But think about the practice. If I'm involved in a scandal, how are patients going to trust me?"

"Aren't they going to know about your money troubles anyway?" I asked. "I mean, the car was just repossessed. What about the house? Are you behind on that, too?" I knew it wasn't my business, but since I'd been dragged into it, I wanted to know.

Packard shot me a look that was pure venom.

"We're not behind on the house, are we Pack?" Sheila asked. Her voice sounded thready. She clutched her throat.

"Of course not, honey." His eyes shifted downward.

"Oh my goodness, we are," she whispered. She looked ten years older now than when we first walked in the room. She'd pulled into herself. All the anger drained out of her and she now sat huddled in the chair.

"I'm so sorry, sweetheart," he said.

"Like I said, I can get the hard drive to Sullivan," I said. "But what about the money?"

Sheila rubbed her arms like she was cold. "Don't we have that in investments? Can't we sell our shares in the market and pay this guy?"

Packard bowed his head. "The market's been crazy this year. I'm not really sure how much we have."

"You already sold them, didn't you?" she whispered.

Packard didn't look at her. "About six months ago."

"We don't have anything left? It's all gone?"

"I'm so sorry." He dropped his head on his desk and began to weep.

Sheila went over to comfort him. She cradled him in her arms, making soothing sounds like she would with a child.

I quietly let myself out of the office.

Chapter 26

I checked my texts on the way to my car. The first was from Jacks. She wanted me to call her immediately. I knew she'd want to talk about my mom's little tantrum this morning. I was going to postpone that talk for as long as I could.

The second text was from Kevin. I ignored it.

The third text, from Eric, said he was at home for a change, and my computer was ready. As I drove to his house, my mind went over all the information Packard told me. Most of it I had already guessed, but it was good to have confirmation.

Axton stole Sullivan's hard drive to get the list of people who owed Sullivan money. Now how could I use that information to get Axton back?

I arrived at Eric's house and knocked the door.

He opened it with a smile. "Hey, Rose."

I stepped inside. "Hi. How come you're not in the office today?"

"I've been averaging sixty hours a week, so I stayed home to fix your computer problem." He pointed to a laptop that wasn't mine. "Ta da."

"What is that?"

"You're new—well, newly refurbished—laptop." He

opened the lid with a flourish. "What do you think?"

"I can't afford this."

"Don't worry kid, I had it sitting around. Consider it a loaner until you can buy a new one." He pressed the power button. "I downloaded your hard drive onto this. Your old laptop was beyond repair. But I was able to salvage all your data."

"Wow." I turned to him and smiled. "Thanks."

"But you might want to invest in more memory, though."

"Eric, I can't afford a new TV right now, let alone money to update my computer."

"Whatever you say. Let me get you something to drink. You want a beer?"

"Got a Coke?"

He went to the kitchen and came back with a cold can of no name soda. "Will this do?"

"Yep." I popped the top and took a sip. "So, let me catch you up on the latest." I gave him the lowdown on Sullivan from last night—minus the handholding—and filled in the blanks where Packard was concerned.

Eric whistled. "You cram more into one day than I do in a week. What's your next move?"

I'd been thinking about that on the way over. "Can I use your phone?"

"Sure. In the kitchen." He pointed down the hall. It was a small space with the original nineteen sixties tile covering the wall, counter, and floor in a weird maroon-slash-dusty pink combo.

Scrolling through my phone, I paused for a second to wonder if I was doing the right thing. I didn't have much choice really. I was out of ideas. Before I could talk myself out of it, I dialed the number on Eric's phone.

Sullivan answered after two rings. "Who is this?"

"It's Rose."

Silence. The kind where you heard crickets chirp. Finally he asked, "Why are you calling from Eric Smith's house?"

"For shits and giggles, of course."

More silence.

I sighed. "Jeez, he was fixing my busted computer, all right?"

"And you're calling me, why?"

I shifted from foot to foot, looked out the kitchen window into Eric's back yard. "I thought we could talk about the weather or football. Halloween's coming up, we could talk about that."

"Rose." It sounded like a warning.

I began opening Eric's cabinets—which were mostly bare—and his fridge—which was mostly filled with beer. Calling Sullivan made me antsy. But at least this time I was speaking to him on my own terms. This felt better, safer, than seeing him face to face.

"I know Packard owes you money."

"I thought we decided you were going to mind your own business."

"Axton is my business."

"I'm not going to discuss this with you."

"What do you want in exchange for Ax?"

"You finally asked the right question," he said softly.

"So what's the right answer?"

"You can't give me what I need."

"Who can?"

"Packard Graystone."

"He doesn't have the money, Sullivan. You can't get blood from a stone, not even a Graystone."

"Ah," he said, "but Packard isn't a stone, is he? He just needs the proper motivation." I heard a click. He'd hung up on me.

"Well," I said to the receiver, "that was helpful." I didn't even have the chance to bargain for Axton with the hard drive.

I told Eric about the call and Sullivan's response.

Eric had a look on his face that was part concern, part exasperation. "Rose, this guy is a dangerous criminal and yet you keep making contact with him. Why is that?"

"I want to get Axton back safe and sound."

"And?" he asked, rubbing his head.

"And what? And nothing. I just want Axton back, that's all."

He tilted his head and raised his brows. "You're into him, aren't you?"

I choked out a laugh. "Into him, as in attracted to him? He kidnapped my best friend," I said, gawking at him as if he had lost his marbles.

"Uh huh." He shook his head. "Why do chicks always go for the bad boys?" he muttered to himself.

"Calm down, Dr. Phil. I do not want to date him or see him or anything else with him."

After a full minute of staring, me looking at him defiantly, Eric looking unconvinced, I was the first to blink.

"Are you sure I can't pay you for the computer?"

"Forget it, kid. Just enjoy all fifty-four of those gigabytes."

I took my new laptop and went home.

My super had put the new mattress inside my apartment, but hadn't moved it to the frame or taken off the heavy plastic encasing it.

It was thicker than my last one and black instead of bright orange. I ripped off the plastic and wrangled it over to the frame. I sat down to give it a test drive. Very comfortable. So comfortable, I decided to kick off my shoes and take a nice long nap.

But fifteen minutes later, my phone rang. It was Sheila and she was incoherent.

"Rose, coming out...grocery...man...Packard...," she sputtered.

"Sheila, calm down. Where are you?"

"Homph," she said. She'd begun to do that thing when you're crying so hard you can't breathe, so you gasp for breath every few seconds.

"It's okay. I'll be right over."

I drove to Sheila's house, and when she opened the front door, she threw herself into my arms, sobbing.

"Come on, let's go inside." I all but held her up as I guided her into the house. I led her to the sofa and tried to pull away, but she clung to me. I gently disentangled myself from her grasp.

"Where's Jordan?"

"He's...at....soc..."

"Soccer?"

She nodded.

"Do you have to pick him up?"

She shook her head and dabbed at her eyes with a soggy tissue.

"Where do you keep the booze?"

She tried to catch her breath, but still couldn't manage a sentence, so she just pointed to the kitchen.

I searched the cupboards until I finally found the alcohol cabinet above the oven. I pulled down a bottle of whiskey, found a glass, pouring two fingers worth.

I walked back to the living room and handed it to her as I dropped down on the sofa. "Here, drink this." I flashed back to Sullivan doing the same for me.

With trembling hands, she took it and sipped as she stared at the large family portrait above the mantle. After she drank half of it, she seemed calmer. "Thanks for coming."

"Tell me what's going on."

She took a deep breath. "I stopped by the grocery store. Not that we have much money to buy groceries. Anyway, I put the sacks in the trunk, and as I was getting back into the car, a tall man in a dark suit was suddenly standing next to me. He was this close." She held her hand about an inch from her chest. "I tried to get into the car, but he held the door and leaned in so that I couldn't move." She covered her mouth with one hand, tears running down her cheeks.

After a couple of minutes she was able to go on. "I was so scared, Rose. I've never been that scared. I didn't know what he would do."

"Did he have a scar right here?" I pointed to the corner of my left eye.

She nodded, her eyes wide. "Yeah, he did. Do you know him?"

Henry The Henchman. "We've met," I said. "So what happened after that?"

"He told me he knew about Packard's life insurance policy. He said his employer would get his money, one way or another."

I guessed this was the motivation Sullivan was talking about. I didn't think he would hurt Packard. Probably just trying to scare the crap out of him. But terrorizing Sheila was just plain cowardly. After all, she wasn't the one who had gotten their family into this mess.

"What are you going to do?" I asked.

She sipped more whiskey. "I don't know. All I can think about is Jordan. I don't want him in the middle of this."

"Is there anywhere you can go? Any family out of town?"

Her fingers fluttered over her puffy face. "My sister lives in Florida."

"Maybe you should go for a visit."

"I don't want to leave Pack." She slouched against the couch and leaned her head back. I think the whiskey had kicked in.

"Pack should go with you."

She looked over at me, her swollen eyes slightly glazed. "He has to work. It's the only money coming in. It doesn't matter anyway. He won't go. He still thinks if he scrapes together enough cash, he can win it back.

"I was going to be the first lady of Huntingford. I bet I could have made vice president of the Junior League if I was first lady of Huntingford." She quietly talked to herself as she stared at the olive green curtains framing the windows.

Sheila had left the building. She couldn't make a rational decision right now if the president of the Junior League asked her to wrestle in Jello at the next fundraiser.

I patted her leg. "I'm going to go. Call me if you see that man again, okay?"

"I would have worn my new pink silk hat to the mayoral inauguration."

It took all my willpower, but I waited until I got back to my apartment before I called Sullivan. I didn't trust my driving while royally pissed skills.

He answered on the first ring. "Yes, Rose?"

"That was cowardly. I don't know why I expected more from you, but I did." I paced the small space of my apartment as I talked to him.

"Should I pretend to know what you're talking about?"

"Sheila, Henry, life insurance policy. Ring a bell?"

There was a long pause. "Sorry, I don't have a clue."

"You ass, you know exactly what I'm talking about. I want to make a trade."

Sullivan sighed. "I hate to repeat myself, but you seem to be a slow learner so I'll say it one more time. You. Don't. Have. What. I. Want."

"Are you trying to piss me off?"

He chuckled. "Goodbye, Rose—"

"I can get the hard drive."

There was another one of those long pauses. "How?"

"Will you trade Axton for it?"

"Do you really have the hard drive? It wasn't in your apartment the first night we met."

I gripped the phone so tight, my fingers tingled. "You searched my apartment? You are such an asshole."

"Do you have the hard drive or not?"

It creeped me out to think of Sullivan riffling through

my personal shit. The next time I saw him, I was going to punch him right in the face. "Let's just say I have access to it."

"What about Packard's end of the deal?"

"I think you're the slow learner. He doesn't have it. Period."

"Then he'd better get creative and find it. When Packard has what he owes me, then we can trade. But no one screws me over, Rose. No one." He hung up.

I was scowling at the receiver when I heard a knock on my door. I hung up the phone and pulled the stun gun from my purse. I had even started taking the darn thing into the bathroom with me.

I looked out the peephole and jerked away from with door like I'd been burned. My dad was here.

Chapter 27

I have three standout memories of my father. He taught me how to ride a bike when I was five, clapping as I rode around our driveway by myself for the first time. I remember he hugged me after my role as Wendy in the eighth grade production of *Peter Pan*, and how proud he looked when I graduated from high school. For the most part though, my father was always working. And even when he was home, he was holed up in his study.

I thought of him as my mom's backup. Whatever my mom wanted, he enforced. I think because he loved her, but mostly just to make his home life easier. My dad would nod vaguely when she categorized my sins, pointed out my flaws, or lectured me on what a bitter disappointment I was, and why, for the love of God, couldn't I be more like Jacqueline?

Consequently, I never felt close to my dad. He was a shadow in my life. A ghostly presence that hovered in the corners of my memories. Really just a piece of scenery. And he certainly never visited my apartment once in the five years I lived here. I wasn't even aware he knew the address.

I tucked the stun gun—or Sparky, as I had started to think of it—back in my purse, tightened my ponytail, and opened the door. "Dad."

He looked as uncomfortable as I felt. "Rosalyn," he said with a nod.

"Hi." After a few awkward seconds, I stepped aside. "Would you like to come in?"

"Yes, thank you." He stepped inside and looked around. "So, this is your apartment?"

I shut the door behind me and leaned against it. "Yep. This is it."

He nodded the whole time like a bobble head, his hands shoved into his front pockets. "Well, this is...uh. Dane Harker called and said you'd been vandalized."

"Someone broke in and stole my computer. Dane likes to exaggerate a bit. Really it was no big deal."

"It is a big deal. How did they get in?"

"I guess my locks were pretty old. They've been replaced."

"You had renter's insurance, right?"

"Already got a new computer." I pointed to the computer Eric loaned me, which sat on the floor next to the futon. Did I feel guilty for misleading my dad? Nope. The last thing I needed was my dad feeling sorry for me. Or worse, thinking I was incapable of taking care of myself and running off to share that news with my mother.

"Good," he said. He glanced around the room again. "You don't have a table. Where do you eat?"

I thought about my little bistro table that had been smashed to splinters. "I've been meaning to get one. I've just been so busy lately."

"That's good." He rocked up on his toes, then back on his heels.

"Would you like to sit down?"

"Oh," he said, sounding surprised, like he'd never heard of this so called sitting before. "Thank you." He hitched up the legs of his pants and folded himself onto the futon. With one hand, he pressed on the mattress. "This isn't quite a couch, is it? What do you call this?"

"It's a futon, Dad."

"Oh, right. Do you sleep on it, too?"

I rubbed my neck. "Yeah, it's multifunctional."

"Huh."

Having exhausted the furniture topic we descended into silence once again.

"Would you like something to drink?"

"It's after five, so why not?" he said, brightening up. "I'll take a scotch, single malt if you have it. Neat."

"I have water."

"No, no. It's fine. I'm fine."

"Oh, okay."

This was the most painful conversation I'd ever had. I lived in the same house with this man for eighteen years. You'd think we'd have something to talk about, for crying out loud.

My eyes darted a glance at him and then bounced away. He was staring at the tips of his shiny black loafers.

"Is there anything I can do for you, Dad?"

"Oh, yes." He looked up at me expectantly. "Well, your mother. You know. She's very upset."

I kept my mouth shut. This was his party, not mine

"Very upset. She had to take a Valium."

"I'm sorry to hear that."

"Well, good. That's good. Now just apologize to her and I'm sure this whole thing will blow over." He stood.

"Wait, what whole thing?"

"Look, you know I don't like to get in the middle of your little…," he shook his head, "but your mother is very upset."

"So you've said."

"Then apologize and all will be well." He smiled, patted me on the shoulder, and walked the three steps to the door.

"Are you kidding me, Dad?" It was a rhetorical question of course, because the man never joked with me in my life.

He turned, confusion marring his forehead. "Kidding? What do you mean?"

"I mean I have nothing to apologize for. She came into my place of employment acting like I was a homeless person she had to step over on her way to Neiman Marcus and scolded me like a three-year old. I am not apologizing."

My father's face became cold, shut down. "You will apologize, Rosalyn, and you will do so immediately. She talked to you like a child because you're acting like a child. From what I understand you were being inappropriately physical with Dane in the middle of the street. Your mother was humiliated."

I flinched. I felt like I saw my father's true character for the first time. The man was weak. In choosing the easy way out, constantly acquiescing to my mother's demands, he diminished himself to me.

I looked him in the eye. "I'm not apologizing."

He frowned at me as if I was speaking Mandarin with a British accent. "Pardon me?"

"I'm not apologizing."

"But Rosalyn—"

"And another thing," I said, stepping around him to open the door. "I prefer to be called Rose."

After he left, I made a piping hot pot of coffee with an extra scoop of dark brown grounds. I refused to think about our conversation, so I called both Roxy and Eric and asked them to come over.

Roxy made it over first. She shrugged out of a hot pink fuzzy jacket, hanging it on the hook next to the front door.

I handed her a cup of coffee, poured one for myself, and curled up on the futon, my feet underneath me. "Thanks for coming."

"Yeah, I was bored anyway."

Eric arrived soon after. He stepped inside, pulling off his blue knit hat and coat. He dropped to the floor, crossing his legs. He took the mug of coffee I handed him. "Thanks," he said. "Okay, what's going on?"

"We need to brainstorm. I called Sullivan again—"

"Goddamn it, Rose." Eric set his coffee cup on the floor next to him and glared at me.

"I wanted to make an exchange for Axton."

"Well?" Roxy asked.

"He won't trade for just the hard drive. He wants the money, too."

Eric rubbed his head. "I thought you said Packard was in debt. Can he get that kind of money?"

"Nope, no way. I think Sullivan's just feeling pissy because of the hard drive debacle. Nevertheless, he won't make a trade. So…"

Roxy grinned. "So we break in."

Eric's eyes almost popped out of his head. "What?"

"Where is the most likely place Sullivan would stash Axton?" I asked. "He owns a ton of properties, but I was thinking the most likely would either be an abandoned building—"

"Right." Eric nodded slowly. "He wouldn't leave him tied up in a working business. Too risky."

"Or," I said, "he's keeping Axton in his own home."

"He could keep an eye on him that way," Roxy said.

"Especially since you've been running around asking questions at different NorthStar businesses," Eric said.

I nodded. "That's what I was thinking. I'm sure Henry took me to Sullivan's house the night he snatched me—"

"Whoa, what now?" Eric asked.

Whoops. Forgot to tell him about that.

"Henry threw her in the back of the car and took her to see Sullivan who threatened her." Roxy blew over the surface of her coffee. "Again."

Eric stood and walked to the window, his hands thrust in the pockets of his jeans. "You didn't think this was important enough to mention?"

Roxy popped her gum. "She didn't tell me about it right away either."

"Can we have 'let's all yell at Rose time' later?" I asked. "I want to narrow down Sullivan's properties."

Eric rubbed his stubble. "But if you know where he lives—"

"I was kind of blindfolded."

Roxy stopped chewing mid-chomp. "Anything else you left out?"

"I saw his decorated library, he threatened me, he served me whiskey, then I came home. End of story."

"Then you have no clue which direction you were go-ing?" Eric asked.

"No, but I know we took the highway to get there, and we drove no longer than thirty minutes."

"Even if we found the place, he probably has it under major surveillance."

I took a sip of coffee. "Probably."

"I can get us in, but not without setting off alarms," Roxy said.

Eric started to look optimistic. "If there's an alarm, I could hack in and disable it for say, twenty minutes. Would that give you enough time?"

"Definitely," Roxy said.

I started to feel a little sick to my stomach. Yes, this was my idea. But breaking into Sullivan's place made me very, very nervous. So many things could go wrong. And knowing me, they probably would.

"I'm going home." Eric shrugged into his coat and put on his cap. "When should we meet back up?"

"How about tomorrow after we close? What about Steve? Will he help?"

Eric nodded. "Yeah, I think so. We'll meet you at the diner at two-thirty. That'll give me time to go over the list of properties. Maybe something will jump out."

"Sounds good," Roxy said.

They left and I was alone in the apartment, going stir crazy.

Chapter 28

The next morning at work, I was such a nervous Nellie that I screwed up orders, spilled coffee, and received very little tippage. I barely noticed. My brain spun with the many ways our plan could go awry. We could break into the wrong house, Sullivan could be home, Sullivan could take us all hostage, Henry could shoot us in the face.

Ma flipped the closed sign and patted my shoulder. "Don't be nervous, toots. Things are going to be okay. Besides, it's kind of exciting."

I didn't find it exciting. I found it scary as hell.

At two-thirty on the dot, the boys walked into the diner. Eric looked like a kid on Christmas morning, Steve looked worried.

"Rose, can we talk for a second?" he asked.

"Sure."

He glanced at the others. "Alone?"

I walked with him outside and crossed my arms against the chilly breeze. "Steve, you don't have to be a part of this. It's okay if you want out."

He looked down at me, his dark brown eyes full of concern. "Eric told me Sullivan kidnapped you, threatened you. Why didn't you tell me?"

I was sort of taken aback. "I didn't tell anyone, not even Roxy at first."

"Don't feel like you have to hide things from me, okay?"

First Kevin, now Steve. I was tired of intense guys who couldn't take a hint. And I didn't have time to worry about Steve's delicate feelings, so I smiled. "Sure. No more hiding."

I walked back inside and moved two tables together and shoved chairs around. Ma served us Rice Krispies Treats and apple juice. Perfect for preschool snack time or when planning a break in.

"This is such a hoot," she said.

"Thanks for coming, you guys," I said. "But I don't want anyone to feel obligated to do this."

Steve pushed up his glasses. "I'm in. Anything I can do to help get Axton back."

"Breaking into Sullivan's house is highly illegal and very dangerous and we might get caught and Axton may not be there—"

Ma touched my shoulder. "Be quiet, toots. We know the risks."

"Okay," Eric said. "I narrowed the properties down to two, both out in the country." He pulled two pieces of paper out of his computer bag and handed them to me. "I looked them up on Google Earth. Which one do you think is more likely?"

One house was close to the street, the other had a long narrow road leading to a circular driveway. I closed my eyes and tried to remember my bumpy blindfolded ride. "I think there was gravel. I remember a curve before the car stopped." I looked back down at the aerial maps. I handed him the one with the circular driveway. "This one, I think." I hoped.

Eric powered up his laptop. "I pulled the blueprints from the zoning commission."

I rubbed my eyes and sighed. "You hacked into the zoning commission?"

He just smiled. "Okay, look at this." He shifted the screen toward Roxy and me. Ma crowded in, squashing my shoulder until I moved my chair over and gave her some room. "This could be the library they took you to." He glanced up. "Do you know if it was on the first floor?"

"Yeah, it was."

"Good. There are six bedrooms. Four upstairs, two down. Axton may be in one of them." He hit a few keys. "Then there's the basement. The door is here, next to the pantry in the kitchen. Any questions?"

"What should we search first?" I asked.

"We should start downstairs," Roxy said, "work our way up and search the basement last." Then she grinned. "It's been too long. Do you feel it, Rose? The rush?"

I shook my head. I didn't feel a rush. I felt the need to hurl. "Are we sure this is the right move?" I scanned their faces. They didn't seem fazed we were about to commit a very serious crime.

"It's your call," Eric said, "but the longer Sullivan has Axton, the more worried I get. And the dean said if Ax didn't show up tomorrow, he shouldn't bother showing up at all."

"He's been gone for over a week," Roxy said.

I took a deep breath and slowly blew it out. "Okay,

let's do it."

"Right," Eric said, rubbing his hands together, "we'll be in Steve's Explorer on the edge of the property. You two," he nodded at Roxy and me, "will have to run through a wooded area, here." He pointed to the aerial map. "I'll hack into their mainframe and disengage—"

To tell you the truth it got very technical at that point. All I knew was the computer geniuses decided to temporarily disable the alarm instead of turning it off completely.

"So you guys will bypass the alarm and Roxy and I will sneak in."

"We'll hook you up with headphones with a microphone attached. You'll tell us if you need a diversion or if you get caught. We'll have your back."

We agreed to reconvene at Eric's house at ten p.m. Project Rescue Axton was a go.

I was about to walk out with Roxy when my phone rang. It was Jacks and she was crying.

"I'll be right there," I said.

I knew Jacks was going to be angry with me, she always was when Barbara and I weren't getting along. It was easier for her to blame me than confront my mom. I'd already been through the wringer the last couple days and wasn't looking forward to any more confrontations, but she was my sister and I loved her. It was time to put on my big girl pants.

For once Scotty didn't answer the door. Jacks greeted me with a red nose, watery eyes, and splotchy skin. She wasn't a pretty crier.

"I heard your talk with dad didn't go so well."

"No, I guess it didn't." I stepped inside the foyer. Sunlight shone through the windows, leaving bright lines of light on the marbled floor. The house smelled like furniture polish and disinfectant, so I knew the maid had been by earlier.

"Dad's very upset," Jacks said, with a sniff.

"I hear that's going around."

She gave me a look. "I thought you'd listen to him."

"You sent him?" I assumed my mom gave him those marching orders.

"I thought he might be able to calm the situation down. Do you want some coffee?" She walked to the kitchen and I followed.

She poured me a cup and topped off her own. She rubbed a tissue against her red nose. "This whole thing has been very distressing."

"I can see that."

"Dad's angry because you were so disrespectful. Mom's barely talking to me. She's mad because I didn't tell her you're dating Dane. Then he calls and he's all worked up about your place getting vandalized. Why didn't you tell me?"

"Jacks—"

"And you know when Mom's pissed off like this, Dad is too. So now he's doubly upset." She took another sip of coffee. "I don't want to be in the middle of this."

I hated when my sister cried. And I hated she was in the middle of this family drama. But I hadn't put her there, my mother had.

Old anger resurfaced. Anger at my mom for holding the family hostage with her icy temper all these years. Anger at my dad for acting like her little lap dog. And anger at my sister for letting my mom control her.

I set my cup down a little too hard and coffee sloshed out onto the counter. "Mom's upset? Dad's upset? Are you freaking kidding me?"

She pulled another tissue from the box by her elbow and delicately blew her nose. "Of course I'm not kidding. I get so stressed out when everyone's like this. Why can't we all just get along?"

I looked at her like she had told me that clouds are made of delicious marshmallow fluff. "Because, Rodney King, we can't."

"Why do you have to be so difficult?"

"How is this my fault? What did I do wrong?"

"Let's not get into this, Rose."

"I think it's the perfect time to get into it, Jacks. How am I difficult?"

She put her hand to her temple. "I don't want to do this."

She wouldn't look me in the eye. So I kept at her, like a little kid picking a scab.

"How am I difficult, Jacks?"

She finally met my gaze. "You always have to provoke Mom. Why can't you just do what she wants? I mean, I did and is my life so bad? I have a husband and a child. What do you have? You live in a hovel. You're a waitress, for God's sake. You have no one to love you. Thumbing your nose at Mom and Dad really paid off, didn't it?" Her voice had gotten louder and louder as she spoke.

Feeling like I had been sucker punched, I left the kitchen and headed for the front door.

Jacks scurried after me. "I'm sorry, Rose. I didn't mean it." Fresh tears ran down her cheeks.

"Yes you did. And you're right."

"No I'm not, Rose. You're just more independent than I am. You live your life your way."

"Bullshit, Jacqueline. You think I'm a loser." I looked around the foyer of her beautiful home. "And you're right. I'm dead broke and don't know what I want to do with my life. I've been pissing around taking random classes trying to figure it all out. And I date other losers because that's all I can attract."

Jacks shook her head and sniffed. "No."

"I know what Mom and Dad think of me, but I never thought you saw me like that." I pulled open the door and left, swiping at a tear as I ran to my car.

I spent the next hour sitting on my new futon feeling sorry for myself. Axton was gone—it wasn't his fault, but I really needed him right now. And I needed Jacks, too. I pushed for the truth, and I didn't have any right to complain, but I still felt abandoned by the people I loved when I needed them the most.

I stood and started to pace. My frayed thoughts took me from Jacks and my broken relationship with my parents, to worrying about Axton and breaking into Sullivan's house. A week ago, I thought my life was boring. Now I prayed for boring.

As I wore down the nubby carpet, there was a knock at my door. I grabbed Sparky before I looked out of the peephole. Two delivery men in red t-shirts stood on my doorstep.

They brought in a small rectangular cherry wood table with two matching chairs. One of the men handed me an envelope before he left.

I ripped it open and read the note.

Hope you like this. If you don't, please notify my secretary and she will arrange an exchange.

Dad

This was the most thoughtful thing my father had ever done for me. Was this a peace offering? Did my mother know about it?

I ran my hand along the smooth cool wood. It was the most beautiful thing in my apartment.

I called his cell and left a message thanking him. It was easier for both of us this way—no awkward pauses.

Chapter 29

Roxy arrived at seven with a duffle bag in one hand and a black backpack slung over her shoulder. I could tell by the goofy grin on her face how excited she was. I, on the other hand, had spent the past several hours chewing my nails ragged.

"You ready?" she asked, chomping her gum fast.

"No."

"Sure you are. This'll be fun." She reached into the duffle bag and pulled out black stocking caps, sweats, leather gloves, and canvas utility belts.

"Where did you get all this stuff?"

"Sometimes it's better not to ask."

"You didn't steal these, did you?"

She looked at me with wide blue eyes. "That would be wrong."

She was right. I didn't want to know.

We took turns in the bathroom getting ready. I looked like a dork with the black sweats and white tennis shoes.

She frowned at my feet. "Don't you have any black shoes?"

"Everything was destroyed, remember?"

"Maybe we can rub dirt on them."

"I am not rubbing dirt on them."

"Fine, okay, whatever."

Ma arrived just before nine dressed in polyester black pants and an orange Halloween sweatshirt covered with bats. Basically, what she wore every day.

Ma held up two Ziploc bags. "I made chocolate chip cookies and more Chex mix." She shook the bags and her bootie at the same time.

We headed off to Eric's early. I guess I was the only one who was nervous. In fact, I was shivering, despite having the heater cranked as high as it would go. Ma and Roxy seemed to be free from the case of nerves that gripped me, as they talked about the zombie game they played at Eric's place. I tuned them out as I drove and mentally ran through the plan one more time.

Eric and Steve were waiting for us with a pile of computer bags by the front door. We each grabbed a bag and headed out to Steve's Explorer. I helped Ma into the front seat and slipped into the back, wedged in between Eric and Roxy.

As Eric gave Steve directions, Ma passed out cookies, and I put my head between my knees so I wouldn't pass out.

Eric bent down and whispered in my ear. "You're doing this for Axton. If I were in trouble, I'd want you in my corner."

"Thanks," I whispered back.

Steve made a sharp turn and I lurched against Roxy.

"Sorry," Steve said. "Now, where do I turn once I get off the highway?"

"Take a left," Eric said.

We pulled onto the side of the road and into a shallow

ditch next to the woods that surrounded Sullivan's house. Or what I hoped was his house. Eric jumped out of the car and stepped around to the back. With Roxy's help he began unloading equipment.

Steve and Eric opened up their laptops and plugged in their wireless drives. Roxy and I stood next to the car, while Ma sat in the passenger seat with the window rolled down.

The night was cold and I could see my breath as I danced from one foot to the other, my pulse racing so fast I thought I might faint. "Okay, are we even sure this is the right house?"

"Rose, shut up and stop hopping around. You're starting to make me nervous," Roxy snapped.

Steve pulled out the headsets. Eric helped Roxy while Steve handed me the wire so I could feed it down the back of my sweatshirt, then he plugged it into the receiver. He duct-taped the receiver to my lower back.

"I'll be here if you need anything, okay?" he whispered in my ear.

"Okay, but I feel ridiculous." I stepped away from Steve and tugged on the hem of my sweatshirt.

Eric squeezed my arm. "Hopefully, Axton is in there." He slipped a black backpack over my shoulders. There might be evidence I needed to take out of the house.

I tucked Sparky, my pepper spray, and a small flashlight into the utility belt, and adjusted the headset. Taking a deep breath, I looked at Roxy. "I'm ready."

"Follow me," she said.

We'd seen the path that led to the house on the aerial map. We would have to climb a small wooded hill before reaching the house.

The night was clear. Stars seemed brighter out in the country. The harvest moon hung low in the sky and I took a deep breath, getting a smoky whiff of someone's fireplace. Old dead leaves crunched under our feet. It seemed unnaturally loud. I fleetingly thought about ticks and snakes and poison ivy and squelched the urge to run back to the car.

Although the moon was bright, very little light penetrated the thick forest of trees. I tried to keep my eyes on Roxy, but found myself tripping over branches and roots jutting out of the ground.

Roxy didn't seem to have that problem. She navigated the terrain like an expert on one of those wilderness shows. If she started drinking her own urine, I was out of there.

Finally we reached the edge of the clearing. Crouching behind a tree to assess our next move, we faced the house, which stood about two hundred feet from the woods. Large and traditional in style, it was comprised of wood shingles and smooth stones. The windows on this side of the house were dark.

Despite the cold night air, sweat trickled down my back. Getting through the woods was the easy part. Now we had to get into the house.

"Okay," Roxy whispered, "we're going to make a run for it." She pointed at the side corner leading to the back. "Ready?"

"No—"

She took off and I scrambled after her as fast as I could. My left side cramped. I made a silent vow to start exercising and tried to control my need to gasp for air.

Roxy must have triggered the motion-activated security lights on the side of the house because they flashed on brighter than the sun. I froze. My gaze met Roxy's and since no one came storming outside with weapons raised, I ran the rest of the way.

Roxy peeked around to the back yard. She reached in her utility belt and pulled out a little pick and an Allen wrench. "Here we go."

We edged around the corner and across the lawn to the back door. There were no interior lights on, and as I scanned the back of the house, I didn't notice any cameras either. Not to say they weren't there, just that I didn't see any.

Roxy, tools in hand, bent down and examined the doorknob.

"You might see if it's unlocked." I twisted the handle and the door opened.

"Damn it, Rose, I was really looking forward to that."

She stood and pushed the door open farther, and we walked into the kitchen. From what I could see in the dark, it had granite countertops and stainless steel appliances. No dishes, no towels, no clutter.

We stood still by the kitchen door and listened. I heard a television from another room, probably the living room, down the hall.

"I'll take the upstairs and you take down," she whispered.

I grabbed her elbow. "That was not the plan. Splitting up was not the plan. Every time they split up in a movie, someone gets hacked to pieces," I whispered.

She shook her elbow free. "Calm down. We'll meet back here in five minutes."

"I don't have a watch," I mouthed silently. I stood in the kitchen and fought the overwhelming need to get the hell out of the house. I gave myself a little pep talk. *Get it together, Rose. You are already here and you can do this. You have to do this. For Axton.*

I pulled the mini pink flashlight out of my utility belt and crept out of the kitchen, hugging the walls as I went. Outside the kitchen door was a hallway hub. One dark hall led to the left, one to the right, and the short hallway in the middle led to the foyer. I craned my head and looked into a darkened dining room to my left. Empty. The stairs took up one side of the foyer. The room on the other side of the foyer next to the staircase, was obviously the living room. It was brightly lit and whoever was in there watched a Seinfeld repeat. I tried to imagine Sullivan sitting on the sofa, watching Seinfeld. Nope, couldn't quite picture it.

I took the hall to the left. I flashed my light over the bare walls. The first door I came to, on the right side of the hallway, was closed. I opened it and swung my penlight over the furniture. A pool table sat in the middle of the room with a small bar to one side, barstools in front of it, and a jukebox on the other side of the room. No Axton. I moved on. The only other room in the hallway was a set of double doors directly in front of me.

My heart began to pound. I wasn't positive until I turned one of the knobs, but then I knew. Sullivan's library. The books, the fireplace, the massive desk, it was all familiar. I'd picked the right house. Yay for me.

I shut the door and dabbed at the sweat on my brow. The laptop was gone. I went behind the desk and tried the drawers. They were locked. Damn, where was Roxy and her mad skills when I needed them?

I hastily looked around for anything else that might be

of use to me, but found nothing. Feeling defeated, I opened the door a crack and peeked out before slipping back into the hallway.

I retraced my steps and made my way down the hall to the right of the kitchen. Only one door in this hallway. Easing it open, I darted in, closing it quietly behind me.

Chapter 30

Sullivan's bedroom smelled like him: oranges, sandalwood, and hot male. I took a deep breath, inhaling his fragrance, and hoped it was lingering cologne not a lingering Sullivan.

But his California King was neatly made and took up most of this part of the room. Small bedside tables sat on either side of the enormous carved headboard. I wondered what he looked like, lying there at night. Did he wear pajamas or go commando?

Opposite the bed was a stone fireplace, a replica of the fireplace in the library, but instead of windows flanking it, there were bookcases. A sofa and coffee table sat in front of it.

To the left of the bed was a door. I opened it and shined my flashlight around, which reflected on a mirror, and I got a quick view of myself. I looked startled. I gazed around, taking in the largest, most opulent marble-covered bathroom I'd ever seen. The Jacuzzi bathtub was big enough for two. Without letting my mind wander down that road, I stepped further into the bathroom and opened the door next to the large steam shower.

It led to a walk-in closet. Row after row of suits, shirts,

slacks, coats—divided by length and color—and shoes stretched out before me. My mother would kill for this room.

Built-in wood cabinets stood along one side, filled with shallow drawers on the top half, deeper drawers on the bottom. I pulled each drawer out, one by one. Time for payback. I was rifling through his shit for a change. One drawer held rolled ties in little cubby holes. Others contained watches, socks, underwear. Sullivan was a boxer-brief man.

None of the clothes belonged to a woman. That didn't mean anything, of course, and it wasn't why I was there, but still, duly noted.

I shut the drawers and the cabinet and walked out of the closet, through the bathroom, back into the bedroom.

In the sitting area I ran my penlight over the fireplace and bookcases. A few books and knickknacks decorated the shelves. I stepped closer, shining the light over the titles, when I noticed a small space between the hearth and the left bookcase. At first I tried pushing the back of the shelf and wound up knocking a stack of books onto the floor.

"Damn," I muttered, then stopped to listen. My clumsiness went unnoticed, thank God. I picked up the books and put them back.

Well, pushing the shelves didn't do anything. I took a hold of a shelf and pulled. When the bookcase opened outward, I landed on my butt. Hard. Mentally cursing, I picked myself up and crept into the secret room. It was approximately the same size as the walk-in closet

As I looked around, my pulse began to race, but this time out of excitement, not fear. Turns out the large library where I met with Sullivan was a fake. This room, this windowless, hidden room, was the real study.

A small desk stood front and center. No books, no tchotchkes, no smooth clean surface. This desktop held neat stacks of papers and folders. Which I quickly began leafing through.

They contained mostly spreadsheets and cost projections—thank you, accounting class. I searched the drawers, starting with the shallow center one and found an old photo. A boy who looked very much like a young Sullivan with a boy-band haircut stood next to a smiling woman with gold eyes. His mom? I ran my finger over the picture. Next to it was an old school ladies Timex, the kind you have to wind. The black imitation leather band was creased and the watch had stopped at eleven forty-seven. These were the only personal items I found in the house. I pulled the drawer out further. There were USB drives. Four of them. I snatched them and stuck them in my utility belt.

The second drawer held three files neatly stacked. I flipped through them. They were labeled Packard Graystone, Axton Graystone, and Rosalyn Strickland. Without taking the time to read them, I shrugged the backpack off my shoulders and stuck the files inside.

I looked in the lowest drawers, which contained hanging file folders. I quickly sorted through them, pulling out files of the most notable people in Huntingford, including Councilman Beaumont and Martin Mathers, the Chief of Police. I shoved those into the backpack as well, zipped it up, and slung it back on my shoulders before stepping out of the study.

Click. I jumped at the sound, my hand flying to my throat. I froze, waiting for more but it was only the heater kicking on. Warm air blew over my head. Crap on a cracker, now I suddenly needed to pee. With shaky hands I opened the door and eased back into the hallway. I paused to listen, but all I heard was the laugh track from the television.

I had no idea how long I had been searching the downstairs. It felt like hours. Roxy should be waiting for me by now.

I snuck back to the kitchen, the backpack weighing on me as if filled with rocks. Every sound magnified. The clink of the USB drives in my belt, the squeak of my left shoe on the tile. I sucked at this. Roxy wasn't there. I opened the basement door and listened, but it was dark and I didn't hear anything.

Panic crept up and the sweat and the heat made me lightheaded. I quickly ran down my options. Go upstairs and keep searching for Axton or stay in the kitchen and wait for a henchman to pop in for a snack. I spoke into the mike on my headset. "I'm in the kitchen and Roxy isn't here. I'm going upstairs now."

I crept back out into the foyer. The television blared from the living room, but I didn't dare peek into the room to see who, if anyone, was there.

Keeping as close to the wall as I could, I tiptoed up the stairs. Once I reached the top, I looked back down to reassure myself no one followed. With my gaze still on the bottom step, I walked forward and ran into Roxy. Literally. We knocked our heads so hard it made an audible thud.

She gasped. "Shit, Rose, that hurt."

"You were supposed to meet me downstairs," I whispered.

"I've already checked this side of the house." She jerked her thumb over her shoulder.

We crept down the other hall, me in front, Roxy right behind. Muffled voices sounded from a room up ahead. I stopped dead and Roxy slammed into me.

"What the hell?" she mouthed.

"Voices," I mouthed back. "Could be Ax."

"Might be Henry."

The door was ten feet away. I couldn't make out words, but it sounded like two men. Henry? Axton? Henry torturing Axton? I'd already come this far. I motioned with my head, and as quietly as I could manage, I walked toward the voices.

I turned off my flashlight and tucked it back into my belt, then pulled out my Sparky. I looked at Roxy and nodded.

Stepping closer to the door I held up my index finger. One. I held up my second finger. Two. When I held up my ring finger I twisted the door handle and burst into the room.

Axton and the bald henchman sat on the edge of the bed with their backs to us. They faced a TV and held controllers in their hands.

All this time I'd been worried about Axton, and here he sat, playing video games.

Irritation, relief, and joy flowed through me as I walked forward and zapped the bald guy in the back of the neck. He gave a little grunt and slumped forward, but I caught him by the collar of his jacket before he fell off the bed.

Roxy shut the door and walked into the room behind me.

Axton, surprise on his face, looked over at the bald man, then up at me.

"Rose," he cried.

"Shhh," I said.

"Rose," he whispered. The controller was still in his hand as he threw his arms around me.

"We're getting you out of here." I turned to Roxy. "We need to tie this guy up and gag him."

She nodded and pulled a rope out of her tool belt.

"You guys are like covert warrior women and stuff," Axton said.

I put my fingers to my lips in the universal shushing motion. "Axton, help me get this guy to the floor."

"His name's Ron," he said.

Together we got Ron down on the ground and flipped him over on his stomach. Roxy trussed him up with her rope while I looked around for a gag. The queen bed was the only piece of furniture in the room, so I used one of the pillowcases. Roxy took another rope and secured the pillowcase in his mouth, tying it tightly behind his head.

"Let's see if he'll fit in the closet," she said.

"Good idea. Axton, help me with his legs."

Ron blinked up at us, dazed, as Roxy grabbed under his arms and pulled. Axton and I each took a leg, and pushed, scooting him on his butt into the empty closet.

After we tucked Ron away, I scrutinized Axton. He looked a little shaggier than normal, but otherwise fine.

"Are you all right? They didn't hurt you, did they?"

"I'm okay."

I smiled at him and he smiled back.

"Enough with the love fest, can we get out of here already?" Roxy asked.

"Okay, right. Do you have your pepper spray?"

She dug it out of a pocket on her belt and held it up.

"I'll go first, since I have the stun gun. Axton, you go second, and Roxy will be behind you."

"Be quiet and stay close to the wall," Roxy told him.

Slowly, quietly, we made our way out the bedroom and down the hall. I peered around the corner at the top of the stairs. We were in the clear, so I motioned with one hand for Roxy and Axton to follow me.

I sidestepped my way down the stairs, my back so tight against the banister, I might be bruised for life. We were halfway down when a man stepped out of the living room and blocked our clean exit. It was the guy who sat next to me in the car when Henry kidnapped me, the one with cold eyes who slipped the blindfold on me.

"Oh no, now we're all captured," Axton said.

"What the hell?" the guy asked. He flipped one side of his jacket and reached behind his back. Probably for a huge ass gun that could blow a huge ass hole through my liver.

"NO!" I screamed. I charged down the remaining steps and zapped him straight in the Adam's apple. His bulk twitched forward as he crumpled and he nearly took me with him on his way down. As it was, I had to struggle to free my right foot from his meaty thigh.

"Rosie, you are kicking ass tonight." Axton slapped me on the back.

"We gotta go," Roxy said.

Body shaking, heart pounding, adrenaline spiking, I stepped over the still conscious but unmoving cold-eyed guy, and waved Roxy and Axton on like a third base coach. "Go, go, go. This guy's won't stay down forever."

Roxy grabbed Axton's arm and dragged him toward the kitchen, me only three steps behind. Then the alarm sounded. Every light turned on and the loudest, most high-pitched wailing blared through the house.

"Go, go," I yelled as loud as I could.

Roxy flung open the back door. Floodlights lit up the backyard like it was opening night at Busch stadium. They flew through the doorway, sprinting across the yard without looking back.

I'd taken just two steps outside, when someone slammed into my back and knocked me to the ground.

Chapter 31

My face scraped the flagstone tile, my right cheekbone taking the brunt of the fall. My earpiece shifted and I felt my shirtsleeve tear.

Cold Eyes hauled me off the ground by my backpack, and with my back to his chest, he wrapped one arm around my neck, the other around my waist, and carried me into the house.

I reached up and smacked at him as hard as I could, but he seemed impervious. I stopped hitting him and clutched the edge of the stainless steel refrigerator, but my puny fingers and the slick surface were no match for his mile-high frame and huge muscles.

He lumbered through the kitchen, the alarm continued to wail, and I kicked back against his shins. I tried to claw at his arms, but had no nails, since I had nervously bitten them off earlier. I shifted my head to the side and tried to bite his arm through his suit jacket, but all I got was a mouthful of fibers.

As we passed through the kitchen and into the foyer, I grabbed a decorative china bowl off the credenza and hit him on the side of the face. He simply grunted and the bowl fell to the ground and shattered. He tightened his hold. Between his arm constricting my throat and the other arm squeezing my ribs, I thought I was going to pass out. Then the front door burst open and Sullivan rushed in, covered in pink and green splotches.

His gaze took us in. Me gasping for air, Cold Eyes squeezing me like a boa. Sullivan hiked his thumb over his shoulder. The henchman simply released his hold on me and I fell straight to the floor, flat on my ass as Cold Eyes made his way out the front door.

I stared at Sullivan, coughing and wheezing, as I rubbed my throat. I didn't run. Blatant fear, excruciating pain, and the mind-numbing shrill of the still blaring alarm kept me rooted to the floor.

When it abruptly stopped, the quiet was as deafening as the alarm had been.

"Rose," Sullivan said. I blinked, as if I had just come out of a trance, like my name was the magic word that set me free.

I scrambled up and ran back to the kitchen and out the door as fast as I could. I sprinted across the lighted yard and into the woods. "I'm coming," I said in a scratchy shout, hoping my headset still worked. "It's Rose. I'm coming."

I tripped over stumps, fell on my already bruised knee twice as I ran in what I hoped was the right direction. When I burst through the trees, I saw Eric standing next to the SUV with the door open. With hands on his hips, his head swiveled from left to right, searching for me. When he finally saw me, he cupped his hands around his mouth. "Come on, hurry up."

No shit. What did he think I was doing, taking a stroll?

I clambered into the car and hopped over the back seat

into the cargo space with Roxy, accidentally kicking Axton in the head. Eric climbed into the car after me.

Steve pulled out of the shallow ditch so fast, Roxy and I tumbled against the cargo door. With a grunt I rubbed my shoulder, but didn't care about the pain. I was just so grateful to have made it out of the house in one piece.

No one said a word until we were huddled around Axton in Eric's living room. He sat on one of the loveseats next to me, with Ma and Roxy sitting on its twin. Eric and Steve copped a squat on the floor.

I told them about playing catch and release with the psycho henchman while Eric grabbed a blanket from the bedroom and draped it around my shoulders. "Thanks." My voice was raspy.

"Sullivan didn't try to stop you from leaving?" he asked as he resumed his seat.

I shook my head. My neck was sore, my ribs bruised, my face was swollen, and my shoulder throbbed, but as I looked at Axton, I was more content than I had been in over a week.

"When we saw the SUV pull into the drive, we set off the alarm," Eric said.

Steve looked up at me. "I grabbed the paintball gun from the cargo space and ran through the woods. The second Henry and Sullivan got out of the car, I nailed them."

"So that's why Sullivan was covered in pink and green splotches. You're my hero."

He grinned his crooked grin and blushed.

I grabbed Axton's hand. "Now your turn. Tell us everything."

"And start from the beginning," Eric said.

"Okay, so, like, I went to this club and the next day I asked you to take my backpack. Remember, Rose?"

"I remember. Where was the club?"

"In this warehouse, well it used to be a warehouse. But now they have poker and stuff."

"Where was located?" Eric asked.

"In the city. And it was a pretty dicey neighborhood. But the people there were dressed up in really nice togs."

"Here you go, honey." Ma handed him a chocolate chip cookie she'd pulled from her quilted tote bag.

"Thanks." He let go of my hand and stuffed the whole thing in his mouth and washed it down with a swallow of beer. "I can't tell you why I was there, you know, for personal reasons."

"It's okay, we already know the trouble Pack is in," I said.

"Really? Because he told me it was a secret."

"Yeah, well, we got it out of him."

"Rose has been working every angle to find you," Steve said.

"Thanks, Rose." Axton tipped the bottle in my direction.

"I had a lot of help. Anyway, back to this club."

"Right. So Pack got me the invite. I went to get info on Sullivan. You know about him?"

I nodded. "Yeah."

"Okay, while Sullivan and Henry watched the poker game, real stealthy like, I sneaked into the back room."

"Clever. Then what?" Roxy asked.

"There was a laptop sitting on this desk, so I removed the hard drive." He leaned back and nodded, a little grin on his face.

"Then what?" Roxy asked. "Are we going to have to pull each and every detail out of you? Just tell us the story already. Jeez." I could tell she needed another piece of gum or a new patch or maybe both.

Axton looked a little hurt. "All right, keep your panties on. So, I removed the hard drive, stuck it in my jacket pocket, and made like the wind.

"Then I drove back to my house and called Pack with the good news. But Pack was, like, pissed. He didn't want me to take the whole thing, he just wanted me to hack into Sullivan's computer. Like I had that kind of time." He looked at Steve and Eric. Eric shook his head and Steve scoffed.

"But then, I noticed this big ass SUV following me around. That's why I gave you the backpack, Rose. After I came home from work that night, I heard a car pulling up in front of the house. I looked out the window and there it was, the SUV, and it was blocking my car. Then I saw Henry." He took a long drink of beer. "So I ran to my room and jumped out the window."

I huffed out a frustrated breath. "I could just slap Joe. I asked him a dozen times about that night and not once did he mention a very large man in a very large SUV looking for you."

Ax shrugged. "You know he's a little scattered. He can't always remember stuff."

"Wait a minute," Ma said, "how did they even know who you were?"

"Sullivan told me his entire club's set up with cameras. So they saw me steal the hard drive. Plus, I think they already knew who I was. I used Pack's invite to the club and they had my stats, you know? It was freaky, them knowing so much about me."

I thought about the files I had stolen. Yeah, Sullivan knew exactly who Axton was.

"Anyway, I ran through the neighborhood and hid behind some bushes. That's when I called you, Rose. But I saw the SUV trolling the street, so I hung up and hopped the fence and lost the phone in a drainage ditch. I decided I better keep moving, in case I was, like, captured, which I totally was, by the by."

"Where did you go?" I asked.

"I hid out in someone's shed, and the next morning, I hitched a ride to Sunset Lake. Packard and I worked that out ahead of time, if I got in trouble, go to the old lake house my family used to own."

I held up a hand. "Whoa. Packard knew where you were?"

"Yeah, he didn't tell you?"

That jackhole. "No, he didn't. Sorry, Ax, finish your story."

"So I broke in and was there four days. I couldn't call you because the phone and electricity had been shut off. But they had some bottled water in the garage and some canned veggies, so I made do."

"How did Sullivan find you, hon?" Ma asked.

"I don't know. Saturday afternoon, I'm on the deck soaking up some rays, next thing I know, Henry's hauling me out to the SUV."

"I saw a picture of you bound and gagged, Ax," I said.

"Did they hurt you?" Eric asked.

"Henry smacked me around a little. 'Where was the hard drive? What had I done with the hard drive?' Then Sullivan played good cop. If I told them where it was, they'd let me go home. But I kept quiet.

"They only let me have water. No food. But then yesterday afternoon, Ron comes in with a sack of burgers and bunch of video games. Wouldn't tell me why."

I squeezed his hand. "I called Sullivan yesterday, told him I had access to the hard drive. I wish I had called him sooner. I'm so sorry, Ax."

He squeezed back. "It wasn't your fault." Ma passed him the cookie bag and he let go of my hand again to eat.

"By the way, look what I found when I searched the house." I unzipped my backpack and pulled out the files, then reached into my belt and snagged the USB drives I'd stolen from Sullivan's desk.

"This is Pack's file," Eric said, taking it from my hand and paging through it. "It has all his financials. How much he makes, what he owes, credit reports. Plus, there's personal info in here. Stuff about you, Ax, and your mom, random pictures of everyone in the family. It wouldn't have been hard to find out about the house at Sunset Lake. People do what's familiar."

Ma angled her head so she could read through her trifocals. "Here's a file on Martin Mathers. And another on Arthur Briggs. "

Eric whistled and rubbed his head. "The mayor? Man." He blinked a few times then looked at me. "What have you done, Rose?"

"She did the only thing she could do," Roxy said. "She took out an insurance policy."

"I thought I could make two or three copies of everything and put them in different—hopefully safe—places."

Steve looked up at me. "That's good thinking."

Eric rubbed his hands together. "Okay then, I guess we should start scanning all this crap."

Chapter 32

"I know I don't have an appointment," I told the receptionist for the third time, "but I need to see him today." I pointed to a chair in the waiting room. "And I'm going to sit there until I do." I flounced away and sat down next to a side table piled high with news magazines.

I had already left Dane four messages. The optimistic side of me said he was probably tied up in court or busy with a client. The rational side said he was avoiding me.

I picked up a magazine and flipped through the pages, but I couldn't concentrate on anything. The copies of the files burned a hole in my bag. I barely kept myself from checking every five minutes to see if they were still there.

They were very detailed, containing financial records, personal stats, and the amount each person owed with coordinating dates, times and bets. It was all very factual and impersonal. I read over my own file twice. It was a little sad how thin and boring it was. But at least I didn't owe Sullivan money.

Ma gave me the day off so I could take care of business. I went to the bank and opened a safe deposit box to hold one hard copy and one set of memory cards. She advanced me a week's salary to pay for it. I wasn't too happy about that, but since I'd emptied my bank account buying stuff like underpants and secondhand sweats, I had to suck it up.

I glanced at the clock every few minutes. The woman sitting next to me gave me the stink eye. Probably because I kept shifting in my chair and clicking my nail nubs against the arm rests.

An hour later Dane walked into the office accompanied by a beautiful blonde in an expensive navy suit. She smiled up at him, laughing at something he'd said. A little bolt of jealousy zapped my chest and I jumped to my feet, wishing I'd worn something nicer than break-Axton-out-of-jail sweats.

When he saw me his eyes widened in surprise. "Rose." The blonde had been mid-hair flick when he stopped. She looked at him in confusion for a second, and then stared at me. And not in a happy way.

"Sorry I'm here unannounced, but I need to talk to you." I looked from him to the beautiful woman now glaring at me. "In private."

"Of course. Is everything all right?"

He took my elbow, his companion forgotten, and steered me toward the inner office door.

"Dane," she said sharply.

He stopped and turned back to the blonde. His hand, still clamped on my elbow, forced me to turn with him. "I'm sorry. Rose Strickland, this is Amy Phipps. Amy, Rose." He nodded his head between us.

Amy smiled. Sincere, professional, with the right touch of warmth. I wasn't fooled for a minute. "Are you a client of Dane's?"

"No, Rose is a friend," he said, answering for me.

"So nice to meet you, Amy," I said.

"Excuse us." Dane led me away again. Over my shoulder, I smirked. Her phony smile turned to a scowl.

He hustled us into his office and shut the door. The office was on the small side, with one window and a large desk. A glass-covered case containing books of codes and statutes stood next to it.

"What's wrong? What happened?" He set his briefcase on the floor and settled me into one ugly green client chair before dropping into the second chair, angling toward me so our knees almost touched.

"Axton's back."

"That's great." He pulled me into a hug. It felt nice. Plus, he smelled good, like cedar and coffee. He finally leaned back a bit, but kept his hands on my shoulders. My knees were wedged between his now.

"How did this happen? Did Sullivan just let him go?"

I cleared my throat. "Not exactly."

"Did Axton escape?"

I took a deep breath and shifted my gaze to his tie. It was navy with little red dots in a diamond pattern. "Not exactly."

He dropped his hands and sat back in the chair. "All right, tell me."

"Roxy and I broke him out."

"What?" He stood, and with his hands in his pockets, he began pacing the length of the small office. Six steps to the window, pivot, six steps to the wall behind me. Rinse and repeat.

"What the hell were you thinking?"

"I was thinking I needed to get Axton out of there. And since Sullivan has the Chief of Police in his pocket… Anyway, I need to hire you."

Dane looked out the window, his back to me. I could see the line of tension in his shoulders. "Yes, of course. But you might need a more experienced defense attorney. One of the partners, maybe."

"Why would I need a defense attorney?"

He faced me then. "I assume you're worried about Sullivan pressing charges."

"Sullivan pressing charges against me? He broke into my place first. And he kidnapped Axton. Wait. Before I tell you anything, Dane, I need to hire you."

He looked at me for a long time. I think he was debating whether or not he wanted me to tell him anything at all. He nodded. "All right. I charge four-fifty an hour."

I pulled a bill out of my pocket. "I'll give you twenty bucks."

He pinched the bridge of his nose. "God. All right." He grabbed the money and tucked it in his pocket.

I took a deep breath and paused before unzipping my bag and pulling out the stack of papers. "I borrowed some files from Sullivan and made copies. I need you to take a set and hide them."

His face blanked, like what I said hadn't even registered. Then his face turned a dull red. He threw his hands in the air. "My God, Rose, have you lost your mind? You stole…" He realized he was almost yelling and lowered his voice to whisper. "You stole files from Sullivan? The man who kidnaps people? The man who broke into your home and destroyed everything you own? That man?" His brows lowered over his eyes and his jaw began to twitch.

"More like borrowed than stole. And I don't think he actually did that last one. Destroyed all my things, I mean. I think that was someone else."

"Who?" he yelled again. "Who else would have done it? That nitwit with the ear holes?"

"Well, I don't think Kevin did it either."

Dane sank back into the seat next to mine and thrust his face into his hands. "Do I have gray hairs yet? Because I feel my hair turning gray."

"Looks all right to me."

He muffled a laugh and sat up. Then he took one of my hands and kissed my palm before looking at me with resignation. "You are so complicated. You are the only person I know who would do something so foolish and so brave."

"I just want to protect my friends. That's how I roll."

When I left Dane's office, Amy Of The Frigid Stare And Nordic Good Looks shot me an icy smile and told me to have a good day. At least that's what her mouth said. The unseen bubble over her head read, "He's mine, bitch. Hands off." Frankly, she scared me almost as much as Sullivan. Just in a completely different way.

I figured it was only a matter of time before Sullivan tracked me down, but I wasn't ready to see him yet. I needed to keep moving. A moving target was much better than a sitting duck, I'd always said. Okay, I'd never said that. But still, my theory was good.

I drove to my dad's office, which was on the ninth floor of the medical building next to the hospital. He had a spacious waiting room with a slate tile fountain on one wall. I glanced around at the three people in the waiting room. Hopefully he wouldn't be too busy to see me.

Sally Jenson had been my dad's receptionist forever. "Rosalyn, honey, it is so good to see you." She came out of the inner office and hugged me. "You look good."

I had always liked Sally. She would sneak peppermint candy to Jacks and me on the rare occasions when we visited the office. Although she had to be in her sixties now, she hadn't changed much. Her blonde hair was styled a little differently than when I had last seen it, but other than that, she looked the same. I wondered what her secret was.

"You look great too, Sally. I like the hair."

Her hand fluttered to it, smoothing back a strand. "Thanks. I just got it cut." Her smile withered around the edges. "I'm not sure I like it."

"Well, I do. It's very flattering."

"You're good for my ego. Now, you want to see your father. Go on back. I think he can squeeze you in." She winked.

The door to my father's office stood open, so I went in and sat down. It seemed my mother had gotten her hands on my dad's office space. I would recognize her bland beige thumb anywhere. Colorless paintings hung on taupe walls underlined by a thick tan carpet. It had been a long time since I had been here. Five years, to be exact. When I told my dad I didn't want to go back to the all-girls school on Cell Block H.

My father walked in twenty minutes later, carrying a green patient folder with him. "What are you doing here?" He was as surprised to see me as Sally was. But I got a much warmer reception from her.

I shifted around in the cognac brown leather chair, uncomfortable, not only in the chair, but in this room. With my father.

He sat behind his desk and waited for my answer.

I squirmed and looked out the window. It was a beautiful day. The sky was a cloudless, brilliant blue. My gaze flitted back to him. "Thank you for the table and chairs. That was very generous of you."

"It's fine. Is that why you stopped by Rosa…Rose? A personal visit wasn't necessary, I got your message."

"No, that's not why I'm here." I shifted in the chair again then forced myself to sit still.

He looked me up and down, frowning. "Are you in some kind of trouble?"

"I've got something to tell you, but I need to know you'll keep it to yourself." I was asking him to keep something from my mom. As far as I knew, he'd never done that before. Taking a deep breath, I blew it out. "Under no circumstances is Mom to know anything about this." I just wanted to clarify.

"I don't know if I can do that, Rosa…Rose."

"Okay." I pulled my purse over my shoulder and stood. "Thanks again for the table."

"Wait." He stared not at me, but at some fixed point over my shoulder. "All right, Rose, I'll keep this between the two of us."

Now I was beginning to have second thoughts. "No, it was wrong of me to ask." I walked toward the door.

"Sit down." The tone was the same one he used when I had been in real trouble, like when I put food coloring in the school fountain and Jenny Truman ratted me out.

I sat.

"I don't have much time. Try to be concise."

I started at the beginning with Axton's disappearance and left nothing out. His expression became tighter and more concerned with each new revelation. When I finished there was a long silence.

"The Police Chief? City councilmen, the mayor? All bought off by this Sullivan?" He tipped his chair back and stared at the framed diplomas on the wall. "You're sure about this?"

I removed the papers and memory cards from my bag and laid them on his desk. It took a while, but he methodically went through them, page by page, muttering to himself. Finally, when he was done, he stared at me with haunted eyes. "My God, what were you thinking?"

I had heard that a lot lately. Seemed not everyone thought highly of my decision making abilities. I straightened my shoulders. "I did what I had to do. And I wouldn't change a thing."

"You could have gotten yourself killed. Why didn't you come to me sooner?"

"What could you have possibly done? No offense, Dad, but you would have either not believed me or told me to go to the police. Which I did, by the way, and got nowhere. And that was before I found out the Chief of Police owed Sullivan money."

"Damn it. What you did was so incredibly stupid and dangerous. I don't ever want you doing something like this again, do you hear me, young lady?"

I smiled at his fatherly concern. It was nice to know he

cared.

"I'm serious," he said, when he saw my smile.

"I need you to keep these copies somewhere safe, Dad, in case, you know, something happens, or Sullivan comes after me. I put down his address and everything I found out about him, which wasn't much."

My father took a deep breath, and after a moment, glanced back at the papers. "Did you make more than one copy, I hope?"

"I made three. They're all in different places. And remember, don't tell Mom."

"Trust me. This is one thing she'll never know about. I'll take care of it, Rosalyn. Don't worry."

I felt such relief when my dad said he'd take care of it. As if a knot in my stomach untangled and I didn't even realize it was there. I wished I had always felt this from him, cared for, protected. It felt nice, like a warm blanket on a cold night.

"Thanks, Daddy."

"You haven't called me that since you were a very little girl." We both stood and stared at each other, then our gazes slid away, uncomfortable with the closeness.

"Well, I'd better get going."

He gestured at the copies I'd given him. "Yes, I have to deal with these." He came around the desk and gave me a brief, one-armed hug, and awkwardly patted my back. "Be careful. No more dealing with criminals, okay?"

I smiled and said nothing as I walked out of his office.

Sally gave me another hug for the road and pushed a couple of peppermint candies in my hand before I left.

Chapter 33

Now for the part I'd been putting off. The part that made my hands shake and my chest hurt. It was time to visit Sullivan.

I could either wait for him and his menacing minions to find me, or I could come from a place of power and go to him. One might argue that going to him was coming from a place of sheer stupidity, a fly dive-bombing a spider's web, but I felt more comfortable with initiative than I did with inertia.

As I drove out of Huntingford and got on the highway, my sweaty hands gripping the steering wheel, I began to feel the enormity of my actions. My dad was right, what had I been thinking? Sullivan must be livid I'd taken those files. No one screwed him over. He told me that. Breaking into his home, not to mention smashing his fancy bowl, attacking two of his employees, invading his private space, stealing personal files. Had to be a worse than owing him money.

Maybe it would be better to just keep driving and not stop until I got a safe distance away. About two thousand miles might do it. But then Sullivan might come after my family, like he did with Axton. Maybe I could offer up my mother. I smiled at the thought of my imperious mother snapping at Henry that he'd tied the rope binding her hands wrong, and that he should do it properly or not at all. But then I quickly sobered and thought of my sister and little Scotty. No, I had to finish this.

I was so lost in thought I almost missed my exit and had to make a hasty lane change to get off the highway. I drove up to Sullivan's beautiful stone house with my heart beating twice as fast as normal. I turned in the circular drive and parked the car. Henry was out of the house and stalking toward me before I even had time to open the car door.

I managed to grab my bag before he jerked me out of the driver's seat and frisked me, patting me down from head to toe. His enormous hands impersonally brushed over my breasts and ass, sliding between my legs.

"Watch it."

"Don't flatter yourself." He unzipped my purse and rummaged around, taking my keys and pocketing them, before shoving it back at me. He grabbed me by my arm and yanked me toward the house. "I wouldn't want to be you right now."

Henry and I had something in common. I didn't want to be me right now either.

He led me through the house, down the hall, and straight to the pseudo library. Henry gave a perfunctory knock on the door before opening it and thrusting me inside. I felt like I had just been thrown into a cage with a very hungry lion.

Sullivan stood in front of the window, his back to me. With the sun washing over him, I could see the blue highlights in his black hair. He wore a navy cashmere sweater and dark slacks, his hands shoved in the pockets. Slowly he turned toward me, his posture deceptively relaxed. His eyes told a different story.

"Rose." His voice was soft. "Have a seat." He gestured with one hand toward the chair in front of his desk.

If he had been screaming or ranting or showing some kind of emotion, I think I wouldn't have been so afraid. The quiet reasonable tone masking his fury made my knees quake, but I wasn't going to let him see that. He'd eat me alive.

I threw back my shoulders and stalked toward the chair, throwing him a haughty look before sitting down.

He slid into his seat behind the desk, and with his hands flat on the desktop, studied me in silence. I stared back with my best bored look. The one I used as a teenager when my mother would chastise me for using the salad fork instead of the dinner fork. I knew which fork to use, but when she insisted on serving salmon, I insisted on using the wrong fork.

"You stole from me, Rosalyn Strickland. And that is not acceptable." His voice dripped ice, but the volume didn't change.

"You and I have different definitions of unacceptable. And I did what I had to do to protect the people I care about."

He stared at me with those angry gold eyes and said nothing. He was waiting me out. He could wait all day. I kept my mouth shut and thought about my homework assignments, my meager grocery list, and the fact I needed an oil change. It had been over ten thousand miles. Way over.

It took a solid fifteen minutes before he got up from the desk and stalked toward me. Grabbing my arms, he hauled me up, his hands warm, even through the long sleeves of my sweatshirt.

My breath came in shallow gasps. We stood three inches apart. That spicy orangey scent tickled my senses. I probably smelled like fear and peppermint candy. I hope he didn't notice.

"I want what you stole from me," he said. It came out more like a snarl and he shook me a little for emphasis.

I casually tilted my head. "Why didn't you just say so?"

"Do you have them with you?" He was so close that if I puckered my lips, they'd touch his.

"Maybe," I whispered. I may have swayed a bit.

He didn't let me go immediately, but kept his hands on my arms while he stared at my mouth. I parted my lips and held my breath in anticipation of whether he would move that half an inch, touch his lips to mine, or pull back.

He pulled back.

I exhaled.

"Give them to me," he said.

When he released me, I sank down in the chair. He, however, didn't go back behind the desk, but instead leaned against it, his leg brushing mine. Boldly, I crossed one leg over the other, bringing my calf to rest against his and raised an eyebrow.

He left his leg where it was and crossed his arms over his chest, to show that touching me didn't bother him. I leaned back and smiled, showing him that I wasn't bothered by his not being bothered.

He held out his hand. "Now."

I wagged my finger. "Not so fast."

His expression shuttered and his nostrils flared slightly. Seeing him lose his shit was a bit satisfying. A lot scary, but a little satisfying.

He scooped up my purse and pawed through it. I didn't like it. I had tampons rolling around in there. But still I didn't protest. I knew it wouldn't do any good.

He threw the bag to the floor. "I'm tired of playing games."

"I am, too, actually. Why did you let me go last night?" I had been wondering about it and it still confused me. I'd told him I had access to the hard drive, but still, he'd made no move to detain me.

"I don't know," he ground out. He glanced back at me, his jaw clenched. "And you broke my antique porcelain bowl."

"Well you could have broken Axton."

"Yes, but the antique bowl had value."

I kicked the side of his leg with my foot. "That's not even funny."

"Do you see me laughing? I want what you stole from me."

"I have the items I borrowed—"

He scoffed.

"And I've made copies. Several of them."

He crossed his arms, his face grim. "Of course you have."

"They'll stay hidden if you leave me and mine alone."

"Or what?" He leaned forward, his hands bracing on the armrests of my chair. He was all up in my personal space. And he smelled so good.

"Or I will put all your business on the internet, send it to all the major papers in the state. It will be on the city council website and any other place I can think of."

His breath fanned my face. His eyes darkened to a rich amber gold. "How do I know you won't do that anyway?"

"You don't." Having him this close made me nervous. I licked my lips and fought the urge to push him away. And draw him closer. The soft cashmere of his sweater brushed against my hand.

His gaze lowered to my lips and stayed there.

"You'll just have to take my word for it," I said.

He pushed off the chair and straightened. "How much?" He walked back behind the desk and sat down.

"How much what?"

"How much is your silence going to cost me?" He was all business now. Gone was the angry sexy expression. In its place was a cold professional businessman making a deal.

"I've already told you. You leave me and my family and my friends and all my acquaintances and anyone I've ever met or talked to alone, and you'll never hear from me again."

"One hundred thousand?" he asked, acting as if I hadn't spoken.

"I just want to know we're safe."

"One fifty?"

"Do we have a deal or not?"

"What's your price, Rose?"

I stood up and leaned across his desk. Why could this man have me hot and bothered one minute then just plain hot the next? "I told you. I want your assurance that we'll all be safe. No more kidnappings. No more threats. Do you understand me? You will leave us the hell alone, and never," I pointed my finger at him, "never mention the name of my nephew again."

He looked at me in silence for several seconds. "Deal."

He stood and held out his hand for me to shake. I ignored it.

I picked up my bag and walked out of his office, my head held high.

I stalked to the front door, past Henry and Cold Eyes, who shot daggers at me. Noticing the bruise on his Adam's apple, I smiled at him sweetly and gave a finger wave.

Keeping my posture stiff like only my mother's daughter can, I walked to my car and opened the passenger door. On the seat was the backpack. I pulled out the textbook that had sustained the least amount of damage from the break-in.

"We already checked the bag. The files weren't in there," Henry said from behind me.

"No offense, Henry, but you're not exactly a brain trust." I flipped my accounting book open to the section I had painstakingly hollowed out with a utility knife earlier that morning. Inside were the folded pages I had stolen and the USB drives. I'd done the same thing to the Tolkien book I'd taken from Ax's backpack. I flipped it open and removed the hard drive.

I handed them all to Sullivan who looked at me impassively. His gaze never left my face. "Henry, go inside."

Henry scowled at me before returning to the house.

"I expect you to keep your word," I said.

He smiled. "I expect you do."

"I'm not bullshitting, Sullivan."

"It's been a very interesting experience meeting you, Rose."

"One I don't wish to repeat." I slammed the door and my garbage bag window rippled, then I walked around to the driver's side. My keys were hanging from the ignition. Without looking back, I got in the car and drove away.

Once I got on the highway, I took a deep, deep breath. My hands trembled so hard, I had to pull over to the side of the road and count backwards from one hundred to keep from sobbing with relief.

It was finally over. His last words hadn't been encouraging, but nothing I could do about it now. I just wanted my life back. I wanted to go back to class and hear Janelle bitch about her ex, Asshat. I wanted to see what crazy outfit Roxy would wear next. I wanted to hear about Axton's defeat of alien warriors from his latest video game. I wanted Jacks to tell me the funny thing Scotty just said. I wanted normalcy.

When I felt steadier, I drove to the college. In the IT office, Eric was in his usual spot and Steve occupied the corner, deeply engrossed in some crazy code bouncing across his screen. But Axton's seat was empty. My heart sank to my stomach.

"Where is he?" I heard the panicked edge to my voice.

"Hey, Rose," Eric said. "He's in the restroom." He stood from his chair and moved toward me. "Are you okay? You look like you're going to faint." He placed a hand on my arm and gently moved me toward an empty chair.

Steve hovered behind him with a water bottle in his hand. "Here, drink this."

I gave him a grateful smile and twisted off the lid, taking a long drink.

"Just breathe." Eric patted my back.

Axton came through the door, his gaze taking in the scene. "What's wrong? Rose, you okay?" He bent down in front of me, placing a hand on my knee.

I burst into tears. Axton pulled me into a hug and I clung to him. I buried my face in his neck and sobbed. I couldn't quit. The tears kept coming, along with little hic-cups.

Axton soothed me. "It's okay, Rose. It's okay."

Finally, the tears tapered off. Eric squatted next to me and handed me a tissue. Steve held the water bottle I must have dropped at some point and rubbed my back.

I dabbed at my eyes with the tissue and tried to deli-cately blow my nose. Poor Axton's T-shirt was drenched. "Sorry," I said.

"No worries." He flashed his goofy grin. "What's a lit-tle snot between friends?"

I laughed a little. "I really missed you."

"I missed you, too. You're my hero, Rose." He kissed my forehead.

"Stop."

"No touchy feely stuff. We'll set her off again," Eric said.

Steve offered me the water bottle. I took it and drained it.

"All better?" Eric smiled.

"Yeah. Thanks." I looked back at Ax. "So, you're not fired?"

"Took my urine test this morning."

"Good. And by the way, I think it's all settled. This Sullivan thing."

Eric frowned. "Did he contact you?"

"I went to see him. At his house."

Gasps all around.

"Rose, what did you do that for?" Axton ran a hand through his swirly, shaggy hair, making it stand on end. "And why didn't you tell us you were going?"

"I didn't want anyone to stop me."

"That was a really dumb thing to do, Rose," Steve said.

"I returned his files and told him it would all go public if he didn't leave me and mine alone."

Eric smiled. "You and yours, huh?"

I blushed. "You know what I mean. My friends and family are off limits if he wants all that stuff to stay buried."

"Did he believe you?" Eric asked.

"I hope so."

Axton looked at me, his eyes wide. "You aren't just a hero, Rosie. You're like She-Ra and Wonder Woman all rolled into one. I love you."

I stared into those blue eyes I'd missed so much. "I love you, too."

Steve cleared his throat. "I'm glad it's over. For your sake, Rose. You'll never have to see Sullivan again."

I glanced up at him and shrugged, thinking about Sullivan's parting shot. "I guess we'll see. I think I need to go home and get some sleep." I stood up and hoisted my purse on my shoulder.

"Sure you don't want to go celebrate, Rose? Let's go to The Carp," Axton said, "and I'll ply you with margaritas."

"How about Friday?"

"You are so on," he said.

Chapter 34

If I could bottle the dull personality that is Assistant Professor Carter and sell him to insomniacs, I'd be a millionaire. And perhaps win some kind of medical award. Sadly, I couldn't do that, so instead I doodled in my notebook during accounting class, in an effort not to die of boredom.

During the break, Janelle filled me in on her kids, Asshat, and his skanky new girlfriend, Flat Ass. Chicken Licker was history.

Same shit, different day. And I loved every normal, routine, ordinary minute of it.

I drove home feeling lighter than I had in days, maybe even months. With Axton, Pack, and Sullivan out of the way, I could concentrate on what I'd been avoiding. My own future.

The last two weeks proved to me how much I can accomplish when I'm proactive. I'd been sleepwalking through the last few years of my life. A big part of it was a screw you to my parents, but it was time to grow up and move on. Time to pick a major and go for it. Get a degree, maybe even a job with a nice perk package, although I didn't want to think about leaving Ma and Roxy. But a bigger apartment with a separate bed and sofa would be nice.

I pulled into my parking lot and automatically scanned for any wayward underlings. All clear on that front. It might be weeks before I dropped that habit.

As I approached the entrance, a man stepped out of the shadows. "Hey, Rose."

I froze for a second, then breathed a sigh of relief. "Steve, what are you doing here?"

"Waiting for you." He pushed at his glasses, the parking lot lights reflecting off the lenses. "I thought you might like to grab a cup of coffee." He walked toward me with a crooked smile.

"It's really late."

Disappointment and anger clouded his features. "You'll never have time for me, will you? Not like Axton or that lawyer or Sullivan. What more do I need to do to get your attention?"

Awareness hit me and in a flash I knew. God, had I been stupid. Steve broke my car window. Steve trashed my apartment. "It was you," I said.

The look on his face scared the crap out of me.

I turned to run, but he jerked me back by my ponytail. "Why not me?" He rubbed his cheek against mine.

I screamed and he slapped a hand over my mouth. "Shhh, be still," he whispered. He let go of my ponytail and snaked his arm around my still bruised ribs and squeezed. He began pulling me away from the building.

I kicked at him with my heels, tried to pry his hand off my mouth, tried to bite his palm. It didn't matter. He was much stronger than he looked. He carried me to his car as if I was no more than a toddler throwing a tantrum. He'd parked around the back of the building where the dumpsters were.

His arm still around my waist, he released my mouth and I screamed. When he slapped his hand over my mouth this time, he wasn't as gentle. "Shut up, Rose," he said, calmly. "I don't want to hurt you, but I will."

Steve-freaking-Gunderson was kidnapping me.

He removed his hand and opened the trunk to grab a bungee cord lying on the floor of the cargo area.

I screamed again.

Then I lost consciousness.

The left side of my face throbbed. I'd never felt pain like that before, and if I had my way, I never would again. He clocked me so hard, I was afraid my jaw was broken.

I slowly opened my eyes. I was bound in a fetal position on a concrete floor. A basement, maybe. My hands, tied tight in front of me, were tingling. My feet were also tied together.

I tried to pry my wrists apart, but the knots held firm.

I struggled to sit up and the pain was blinding. Bile rose up, but I choked it back, trying not to pass out. Gray concrete walls and floor surrounded me. There was a cheap wooden door on the wall in front of me and a bare half window to my left. A furnace and hot water tank sat in one corner. The only light in the room came from a single old fashioned bulb dangling above my head. The basement was completely bare of furniture, appliances, boxes, or tools.

I didn't see my bag anywhere, either. So no pepper spray or stun gun to subdue Steve.

The floorboards above me squeaked. A minute later

the door in front of me opened and Steve stepped into the room with a plastic container in his hands. He walked gingerly, so as not to upset whatever was in the bowl.

He squatted before me, setting the bowl down next to him. It contained water and a washcloth. He squeezed water out of the rag and brought it toward my face.

I flinched and backed away. Then I steeled myself, vowing I wouldn't show my fear again.

"I just want to put this on your jaw, Rose. I'm so sorry I had to hit you." He applied the cool cloth to my face.

"You didn't have to," I said. My jaw ached with every word.

"You didn't leave me any choice. I couldn't let you scream, now could I?" He sounded so calm and reasonable. He wasn't hiding anger the way Sullivan had. Steve was perfectly pleasant—it wasn't an act. Chills crept up my spine.

"Why am I here, Steve?" I had nothing to fight him with, not even my body at this point. The only thing I could do was keep reminding him that I was Rose, a person, someone he knew and kind of liked.

"Because this is the only way I can get your attention. With Axton back, I knew I wouldn't see you anymore." He wet the rag, wrung it out, and reapplied it to my bruised, swollen skin.

"You could have gotten it another way, Steve."

He pulled the rag away and gave me a cold look. "Don't pull that bullshit, Rose. I asked you out and you kept turning me down."

"So you kidnapped me instead?"

He brought the cloth back to my jaw. "I tried to get your attention other ways. But you always ignored me." He used a little more force when he said the words, causing me to groan and pull back.

"Sorry." He immediately regulated the pressure.

"What ways?"

"I saw Sullivan come out of your apartment. Be honest, Rose, you had more of a relationship with him than you let on. And that lawyer was up in your apartment for a long time. That's the night I broke your car window. I didn't want to, but knowing he'd touched you made me so angry."

"We just talked. And I've never had a relationship with Sullivan."

"I won't tolerate lying. Be honest with me."

"I'm serious, Steve. I never even kissed Sullivan."

He continued to stare at me before smiling once again. "Okay then, but you let the lawyer fuck you, right?" He dipped the rag and brought it back to my jaw.

Oh my dear Lord, I was dealing with a psycho. How could I have not seen that he was crazy pants? He'd seemed like a perfectly nice guy.

"Rose," he said in a conversational tone, "did you fuck him?"

I shook my head. "No."

"Good." He dropped the rag back into the bowl with a plop. Water splashed over my knee and onto the floor. "What about that guy from the band, the one with the holes in his ears? I saw him outside your apartment, along with the lawyer the other night. Were you doing both of them at the same time?"

"No."

He reached out and stroked my hair. "You're so beautiful. Every man wants you, Rose. Even Eric."

"Steve," I said, phrasing my words carefully. "Eric is just my friend."

His hand left my hair and strayed to my neck, which was still bruised from the other night's fiasco. "I know. But he wants to be so much more." He brushed his thumb over my collar bone. "I drove by and saw you at his house. I looked through the window and watched the two of you hug and kiss."

"I don't remember—"

"That was the night I broke into your apartment. I was so upset you let him hold you like that. I regret my lack of self-control."

I suddenly felt very cold. Kidnapping me, hitting me, tying me up in his basement—that wasn't a lack of self-control?

"I forgive you. Maybe if you untie me, we can talk like two people. Like Rose and Steve," I said, as casually as I could manage.

"Right. I went to all this trouble to get you here and I'm just going to untie you?" He pushed his face toward mine, his eyes hard behind his lenses, his lips compressed. "Do not treat me like a fool."

Panic started to rise and I thought I might start hyperventilating. I inhaled as slowly as I could, then exhaled. "I won't. But why am I here, Steve?"

He ran a finger along my bruised jaw. "I want to give you the chance to get to know me. You never gave me a chance. There are things I want you to know. Things I want to say to you."

"I want to get to know you," I said as sincerely as I could muster.

He smiled. "Good. We'll have lots of time together."

It hit me then that he didn't intend for me to ever leave. He would never let me go. He'd either kill me or keep me a prisoner in this basement forever. I felt tears sting my eyes and blinked rapidly to keep them from falling.

I wanted to keep him talking. Knowledge was power, I reminded myself. "You can say anything to me, Steve."

He sat back on his heels and regarded me with steady eyes. "No," he said after several minutes, "I don't think you're ready to listen yet." He picked up his bowl and left. I heard a lock slam into place.

Hours passed. The pain in my face dulled to throbbing ache. When he came back it was still dark out. This time he brought a bottle of water, a handful of tissues, and an empty bowl. "I figured you might need to go to the little girl's room," he said, setting the bowl on the floor.

I held out my hands for him to untie me. My stomach clenched. How was I going to subdue him and get out of here with my feet bound? I didn't know, but this might be my chance to get free.

"No." He smiled. "I'll help you."

I didn't want him touching me, let alone see me with my pants down. But I had to pee, so I decided to suck it up. Since he'd last left, I had resolved to do whatever it took to stay alive. I knew it would get much worse than this. My only goal was survival.

I focused on a crack in the wall as he unfastened my jeans and yanked them down. Although he seemed clinical and detached from the whole process, having him touch me like that was the most humiliating moment of my life.

When it was over, he unscrewed the water bottle and

held it to my mouth. I eagerly drank a third of the bottle, dribbling a little on my chin. He wiped it away with the back of his hand. Then he left, taking the bottle and the pee bowl with him.

I managed to doze off and on, but awoke every time my chin dipped toward my chest.

I kept an eye on the window. It was too small to crawl through, and we were too far below ground to actually see anything but tall grass, but I could tell it wasn't as dark now, and slowly, light crept into the room.

Steve came down again with the bottle of water in one hand and a small white pill in the other. "This is a sleeping pill. Open up."

I clamped my mouth shut, my jaw screaming at me the entire time.

"If you don't take this I'm going to have to knock you out again."

I quickly thought about another knock to my jaw and decided to take the pill. I opened my mouth and he gently placed it on my tongue. Then he gave me a sip of water and pinched my nose. I held the water in my mouth until I ran out of breath. I swallowed, then sputtered and coughed.

"I'm going to leave the bottle here with the cap off," he said, setting it down next to me. "Do you need to use the restroom before I leave?"

I hastily shook my head. "Where are you going?"

"To work, of course."

He left and slid the lock into place.

Fifteen minutes. That's about all I had before the pill

would hit me. I scooted my butt backwards until my back hit the wall next to the door.

Sharp needles dug into my hands and feet. Ignoring the pain, I pressed my back against the wall, and using my feet, pushed myself to a standing position. Then I began bending my legs, shaking my bootie, straightening my bound hands over my head. Anything to keep the pill from working. I did this until my muscles ached. A thin film of perspiration covered me, sweat pooling around my bound wrists. I felt the drug making me sluggish, sleepy.

I needed to keep my body moving.

Out of breath, I slid back to the floor, sitting in the butterfly position, with my bound feet pulled as close to my butt as I could manage, my knees slightly spread. I began trying to work the knot at my ankles. Whenever I felt myself drifting off, I hit my face. Hard. The pain helped keep me focused.

I drifted between a groggy state of exhaustion and a jittery state of panic. The shadows moved over the floor and I knew it must be afternoon. I didn't know how much more time I had left, but I had to get these damn knots undone before Steve came back.

I needed to break the glass in the window and use a shard to cut through the cords, but I had nothing to stand on. The light bulb, however, wasn't that far above my head. If I jumped, I could reach it. Maybe bat it with my hands. Whack hard enough, maybe I could smash it against the ceiling.

I shimmied my way up the wall again and took a second to let my legs and feet get past the pain and prickling sensations. Then with all the concentration I could muster— which was not much, because, dear Lord, I was so tired—I hopped to the middle of the room and jumped as high as I could, my arms over my head swinging at the light bulb piñata.

It took four tries, but I got it swaying back and forth. Like playing tether ball in grade school, I had to jump and swat at just the right time.

It was so close to hitting the ceiling, but missed by just a hair. I kept at it. Jump, hit, jump, hit. Over and over.

I didn't break it against the ceiling. It finally broke by banging into the metal hook on the bungee cord. Sparks flew, and so did little shards of glass. Turning my head, I covered my face with my upraised arms to avoid getting cut.

Yes, I had done it! Now I just had to saw the cord off my wrists. I sank back to the floor and found a shard that was about an inch and a half long. Sitting in the butterfly position again, I wedged the shard in between the coils around my ankles. I cut my hand in the process, but didn't care.

I tried to saw through the cord at my wrists quickly, but broke the delicate glass. Muttering a string of swear words, I picked up another shard, and pulled the bungee cord against it more slowly this time. I checked my progress. The cord was slightly frayed. It took patience, but eventually, I made it halfway through the cord.

With every ounce of strength I possessed, I tried to pull my hands apart. Still, nothing. Back to rubbing.

I had no concept of time, but the sunlight faded and shadows lengthened across the room. I prayed I would get free. I made deals with God as I continued to saw through the cord.

Minutes passed, maybe an hour, and then the small area I had been working on severed. I was so relieved, tears stung my eyes.

I again tried to pull my wrists apart. They moved maybe half an inch. Still, success.

A door slammed in the distance. Panic bolted through me. Steve was home.

Chapter 35

My whole body trembled. What would he do when he realized I tried to break free?

I looked around the dim room for the largest piece of glass I could find. There was a curved piece about two inches wide lying close to the door.

I scooted my butt across the floor. I reached for the glass, but my hands were shaking so badly, I dropped it twice. On the third time, I held it tightly in my right hand. It felt awkward, thin and fragile, and I was so afraid I was going to drop it again. Then I heard the floorboard above me creak.

Holding the glass as tightly as my bloodless fingers would allow, I quickly scooted next to the door, positioning myself behind it, and slid up the wall. I clung to the piece of glass, knowing it could be the only thing between me and death. And seeing Steve Gunderson's stupid face was not going to be the last thing I saw before I died.

I heard the lock slide, and I prepared myself. I'd only get one shot. The door opened and he walked into the room. "Rose?"

I shoved the door with my forearms as hard as I could, knocking him off balance. He stumbled forward and before he could straighten, I hurled myself at him, my weight pushing him to the floor. I landed on his back, slashed it with the shard.

Steve screamed and tried to buck me off of him.

I dropped the glass.

But I was in a frenzy of anger and fear. I bit the side of the neck. Hard. I tasted blood.

He reached back and pulled my hair. I retaliated by grabbing his hair, as much as I could anyway, in my numb, bound hands.

When he tried to stand up, I pulled a Mike Tyson and bit his ear as hard as I could. A chunk of cartilage came off in my mouth. I gagged and spit it on the floor.

He flailed and screeched. I didn't let go of his hair, but he let go of mine as he covered his bloody, severed ear with one hand.

Using his hair as leverage, I pounded his forehead into the cement. Over and over and over until he stopped moving.

I stretched out on top of him, panting and wheezing. I rolled off of him and sat up. I kicked at him with my feet to make sure he wasn't going to hop up like Michael Myers in the *Halloween* movies.

Steve was unconscious. And bleeding. Blood pooled around his head.

I scooted toward the door, which was still half way open. Using the doorjamb, I managed to stand. I grabbed the knob with my hands and hopped backward. I fell on my butt twice, my eyes never leaving Steve's prone, bleeding body. I shut the door and slid the lock in place.

I leaned against the cement wall of the stairwell. My chest heaving, I gagged, and threw up what little I had in me.

I lifted my arms and twisted my head, wiping my mouth on the sleeve of my sweatshirt, before I turned around and sat my butt on the first stair. Leaning my head against the wall, I just sat there, every muscle in my body aching. I knew I was going to have to get up those steps, but it looked like Mount Everest to me.

I'm not sure how long it took, but I finally I gathered my strength to move and slowly climbed the stairs, using my legs to push my ass to the next step. Just make it up the stairs, I told myself over and over.

I took a few minutes to catch my breath when I finally reached the top. Then, as best I could, I clung to the wrought iron railing, and hopped up the last stair. The door to the family room was open.

I rolled over on my side and tried to catch my breath. Steve's house was small. It looked like it had been built in the seventies. Or at least that was the last time it had been updated. Brown shag carpeting and ugly flocked wallpaper. The family room held a flat screen TV and one recliner.

Gathering my strength, I crawled like an inchworm across the floor to the kitchen, but the carpet burned my belly and arms, even through my sweatshirt. I flipped over, sat up, and went back to the old butt scoot.

I made it to the kitchen and stood up using the refrigerator as leverage. I glanced at the harvest gold stove and the wallpaper covered in red and green mushrooms. On the gold laminate counter next to the phone, I spied my purse.

Hopping a couple of times, I unzipped the bag with my teeth, and upended it on the countertop. My wallet, keys, lip gloss, tampons, and various receipts went flying. I leaned down and managed to grab a pen with my tongue and work it into my mouth, then reached for the phone. It skidded out of my hands, landed next to the garbage can. Sinking to the floor, I snagged for it and struggled to sit back up. It was difficult trying to flip open the phone with my hands still tied, but I managed. With the pen clenched between my teeth, I dialed and hit send. I spit the pen out on the floor.

"Help me."

Within fifteen minutes Sullivan kicked in Steve's front door. "Rose?"

"In here," I said. My voice sounded scratchy and faint.

Seconds later, he was in the kitchen. Shock marred his handsome face as his gaze swept over me. He bent down next to me on the floor, his hands probing my head and torso. "Where's the bleeding coming from?" His elegant fingers glided over my jaw. I winced.

"It's not my blood. It's Steve's. He's in the basement."

"Henry," he said. His attention to me never wavered.

"I'm on it."

I heard Henry stomp through the family room.

"Untie me," I said.

He looked strange, swallowed a few times, and seemed like he wanted to say something, but didn't. He went to work on the cords. Once I was free, he rubbed my wrists and hands. Tingling was too mild a word for what I felt when the blood started flowing back into my fingers and toes.

"Did you kill him?" he asked.

"I don't know."

Henry walked into the kitchen. Eyes on Sullivan, he shook his head.

"I bit him. I bit off his ear," I whispered.

Sullivan smoothed a hand over my hair.

He stayed with me, crouching in front of me, petting me. Then he sat down next to me, pulling me onto his lap, and wrapped his arms around my shoulders. I buried my head in the crook of his neck, while he murmured into my hair and continued to stroke my head.

"I have to go to the bathroom," I said after a while.

"Do you need help?"

"No," I snapped.

"Okay. I'll wait right here for you."

He helped me up. My muscles were stiff and achy, and I shuffled like a little old woman down the hall.

I turned on the overhead light in the bathroom, realizing for the first time it was fully dark outside. I looked at myself in the mirror and gasped. I looked like Ma's video game zombie who'd gone on a feeding frenzy. Steve's dried blood smeared my pale face, and there was a dark bruise covering my jaw.

I bent over the sink and scrubbed at my face with hot water. It floated through my mind that I would need an AIDS test. Probably other STD tests as well. It's not every day you take a bite out of someone. The thought made me giggle, hysteria started to creep up, but I quickly shook it off. I wiped my hands and face on a blue towel hanging next to the sink, used the toilet, and washed up again.

As I walked out of the bathroom and down the hall, I heard Sullivan and Henry whispering. They stopped talking when I walked into the room. Henry turned and went toward the family room again and Sullivan took both of my hands in his.

"Tell me what you want to do, Rose."

"I want to go home."

"About Gunderson."

"I just want to go home."

He let go of my hands and rubbed up and down my arms. "I know, sweetheart. But what do you want me to do with Steve?"

I shook my head. I still didn't understand the question. All I wanted to do was fall onto my futon and pull the covers over my head.

"I can make his body disappear. Is that what you want, Rose?"

"What? What are you talking about?" I understood the words but I didn't comprehend their meaning.

"Steve's dead."

Wordlessly, I shook my head.

He pulled me close, wrapped his arms around my shoulders. "You did the right thing. You were protecting yourself."

I'd killed a man. I'd pounded his head into the concrete and killed him. I should have felt guilty, horrified. But I felt numb. I survived. I was still standing and Steve was dead.

Sullivan drew back. "I'll call someone I know on the police force. But listen," he gave my arms a little squeeze, "you got away from Gunderson, you made it to the kitchen, and you passed out. Do you hear me? You passed out before you called me."

It finally dawned on me what he was saying. "How long has it been since you got here?"

"Four and a half hours. Now, repeat what I said

Rose."

Had Steve died because of the delay? If I'd called the police instead of Sullivan, would he still be alive?

Sullivan shook me. "Repeat."

"I passed out in the kitchen before I called you."

"I told you not to do anything until I got here. Say it, Rose."

I repeated everything he told me, like a robot.

He led me to a kitchen chair, knelt down, and hugged me while we waited for the police to show up.

Yesterday I felt nothing but anger for this man who used the police and political figures for his own purposes. Now I was relieved he had so many connections.

Grateful he was here.

Two detectives, uniformed officers, and four EMTs arrived.

The paramedics checked my vitals and pronounced that I was in shock. The detectives questioned me briefly as the paramedics bundled me onto a gurney. Sullivan climbed into the back of the ambulance and held my hand the entire way to the hospital.

"Do you want me to call your parents?"

I swallowed and shook my head.

"What about Axton or your friend Roxy?"

"No." I didn't want them to see me like this.

"What can I do for you, Rose?"

"Don't leave me," I whispered.

Chapter 36

It took four days of being questioned by the police, a two night stay in the hospital for observation—my jaw was only bruised, not broken—and three visits with an attorney my dad insisted on, before I finally got back to my life.

I don't know how Sullivan managed it, but my name stayed out of the news. I watched the coverage from my hospital bed and my name was never mentioned. The helmet-haired reporters said Steve Gunderson had kidnapped an unnamed victim and died during an ensuing altercation.

Altercation. Right.

When my parents visited me in the hospital, my mother was slightly less rigid than usual. We chatted briefly before my father asked to speak to me alone. My mother glared at him, but left the room.

"Did Sullivan have anything to do with this?" he asked, once she was gone.

"No, Dad, absolutely not. In fact, he helped me."

I saw doubt on his face. He scanned my features, checking to see if I was lying, I guess.

"It's true. I called him for help. He came to Steve Gunderson's house and called the police. He even rode to the hospital with me."

"Where is he then? I haven't seen him."

I hadn't seen him either. He stayed that first night, but when Roxy, Axton, and Eric arrived, Sullivan disappeared faster than a pot brownie around Stoner Joe.

My dad kissed my cheek and left.

When my sister and Allen came to the hospital, they brought flowers and a card that Scotty made. Eventually Jacks sent Allen to get me some ice chips, but really, she just wanted some privacy.

"I'm so sorry for those things I said, Rose." I could tell by her puffy, red eyes she'd been crying.

"No, Jacks, it's okay. I love you. You're the best sister in the world." I think I was feeling a little loopy from the sedative the nurse had given me.

"I love you, too, Rose, just the way you are. And you're not a loser." She laid her head on my stomach and began sobbing.

I patted her hair until I fell asleep.

Ma didn't let me work for a week. I told her I needed the money, but she insisted it would be a paid sick leave. That was really generous of her.

After I got home from the hospital, Axton bought me a new TV and a DVD player. He christened it with *Mars Needs Women*—which according to him was a classic. He and Eric stopped by every night for a week and usually brought pizza.

Ma and Ray came in the afternoons and brought real food. Jorge's wife, Marisol, sent enchiladas.

Roxy came bearing anime DVDs and nail polish. My toes never looked better. And I was hooked on *Eden of the East*. "Told you," she said smugly.

Jacks stopped by every morning with a latte and a fresh

danish.

Even Janelle dropped in, bringing my graded assignments with her. I looked them over and knew my major would never be in accounting. She also brought me a gift from Tariq, something called a Knuckle Zapper. It looked like brass knuckles, but acted like a stun gun. It was very cool.

Dane came as well and brought flowers. "Rose." He dropped next to me on the futon. "I should have stuck to you like glue throughout all this. I feel responsible."

I patted his leg. "You're not responsible any more than I am. Steve Gunderson was a nutball. No one knew. Apparently he pulled this stalker shit on his ex-girlfriend and she was too scared to report it."

He picked up my hand and kissed the back of it. "As soon as you're feeling up to it, I want to take you out. Anywhere you want to go."

I smiled, gently pulling my hand from his grasp. "I can't."

"Why not?"

Because I'd killed a man and it had changed me. I'd do it again. It was Steve or me and I chose me. I didn't feel guilty about it, not exactly. But I didn't feel okay about it, either. And I couldn't just go back to my life like nothing had happened. I certainly couldn't think about dating.

"I'm a mess, Dane. I can't be with anybody right now."

"Is it Sullivan?"

God, I was so tired of men and their fragile egos. "No, Dane. But it's not you, either. I'm not what you want and I don't know if you're what I need."

"You are what I want and I'm not going to give up on you, Rose Strickland."

"Now you're starting to sound like Kevin."

"That was cold."

I nodded.

That was the first week. On day eight at five a.m. on the button, I threw on jeans and a Ma's Diner t-shirt and went back to work. Ma protested, as did Ray. But Roxy set the salt shakers in front of me. I ignored everyone and re-filled them.

By the middle of my shift, I was exhausted. All the sleepless nights and the stress had taken their toll. Ma made me sit down and eat. I felt weird, sitting at the counter with the customers, eating breakfast. But I did it, then finished my shift.

They wouldn't let me help clean up, though. Ma sent me packing just as soon as she flipped the closed sign.

I drove home, and when I pulled up to my building, I saw him standing there, waiting for me. He leaned against the hood of a black Lexus sedan.

After I parked, Sullivan walked toward me. I met him halfway and we stood awkwardly in the middle of the parking lot.

The autumn sun made his skin seem more honeyed than usual. He looked handsome in his dark tailored suit.

"How are you, Rose?"

The wind picked up a strand of my hair and blew it across my cheek. Sullivan reached out and tucked it behind my ear. His fingers brushed lightly over my still bruised jaw.

"Better. You?"

"I wanted to make sure you were okay."

"I'm fine."

"No you're not. But you will be." He dipped his head toward mine, his lips grazing my cheek. "If you're ever in trouble again, promise you'll call me."

I wasn't about to promise him anything. I had just rescued Axton, outsmarted Thomas Sullivan, and survived a psycho. I was Rose Freaking Strickland, and I was a badass.

Reader's Discussion Guide

1. Rose went to great lengths to rescue Axton. Would you have done the same? How far would you go to save a best friend? Would you put yourself in danger?

2. Which secondary character was your favorite and why?

3. Some of the characters have questionable ethics. Roxy used to steal, Axton uses drugs, and Sullivan is a criminal. Do the positives outweigh the negatives in these characters?

4. Compare and contrast Rose's "adopted" family with her real family. What are the positive and negative traits of both?

5. Rose's mother, Barbara, repeatedly tells Rose to do something with her life. Is she wrong to pressure Rose to get a degree and find a better job?

6. Did Rose evolve over the course of the book? Why or why not? If so, what brought about the change?

7. Who is more successful, Rose or Jacks? Why?

8. Do you think Rose regretted her decision to break away from her family and gain her independence?

9. What were the major themes throughout the book?

10. Which character do you relate to the most and why?

11. Do you wish the characters had done something different or made a different choice?

12. Describe what you liked about the writer's style.

Terri L. Austin

When Terri isn't writing, she enjoys eating breakfast at her local diner, watching really bad movies, and hanging out with her kids when they're home from college. She lives in Missouri with her funny, handsome husband and her high maintenance peekapoo.

Visit Terri at www.terrilaustin.com to see what's next or drop her an email (terri@terrilaustin.com), she loves to hear from readers!

IF YOU LIKED THIS BOOK, TRY THESE MYSTERIES FROM
HENERY PRESS . . .

PORTRAIT of a DEAD GUY

by LARISSA REINHART

In Halo, Georgia, folks know Cherry Tucker as big in mouth, small in stature, and able to sketch a portrait faster than buckshot rips from a ten gauge -- but commissions are scarce. So when the well-heeled Branson family wants to memorialize their murdered son in a coffin portrait, Cherry scrambles to win their patronage from her small town rival.

As the clock ticks toward the deadline, Cherry faces more trouble than just a controversial subject. Her rival wants to ruin her reputation, her ex-flame wants to rekindle the fire, and someone's setting her up to take the fall. Mix in her flaky family, an illegal gambling ring, and outwitting a killer on a spree, Cherry finds herself painted into a corner she'll be lucky to survive.

AVAILABLE AUGUST 2012

MORE DETAILS AT HENERYPRESS.COM

Lowcountry BOIL
by Susan M. Boyer

Private Investigator Liz Talbot is a modern Southern belle: she blesses hearts and takes names. She carries her Sig 9 in her Kate Spade handbag, and her golden retriever, Rhett, rides shotgun in her hybrid Escape. When her grandmother is murdered, Liz high-tails it back to her South Carolina island home to find the killer.

She's fit to be tied when her police-chief brother shuts her out of the investigation, so she opens her own. Then her long-dead best friend pops in and things really get complicated. When more folks start turning up dead in this small seaside town, Liz must use more than just her wits and charm to keep her family safe, chase down clues from the hereafter, and catch a psychopath before he catches her.

AVAILABLE SEPTEMBER 2012
MORE DETAILS AT HENERYPRESS.COM

CPSIA information can be obtained at www.ICGtesting.com
Printed in the USA
BVOW022152270513

321756BV00006B/22/P